She made it out of the tub with an ungraceful splash and threw her robe on. She didn't hear it until she stepped into the hallway.

Tick.

Tick.

Tick.

Her body shook with fear, her fingers so badly, she didn't think she could dial the police if she tried. *Someone was inside her house.*

DEADLY SECRET

TARA THOMAS

St. Martin's Paperbacks

DEADLY SECRET

Copyright © 2018 by Tara Thomas.
Novella *Hidden Fate* Copyright © 2018 by Tara Thomas.
Excerpt from *Broken Promise* Copyright © 2018 by Tara Thomas.

All rights reserved.

For information address St. Martin's Press, 175 Fifth Avenue, New York, NY 10010.

ISBN: 978-1-250-13796-8

Our books may be purchased in bulk for promotional, educational, or business use. Please contact your local bookseller or the Macmillan Corporate and Premium Sales Department at 1-800-221-7945, ext. 5442, or by e-mail at MacmillanSpecialMarkets@macmillan.com.

Printed in the United States of America

St. Martin's Paperbacks edition / April 2018

St. Martin's Paperbacks are published by St. Martin's Press, 175 Fifth Avenue, New York, NY 10010.

10 9 8 7 6 5 4 3 2 1

TO EMILY,
I'M NOT SURE WHERE I'D BE WITHOUT YOU,
BUT I'M PRETTY SURE I'D HATE IT.

ACKNOWLEDGMENTS

New ventures, at least for me, are always half exciting/half scary. I've found that to be the case, even when they're as much fun as this series has been to write. And this series has been the most fun. Alex, so much of why I've enjoyed this the way I have is because of you. I don't want to think about what these books and novellas would be like without you. You have been a dream to work with. Every author should have an editor like you.

Mr. Sue Me Thomas, thank you for taking this all in stride, for doing a lot more than your share, for letting me change your name, and for never complaining. Every author should have one of you, too, but I'm not sharing.

To my readers, you're the best; don't let anyone tell you otherwise.

CHAPTER 1

Bea had to get out of the conference room before the man across the table tried to kill her.

Logically, she told herself he wasn't dangerous. Even though she knew better than to judge people based upon their appearance, the man in question was short, on the stocky side, and, unless he pulled a gun on her, she could probably take him, thanks to the self-defense course she'd completed last week. It was the pen he kept tapping on the table that tested her sanity. The *tap, tap, tap* that wouldn't stop and she couldn't get out of her head because it brought back thoughts of the man who almost *had* killed her.

Tap. Tap. Tap.

Sweat trickled down her spine.

Tap. Tap. Tap.

Her stomach began to feel sour.

Tap. Tap. Tap.

She closed her eyes, took deep breaths, and tried everything she knew of to make it stop. None of it worked. Not counting backwards. Not running through multiplication tables. Not even picturing herself relaxing on a deserted beach. Damn it, she was going to have a full-blown panic attack sitting in the middle of her senior partner's meeting with a client he wanted her to co-represent.

Tap. Tap. Tap.

She took another deep breath. This was not happening. She wasn't going to let it. But her heart began to race and she knew she was fighting a losing battle.

"Ms. Jacobs?" Skip, the senior partner, asked. "Your thoughts?"

Shit. "I, um, agree with your analysis."

The pen stopped tapping and she was able to suck in another breath. Deep even breaths. Surely the meeting wouldn't go on much longer and she'd be able to get up and walk. Splash some water on her face and maybe go outside for some fresh air.

Skip raised an eyebrow. "Really? You were most forceful in your opposition yesterday."

The pen started tapping once again.

Tap. Tap. Tap.

Tap. Tap. Tap.

She was going to be sick. She pushed back from her chair and stood on wobbly legs. "If you'll excuse me."

Without waiting for a reply, she darted from the room as quickly as possible, managing not to crash into Vicky, the office admin, who was bringing coffee into the conference room.

"Ms. Jacobs?" Vicky called as she raced by.

Bea didn't slow down or turn around. She made it to the bathroom and shut the door, sagging against it, and forcing herself to take deep breaths. For a brief second, she thought she was going to be fine, but the panic she'd tried to hold back clawed its way up her throat. Her stomach lurched in response and she stumbled forward, desperate to make it to a toilet before losing her breakfast.

After, she rinsed her mouth out and leaned her head against the cool tile on the wall. She was still breathing heavy and she balled her fists in defiance, even as her mind replayed the seconds leading up to her attack: the sudden shift in the air that alerted her something was wrong and the feel of rough hands pushing her against a brick wall. In what she thought was a cruel mind trick, all of her senses had been super-heightened and now, almost six weeks later, she could still feel him breathing on her, still smell the stench of human waste in the alley he dragged her into, and through it all, still hear the *tick tick tick* of his watch that haunted her.

She stood up with new determination. The assholes who hurt her weren't going to win. She'd be damned if they were going to get the best of her.

If she had to force herself to listen to pen tapping for hours on end, she would beat this. Maybe she should get some professional help like they'd recommended at the hospital after her attack. At the time, she'd thought she'd be fine if she could only get home and she'd thrown away the business cards they'd given her.

Little did she know that getting home was only one step in the seemingly three thousand needed for recovery. And in no way had it ever crossed her mind that she'd still be having panic attacks weeks later. Knox would be upset if he knew.

Knox . . .

He was an entirely different problem. Her gaze dropped to her bare left hand and she had to squeeze her eyes closed so the tears that always seemed to follow thoughts of him didn't fall. But trying not to think of his devilishly handsome grin, his tousled dirty blond hair, and his utterly devastating charm only made her think of them more.

Someone knocked on the door.

"Ms. Bea."

It was Vicky, bless her heart.

"Just a minute." Bea splashed water on her face and wiped her eyes. A quick glance in the mirror told her she looked like shit, but there was little she could do to fix it at this point.

"You okay?" Vicky asked when Bea finally opened the door.

"Getting that way."

Vicky pressed her lips together. Probably because she knew a lie when she heard one. Bea wasn't getting better. Some days she felt as if she were barely functioning. And it didn't help that Vicky was a mother hen and had sharp eyes.

"I don't feel so good," Bea said. "I'm going to work from home. I'll call Skip when I get there."

Vicky nodded. "I'm going to let you go, but I don't like you being alone so much."

Once she made it home and she called and left a voice mail for Skip, she pulled on her pajamas and curled up on her couch with her comfy blanket. It was absurd to even have a blanket out this time of the year, much less to use one. But for some reason, it made her feel safe to have it wrapped around her. Silly, of course, the blanket being a thin piece of fabric.

It was probably because *he* gave it to her. She snorted at the way her brain worked. Of course it was because he gave it to her. For what other reason would she bring the soft material to her nose in order to see if some small trace of his scent still lingered there?

But the softest of fabric was nothing even close to him and she shrugged the blanket from her shoulders. She turned her laptop on so she wouldn't think about him anymore, only to have the project she'd been working on with him before the accident pop up. She shook her head, hating that she now kept track of time and events that way.

The Johnson case? Oh, yes, that was *before*.

The Turner case, however, that was *after*.

Another thing she needed to take care of and fix. Thinking that way gave her attackers too much power over her, her life, and her future. She would stop that type of thinking today. Right this minute.

She thought about opening the file containing the project, but with the memory of her recent panic attack still fresh in her mind, she didn't dare. Too afraid that thinking about anything having to do with the Benedicts would stir up a pot of trouble she wasn't prepared to deal with.

It shouldn't bother her not to work on the case. After all, it wasn't a case for work. It was a personal matter, from Knox. He asked her privately to look into some issues his family's company had years ago. His older brother, Kipling, had thought the human resources records looked off. She had gone to work, looking into the personnel files he gave her for any kind of clue she could find, and in the end, she got attacked for it.

That last bit had come to her days later in the hospital. When she remembered the man she associated with the ticking telling her to stay away from Knox. Or else. She still recalled the cold sweat that covered her body the moment she remembered and the way goose bumps rippled her skin. But most of all, she remembered the despair she felt, knowing she had to end her relationship with Knox. Because she knew the next time she met the ticking man, he wouldn't leave her alive. And Knox would be his next target.

Her phone rang and she grabbed it, thinking it was Skip.

"Hello," she said, not looking to see who it was.

"Ms. Jacobs, this is Mandy at Dean Family Law. Your divorce papers are here and ready to be signed."

Someone else might have described it as being watched. Jade was being hunted. *Watched* was much too mild of a term to describe what he was currently doing to her. There was no doubt in her mind, she was being hunted. She was the prey. He was the lion.

Perhaps if she were smart, she'd have stayed away from South Carolina, but she'd learned early in life that running from your problems got you nowhere. In fact, that had been what killed her mother. When she had time to think about it, the irony didn't escape her.

The Gentleman had found her after her mother's death and now it seemed he'd be the instrument for hers.

Did she hate him? Of course.

But without him, would she be alive?

The answer to that only made her hate him more. But that hate did something she didn't think he'd counted on. It moved her forward. Consumed her with the need to bring him down. And that's why she'd come back.

Now, if she could only stay alive to see her plan finished.

Knox Benedict knew he was pushing his luck with the Charleston Police Department, but surely they had more information than they were telling.

"Come on," he told the lead investigator, Alyssa Adams. "You have to have more than you're letting on." After all, she'd been involved in every aspect of the threats directed to the Benedict family.

"Even if I did, Mr. Benedict," she said. "I'd hardly share it with you."

What Knox needed was his older brother, Kipling. Out of the three Benedict brothers, Kipling was the player and he'd often got into verbal sparring matches with Officer Adams a few months ago when she was investigating a series of murders that touched the Benedict family. Hell, she'd arrested Kipling for one of them. Of course, all charges had been dropped, but still, to say his family had history with the police officer was an understatement.

Besides, she'd shared information before. Why wouldn't she do the same and fill him in with the latest on how close they were to finding Bea's attacker? He'd worked in Afghanistan during the summers while he was in college. One of the skills he'd honed while there was IT security. Or to be more exact, how to get around it. He didn't want to hack into the police department's systems, but he would if he kept getting the run around.

"You do not have access to privileged information in an active police investigation."

"So you're admitting that you do have more information, but you're just not sharing it at the moment."

He thought he had her until she gave him a sarcastic smile. "And here I was under the impression it was your wife who was the practicing attorney and not you."

His smile faltered for a moment, but he finally decided she'd misspoke. "I don't know what you're talking about."

"You know when I first investigated the attack on Bea, I did a thorough background on her." She said it so matter-of-factly, he almost didn't grasp her meaning.

"You mean, you knew? This entire time? And you didn't say anything?" He was stumbling over his words, but he didn't care. He was shocked to find out that she might be privy to information he and Bea thought was private.

"That you and Bea are married?"

He was so stunned, he didn't answer her question, but his shocked expression must have been the confirmation she needed.

"I only reveal what is needed, Mr. Benedict. And your marital status had no bearing on the case."

"In that case," he said, "is it safe for me to assume that you will not divulge our secret?"

"Absolutely, Mr. Benedict."

He thought so, but he had learned the hard way it was never a good idea to assume anything.

"I'm not getting anything out of you today, am I?" he asked.

"Or tomorrow or the day after."

Not ready to give up, he flashed her a smile. "How about I invite you over to Benedict House for dinner?"

She raised an eyebrow.

"I could make sure Kipling's there," he added.

She laughed. "That especially won't work."

"Then I'll make sure he's not there."

"Good-bye, Mr. Benedict."

Her tone was light, but her meaning was clear. He knew better than to keep trying. Best to wait for another day. He tipped an imaginary hat and left.

Once he made it to his car and pulled out of the parking lot, he headed in the direction of Bea's office. She would hate it if she knew, but he drove or walked by her office or apartment at least once a day. He couldn't say exactly why he started. He never spoke to her and rarely saw her. Yet somehow just being in her space seemed important. Even if it was an odd one-sided attachment. He couldn't help but wonder if she ever thought of him. What he wouldn't give to know exactly what she was thinking.

He couldn't accept that their marriage was over. How could he when she'd not once given him a reason for why she felt that way? Even though Bea had been very adamant the few times they had spoken since her accident, he wasn't ready to give up hope yet. He'd never thought he'd find love, not the all-encompassing type that he had found with Bea. As such, he could not imagine not living without it.

For now, he would give her space. He'd only surrendered the battle, he had no intention of losing the war.

He drove by her office, but didn't see her car. Pushing back the uneasy feeling that always seemed to be simmering just under the surface since her attack, he told himself he wouldn't worry until he had a reason to do so.

A short drive down the road and five minutes later, he should have been able to relax since her car was in its spot. He pulled into an empty spot and debated on knocking on her door. Just a glimpse of her would do. Even if all she did was tell him to go away and not come back like she had the last time.

He decided not to knock on her door in the hope that if he abided by her wishes maybe she'd come to her senses quicker. It still made no sense why she didn't want him. He was her husband, he was supposed to protect her.

He remembered when they had first met. A local corporation didn't like the Benedict Industries plans for the expansion of their docks, and had threatened legal action. Knox had spoken to the family lawyer, Derrick, who had assured him that the corporation didn't have a case. Knox requested a meeting with them and told them to bring their attorney. He knew he was screwed when Bea Jacobs walked into the room.

Her reputation had preceded her and she was truly a sight to behold. In under two minutes, it became very clear that this was not an open-and-shut case. In fact, it soon became a real possibility that the expansion would be shut down. Sure she was beautiful, but she was also brilliant. When he'd finally made it home after that first meeting, he put his computer hacking skills to work and discovered she also did a lot of pro bono work. He ended up falling hard and fast. It took a lot of compromise and considerable expense, but an agreement was eventually reached, and the expansion proceeded.

He knew the smart thing to do would be to leave her alone. But he found he couldn't do it. He showed up at her office, with coffee made just the way she liked, and asked her out. He thought she'd be impressed that he'd paid such close attention to her. He'd thought wrong. She turned him down, but he was persistent. Even though he believed she only went out with him to get him to leave her alone.

And yet, much to his surprise, one date led to two, two led to three, and after that he stopped counting. He couldn't pinpoint exact when he had realized that he couldn't live without her anymore. Yet he remembered very well the day he had asked her to marry him. He wasn't sure who was more surprised she said yes, her or him.

After she'd accepted him, they both stood there silent for several long seconds, then they both started laughing. The laughing ended in a kiss. But all too soon reality descended upon them. For starters, her father hated him. He'd made that very clear the only time they had seen each other. Usually the Benedict name opened doors, but her father only saw him as a wealthy and reckless playboy, unworthy to serve soup to the homeless. Not only that, but Knox wasn't sure how his family would react to her being his wife. Especially after the expansion case.

With the potential of her father's ability to create a shit storm neither one of them could withstand, coupled with his family's ability to do the same, they decided to keep their marriage secret. They went to Vegas next weekend, and eloped.

Neither of them had ever regretted not telling others. Or that was what he'd thought. Now he wasn't sure.

Bea was working late in the office the next night. It was easier to work late at night, because she was alone. There was no one there to watch her if she had a panic attack. It didn't escape her that alone meant she was *alone*, with no one else in the building to protect her.

Or even to call the police if she shouted for help. And yet, she still found it preferable.

She had arrived at work early that morning, only to find Skip in her office.

"Good morning," she greeted the senior partner. "What's going on?" She decided to go for the direct method, even though she knew there was only one reason he would be in her office.

"Bea," he said. "I'm concerned."

She resisted the urge to sink in her chair. She would stand up to him. Be strong. Fight the battle she knew she could fight. And she could fight this one.

"I understand." She didn't need to let him finish what he was concerned about. She knew. "There will not be a repeat of yesterday."

"Good." He nodded. "You need to get your act together. Goodbye."

And with that, he took off. Walked out of her office without looking back. She waited until he got into the hall and closed his door before she sank onto her chair. She truly had to get her act together. She didn't need anyone to tell her.

If she didn't, there was no way she could run for Congress. It had been a dream for so long, and she'd worked so hard for it. She wouldn't let the attack stop her from achieving her dream. Not when she was this close. Not when she could taste the seat on the Congress. Could almost see herself making a difference for her state and community. Her passion for underprivileged children made her work harder and longer. If she could make it to Washington, she knew it'd be worth it.

If it required her to work doubly hard, she would.

And if that meant saying good-bye to Knox to keep him safe . . .

She turned on her computer, not ready to face the rest of that statement just yet.

Tonight, to make up for running out of the meeting early yesterday, she was looking through case law for him. She planned to present it to him tomorrow.

Picking up her cell phone, she decided to call for some takeout. She was going through the menus in her desk when a knock on the door caused her to drop them. Her heart pounded and her chest felt tight as she looked at the clock. It was much too late for anyone to be coming by on business. She thought about calling the police, but how stupid would that sound? "Someone knocked on my door."

What the firm needed were security cameras. She put that on her list to talk to the senior partner about tomorrow. She went to one of the far windows and looked outside, her fingers trembling as she peered through the blinds. It wasn't anybody she recognized. It appeared to be a young woman, or maybe an older teenager. She was very thin and carried a backpack. Perhaps looking for handouts?

She shouldn't have been scared open the door, but she was.

"Who is it?" she asked through the door.

"I'm looking for a Bea Jacobs," the unknown woman's voice said.

"Why?"

"I need help." It was the fear in her voice that swayed Bea. "He can't find me. Please."

Bea sighed. She was crazy to even think about

opening the door. But whether it was her own personality or growing up as a preacher's kid, she couldn't leave anyone in need outside in the dark.

She opened the door. Before her stood a young woman, biting her lower lip and glancing around as if expecting the bogyman to jump out at her any second. She wondered if she looked the same, but then schooled both her expression and her thoughts. She couldn't afford to walk down that path right now. Not with her job being on the line. And especially not with her life being threatened the way it was. "I don't offer that kind of help," Bea said as gently, but as firmly as possible. "There's a shelter down on—"

"He'll find me there." There was such sorrow in her voice and her eyes looked so full of fear, Bea's heart ached for her.

She had a feeling she'd regret it, but she heard herself saying, "Come on in." Before she closed the door she looked around the property to make sure all was quiet.

The young lady looked even younger when she was inside and under the lights. Bea tilted her head. There was something familiar about the young woman. She couldn't quite put her finger on what it was, but somehow underneath the dirt and the fatigue through her features, there was something she almost recognized. She just couldn't say what. Of course, she also looked horribly frightened. Bea wished she'd had time to order the takeout; it didn't appear that the woman had eaten recently.

Bea asked, "Can I get you anything? Water?"

"Water would be wonderful. But don't go through any trouble."

Bea was already making her way to the break room. "No trouble. I was just getting ready to order some takeout. You're more than welcome to join me. Pizza or Japanese?" Old Southern manners died hard.

She thought she was going to be turned down, so she was surprised when her guest made a request for pizza. Bea called it in, all the while aware of the set of eyes that followed her every move.

"There we go," Bea said, hanging up. "It'll be here in twenty minutes. Let's sit in my office and you can tell me how I can help you."

Once inside, they each took a seat. The young woman sat at the very edge of the chair, clearly poised to take off if needed.

"What's your name?" Bea asked. "And what can I do for you?"

"People call me Jade. I'm twenty. I don't go to school and I can't pay you."

"I don't care if you can or can't pay me," Bea said. "I've done pro bono work before. But I do need to know what I'm helping you do."

Jade nodded and licked her lips. "It's tricky. I've been involved in stuff. Illegal stuff, and I want to know how to make amends. I can't go to jail. If I go to jail, he'll know and he'll kill me or have someone else do the job for him." She added under her breath, "He likes to do that."

"He likes to do what?" Bea immediately thought domestic violence. Just because there weren't any visible signs didn't mean they weren't there.

"My guardian," Jade said in a whisper. "He likes to have people do his dirty work."

"Why are you so worried about your guardian?

You're of legal age. You don't have to stay with him and
he can't force you to stay."

Jade didn't quite meet her eyes. "I've been living
with him, and he had a job he wanted me to complete.
I've done lots of jobs for him in the past, but this
one . . ." She shook her head. "I couldn't finish it."

There was more to it than that, but before Bea could
formulate a question, Jade spoke up. "I don't want to
be a pain, but do you have a bathroom I could use?"

"Yes, of course." She probably should have asked her
when she first came in if she needed one. She pointed
down the hall. "Right down there, second door on
the left."

Jade thanked her and left to go to bathroom. She still
hadn't emerged when the pizza came. Bea paid the deliveryman and took the pizza into her office. "Jade," she
called. "Pizza's here."

Jade entered her office moments later. Her hair was
wet, and it looked like some of the dirt had been washed
off of her face. "Sorry it took so long," she said. "It's
been awhile since I've been in a clean bathroom."

"Don't worry about it." Bea waved to the conference
table where she'd placed the pizza box. "Have a seat
and dig in."

Jade didn't have to be told twice. She took a seat and
devoured a slice in what looked to be three bites. She
gave Bea a shy smile and wiped her face. "That was so
good."

"There's plenty more."

They didn't talk about business at all while they ate.
Bea only ate one slice; she didn't feel very hungry after
seeing how starved Jade was. When Jade pushed back

and said she was finished, Bea boxed up the leftovers and gave them to her.

"Now," Bea said. "Tell me about your guardian and what you need help with."

While she'd been eating, Jade appeared to have relaxed a bit. Now, at the mere mention of her guardian, she tensed back up. Bea wanted to assure her that it was okay and she was safe, but there was no way she could give that assurance. Instead, she waited for Jade to continue.

"He's evil," she finally said. "And he does horrible things. He's made me do some." She looked to Bea, as if waiting for her to say something, but Bea wasn't about to interrupt or attempt to know what she wanted in coming to her office.

"He's done things the police know about, but they don't know it was him." Jade glanced quickly at the window. Bea had closed the blinds when it became dark, so there was no one watching. "I'll tell you about them, give you everything you need to put him away, but I have to know that I won't get in trouble."

"I suggest we call the police," Bea said. "I know just who to call. She'll arrange a place for you to stay and ensure your safety. I'll agree to act as your counsel and I'll do anything in my power to keep you out of trouble." Bea thought it was a reasonable plan, but no sooner were the words out of her mouth than Jade had pushed back from the table and stood up. Bea forced herself to remain sitting.

"No," Jade said and her voice shook. Not only that, but her body trembled. "No police. I'll leave as soon as you call. You can't keep me here."

Bea held her hands up. "Whoa. Whoa. Whoa. Sit back down. It was only a suggestion."

Jade didn't budge. "No police."

"No police," Bea agreed.

Jade sat back down, but didn't seem to be anywhere near as comfortable as she'd been moments before.

"Can you at least tell me what he's done?" Bea asked.

"Not until I know that I won't go to jail," Jade said.

Bea wished that she could give that assurance, but unfortunately it was not in her power to do so. She couldn't even give her the probability of such a thing at this point. She shook her head. "I need to know exactly what we're talking about."

Jade looked torn. Bea didn't miss the way her hand trembled. Seeing she was being watched, Jade placed her hands in her lap and kept her head down.

When she looked up from her lap, there was a fierce determination in her eyes. "I can't tell you tonight. I have to think about it some. I might just leave here and not come back. No one will know. The only reason I don't want to do that is because I want to stop him."

Bea had worked with enough people to know when to push and when to back down. She knew beyond a shadow of a doubt that Jade was not giving out any more information tonight.

"I understand," Bea said. "My door is always open if you need me."

Jade stood and picked up the pizza. "Do you mind if I leave out the back door? I don't want to use the front one again."

Bea could certainly understand her worry; it was a feeling she knew all too well. The feeling of always being watched and not knowing what to do about it. Knowing there was nothing you could do about it.

"Sure." Bea stood up and unlocked the door for her.

Before she walked out, Jade looked over her shoulder. Tears filled her eyes. "I knew you were the right person to come to, but now I see that it was selfish to come to you. And the worst of it is, I probably haven't done anything but put you in more danger. I'm sorry."

It took a few seconds for Bea to understand what she said. "Wait," she called, but Jade had already disappeared through the darkened alley. She couldn't help watching the shadows as well, just to make sure nobody was looking. Everything looked clear, but she knew all too well how looks could be deceiving.

Tom took a step back into the shadows in order to process what just happened. He was under direct orders to bring Jade back to The Gentleman, alive. Tom had been following her for a week.

She was good, he'd give her that much, but he was better. Which was why he was taking his time. He wanted her to feel hunted. To know what it was like to be prey, and for her to experience the sense of failure that came the moment she realized she'd been bested. He wanted to see the look in her in eyes when she realized all was lost.

He'd followed her from the numerous spots she slept at to her forays around Charleston. He was pretty sure she knew she was being followed. He'd never imagined she'd have gone to Beatrice Jacobs for help. Especially since Jade knew The Gentleman's plans for her.

Which led to his current quandary. With Jade and

Bea together, he could accomplish two tasks in one. At the last meeting, The Gentleman had stated he wanted to take Bea out of the picture completely. Originally, the plan had only been to hurt her enough to scare her away from looking into the files Knox had given her. But that plan went straight to hell when Knox raced to the hospital. It was then The Gentleman knew Bea meant more to Knox than just a lawyer reviewing the files. After that, it quickly became obvious that Bea had no intention of ignoring the files and that if she suffered, a Benedict would suffer. That sealed her fate.

That task should rightfully fall to Tom since he was the one who originally roughed her up. The Gentleman had told him that the hotshot lawyer was in possession of information that might be crucial to the running of his organization. It was unclear if Bea knew what she had, but until it could be proven one way or the other, they had to assume she did. Especially since she refused to stop digging into them.

Now that Jade had connected with Bea, maybe he should put off doing anything until he was certain the information had been dealt with. Not to mention, he was very curious about what the two women were discussing. What he wouldn't give to be a fly on that wall.

In the meantime, he could put both women on the defense. Which might be fun. When the time was right, he'd shoot Bea and hand Jade over to The Gentleman. He'd turn her over gladly because The Gentleman had promised Tom could have her when he was finished with her. He ran a finger over the puckered skin of the scar he'd received recently when he'd been tied up and beaten in her place. Oh yes, when The Gentleman gave her to Tom, he would take great pleasure ensuring her currently nearly flawless skin was covered in scars that matched his.

The next morning, Bea did something she thought she wouldn't do for another six months: she called Knox. She hadn't planned on it. She hadn't woken up that morning telling herself, *Today I'm going to call Knox*.

After making it home the night before, she'd found it nearly impossible to get to sleep. Of course, insomnia had bothered her since the attack, but this was something different. This time it was because of Jade's parting words.

The more she thought about them, the more she believed they could only have one meaning. Jade's problems were somehow tied to her attack. She tried to remember if she'd ever seen her name in any of the files Knox had given her. She didn't think so, but would not allow herself to get out of bed to check. There would be plenty of time in the morning.

When she entered the office, Vicky had said Skip would be out of the office for the next week. It was a relief in a way. When he was around, she was self-conscious about her panic attacks, because they made her feel weak. Stupid, she knew. It was a medical condition. She thought perhaps it was the pity he looked at her with. She couldn't stand the look of pity.

For the next week she was blessedly senior-partner free. She turned on her laptop and pulled up the project she'd been working on with Knox. She couldn't find a reference to Jade, but she only had a fraction of the files. Taking a deep breath, she picked up her phone and called him.

"Bea?" He asked in lieu of saying hello on the first ring.

"Hey, Knox," she said and suddenly the enormity of the call hit her. Her heart began to race, because with just that one word, her name, every feeling for him she tried to hide, every passion she pretended to ignore, rushed back at her with the speed of a tidal wave.

"Are you okay?" he asked, his voice worried.

How was she supposed to answer that question? Did he really want the truth? Should she be honest and tell him about the panic attacks? That even though they often slept apart before her attack, it was still hard to sleep without him?

Yes, he probably did want the truth. She was the one who wasn't ready to face it just yet. So instead of telling him the truth, she lied. "Oh yes, everything's fine."

He didn't say anything else and after a few seconds it occurred to her that either he knew she was lying or else he was waiting for her to speak. Because the last time they talked, she told him not to contact her again.

"I've opened up the file on Mr. Brock today," she said. "I was looking at it again." She took a deep breath. It was time to tell him everything. "There are several things I need to discuss with you and I don't want to discuss them on the phone. Can we get together soon?"

She was panting as if she had run a race. Perhaps that's what talking to your estranged husband did to you. She closed her eyes. He was going to talk, wasn't he?

"Knox?" she asked. "If you don't want to, I understand."

"No," he said and cleared his throat. When he spoke again, his voice wasn't as rough. "No, that's not it. I wasn't expecting to hear from you."

I know, she wanted to whisper. *But I had no choice and I need to tell you why.*

"Are you able to meet?" she asked.

"Yes," he said and she hated that they were talking over the phone because she couldn't get a grasp on what he was feeling or thinking based on the sound of his voice. "Does after lunch today work for you?"

"That will be fine. See you then." Knox had turned away from his brothers once he recognized Bea's voice. There was no way he was going to let them know who was on the phone or how much she meant to him.

He stared at the phone for several long seconds after the line went dead, wanting to make sure his expression was as neutral before facing his brothers. He squeezed his phone and blinked back tears. God, it had been good to talk to her. It wasn't until his older brother, Kipling, coughed that he realized how much time it passed. He turned around.

"Was that a woman?" Kipling asked. "I bet it was the way you were standing, turned away from us and like you were in hiding. Tell us about her."

Knox just stared at him.

"Honestly," Keaton, his younger brother, said. "Cut him some slack."

Knox wasn't sure which brother was the most annoying. The blunt, hard-ass Kipling, or the *I'm so in love, everything's sunshine and happiness* Keaton. Frankly, at this moment in time, they were both obnoxious and getting on his last nerve.

"You look upset. You should go see her," Keaton said. "Tell her how you feel."

Right, like number one, he'd never thought of doing

that, and number two, that he hadn't told her how he felt. It was difficult to get Keaton to see anything his way, though, since he was the self-proclaimed Benedict brother expert on relationships and love. Knox thought that was mostly his fiancée's doing. If he needed advice from anyone, it was probably Tilly. In his experience, women were much better with talking about emotions. Or at least he had felt that way when it came to his mom and dad.

"Forget that shit," Kipling said. "You should go get laid. If you're interested, I have several—"

"Ick!" Tilly interrupted, coming into the conference room at the worst possible time and covering her ears. "I do not want to hear this."

If it had been him or Keaton who'd asked Kipling to stop, he'd have laughed and kept right on talking. But Kipling liked and respected Tilly too much to offend her, so he simply winked at her and said to Knox, "Come by my office later. We'll talk."

The very thought of going by Kipling's office and having him talk about his numerous exploits, and worse, for him to try to hook him up with one, turned Knox's stomach. "No," Knox said. "We won't."

"Why not?" Kipling asked.

"Because when this meeting is over, I'm going to go see her." Knox spoke it like he'd made his mind up hours ago, but in reality, he'd just decided a few minutes prior.

"Are you talking about Bea? If so, I think that's a good idea." Tilly looked at him cautiously while taking her seat beside Keaton. "I talked to Janie this morning."

By some stroke of fate, Tilly was friends with Bea's half brother, Brent, and his fiancée, Janie. Though they resided mostly in DC, they were both from Charleston and they talked with Tilly regularly. Brent and Bea had the same mother. She'd remarried after Brent's dad died.

Knox wrinkled his forehead, not liking the look Tilly had on her face. "Did Janie say something about Bea?"

"Bea's still having panic attacks. Apparently, she had a bad one a few days ago." Tilly dropped her voice. "I'm sorry."

Knox was so pissed, he could punch something. Bea was still dealing with the aftermath of her attack and there was nothing he could do. Hell, she'd told him to stay away from her.

He took a few deep breaths, trying to control his anger at the situation. "I bet she hasn't seen those therapists the hospital recommended, has she?"

Tilly shook her head. "Janie wasn't sure, but she said Brent didn't think she was. In fact, he told her that he was going to suggest to Bea that she come to DC for a few weeks the next time she called."

He'd be damned if his wife was leaving the city without him. Especially since she was still having panic attacks and had thus far refused any sort of medical help. He pushed back from the table. "You guys are smart. You can do without me for a bit. I'm going to see Bea."

Keaton clapped. "There you go. That's the spirit."

But Kipling only shook his head. "You should have done it my way. It's a lot more fun."

Knox wished he could have half of Keaton's positive outlook, but he feared all he was going to do was make Bea even more upset at him. In which case, he'd probably wish for half of Kipling's "who gives a shit" outlook. Unfortunately, he was neither of his brothers.

And yet he didn't quite fit the mold of saint, either, despite what the society pages said. He'd always felt he only got the nickname because he wasn't as outgoing as either of his brothers. For the most part, he was a quiet man, who lived a quiet life.

In the end, it was Tilly's softly spoken, "Be gentle" that got to him the most. Tilly who probably knew better than any of the three brothers what Bea was going through.

He thought about that as he drove to Bea's office. Tilly hadn't been assaulted, but she'd been threatened by someone they'd never found and held at gunpoint by a woman she once called a friend. As far as he was aware, Tilly never had panic attacks, and since they all lived in the same house, he'd have thought he'd know if she did.

But Tilly had a large support group of people who'd rallied around her afterward. It chilled him when he realized Bea had no one. Even her half brother and his fiancée had been out of the country. Who did she have nearby? No one other than her father, and he didn't count in Knox's book. It was more than the way he treated Bea, though that was enough. It was his entire philosophy toward people in general. He was quick to judge and slow to forgive, and if he found you lacking in any way, just one time, he would never like you, because his perception of you would never change. How the man ended up a member of the clergy was beyond him.

The closer he got to her office, the more determined he became. This time he wasn't backing down. It was time for him to step up and be the man—the husband—Bea deserved. Even if she didn't want to admit it.

He'd been patient. He'd given her time. And he'd

played by her rules. It was plain as day that her way wasn't working. Not if he had to find out secondhand that she was still having panic attacks.

He pulled into the parking lot of her office building, pleased to see her car parked outside. He knew for a fact that the office admin, Vicky, liked him. He'd walk inside and sweet-talk her into putting him on Bea's schedule so she had to see him.

If nothing else, Bea could spare him half an hour.

"Here goes nothing," he muttered to himself.

He walked inside and found it oddly quiet. He waited in the foyer for Vicky, not wanting to bust in on Bea if she was in the middle of a meeting. He didn't have to wait long before he heard Vicky walking to her place up front.

Her worried expression didn't change when she saw him. "Mr. Benedict, what can I help you with?"

He gave her a smile that typically opened doors for him. "I'm so sorry to be stoping by unannounced, but I really need to see Ms. Jacobs and I couldn't help but notice her car is outside. Is there any way you could put me on her schedule for fifteen minutes?"

Vicky squared her shoulders. "Ms. Jacobs isn't here. She's stepped outside."

She held something back, he saw it in her eyes. He motioned to a chair. "I'll just wait for her then."

"Mr. Benedict," she started, but didn't continue.

"Yes?"

She took a deep breath. "I don't know where Bea went. A courier dropped off a letter for her. I gave it to her and minutes later, she comes flying by me on her way out. I called out to her, but she wouldn't stop. I called her cell, but she's not answering it."

Unease began to seep inside Knox's body. He wondered who the letter was from, but that could wait. First they had to find Bea. "Her car's still here, so she can't be far. Have you been outside to look for her?"

"I went outside right after she left to look around. I came back in for a minute to decide what to do next."

Something felt wrong about this.

He wanted to get his hands on the letter she'd been sent, but that could wait until after they located her. His first priority was to find her and make sure she was okay.

"Why don't you stay here in case she comes back or calls?" he told Vicky. "And I'll go look around outside to see if I can spot her."

Vicky looked close to tears. "You'll let me know if you find her?"

"Yes," he assured her, wishing he could give her more hope. "And you do the same for me. Let me give you my number."

With that settled, he slipped his sunglasses on and stepped outside. He'd parked near her car, so he knew she wasn't sitting in it. Nor was she at either of the benches along the front of the building.

The office was near the historical section of the city. All things considered, she could be just about anywhere. However, even if she would be loath to admit it, he knew her. In some ways he knew her better than she knew herself. Armed with the knowledge he had of her, he narrowed down the possibilities to either the battery or the small neighborhood park nearby. Those were the two places she went when she needed to think.

He headed toward the park because it was closer. He walked quickly, eyes scanning everyone and everything, but he found no trace of her. He passed a few tourists, a college-aged couple, and a woman running with a dog, but no Bea. From what Vicky said, Bea hadn't left that long before he got there. He'd have thought he'd caught up with her by now.

He was almost to the entrance of the park when a movement off the side of the walkway caught his eye. Looking again, he discovered it was a woman and though he could only see her from the back, he knew it was Bea. If he had only seen her red hair, he'd have known. He'd recognize her hair anywhere.

But what was she doing and where was she headed?

He waited until he was almost upon her before he said something.

"Bea?" he called.

Immediately, she stiffened, but she took a deep breath and relaxed. She turned. "Knox?"

The sight of her punched him in the gut. She'd been crying, her cheeks were still wet. Her entire body trembled and in her hands was a crumpled sheet of paper. That damned letter, if he had to guess.

"Yes, baby." He held his arms out to her, knowing it had to be her choice to come to him. "Come here. Let me keep you safe."

He could have wept when she took a step toward him with no hesitation. The fact that she went willingly into his embrace spoke volumes about her frame of mind, he believed. After all, since her assault, she'd refused to simply talk to him and now she allowed him to hold her? He'd worry about getting to the bottom of what happened in in bit. What mattered was that she was scared and troubled, and she turned to him.

She wasn't crying anymore, but every so often she

gave a little hiccup of a sob and each time she did, it was like a knife in his heart. His ire at whoever caused her to feel this way increased. It had to have been triggered by the letter. He vowed to track down whoever sent it.

"Let's go to the park," he suggested. This time of day, it should be relatively empty. He wanted to take her to Benedict House. Not only because she'd be with him, but also because of the security Kipling had insisted be added after Tilly's incident.

Bea gave one last sniffle and nodded. He was loath to have her step out of his arms, but he took her hand and she didn't pull away. He'd take every victory he could, no matter how small.

By the time they reached the park, about five minutes later, Bea looked more composed. Her cheeks had color once again. Even when they sat on an empty bench and weren't holding hands anymore, she remained pressed against his side.

She glanced down at the paper in her lap and tried to straighten it out. Unfortunately, she had it flipped so the words weren't visible.

"I need to call Vicky. She's worried sick." He shifted so he could get the phone from his pocket. She answered on the first ring with, "Tell me you found her."

He looked at the woman at his side. The woman he loved. His wife. "Yes," he said. "I have her. And I'm going to be with her for the rest of the day. She's not going back to the office."

"Thank you," Vicky said, her relief obvious. "I know she's safe with you."

They said their good-byes and he noticed Bea eyeing him as he slipped his phone back into his pocket.

He wasn't sure how to go about saying what he needed to say. Direct and honest was probably the best route to go. But first he had to see the letter that had caused all the trouble. He held his hand out. "Can I see the letter?"

She only hesitated for a second before handing it to him and then turning away as if she couldn't stand to read it again. After reading the message, he completely understood why.

I'm coming to finish what I started.

Typed in black, the large font used might as well have been a billboard. He swallowed his anger at the fact that someone was threatening his woman, and took a deep breath.

"I didn't see who dropped it off. I don't know if Vicky did or not."

"She said it was a courier. No help there." He lowered his voice. "How often are you having panic attacks?"

She looked at him in shock. "How'd. . . ."

He shook his head. Not wanting her to get mad at either her brother or Janie for passing along that information. "How I know isn't important. It's you and what this is doing to you."

"Not too often. I usually know what's going to trigger one, so I stay away from those situations."

It didn't escape his attention that she didn't answer the question. "How are you sleeping?"

She didn't answer, but bit her lip and looked away. "Bea?"

"It's hard to avoid the triggers when your subconscious brings them to you."

He swore under his breath. "I'll take that to mean you're not sleeping."

"I'm fine. Really."

When she ducked her head, the sun struck her hair, showing off all the colors. Lord, he loved this woman, but he wanted to shake some sense into her. No. What he wanted to do was drag her to bed and keep her there for days on end. He'd bring her so much pleasure, she'd forget her own name, much less the asshole who kept threatening her. And he'd ensure she was so exhausted, she would fall asleep in his arms and would sleep like the dead for at least ten hours.

But none of that was going to happen anytime soon, so until then, he'd have to talk some sense into her. "Bea," he said, much calmer than he felt. "What part about any of this is fine? Are the panic attacks fine? The threats? Us?"

"Don't bring us into it, Knox," she said and even though it was directed at him, he was glad to hear the steel reenter her voice.

"Why shouldn't I?" He took her hand and she didn't pull away. "If you hadn't been attacked. . . ." He trailed off.

The truth was they'd never had a conversation about why she didn't want him around. He'd shown up at her side at the hospital and when she woke up, she took one look at him and told him to get out. He hadn't pushed her on it or asked her to explain.

But what if it hadn't been either of those reasons? What if it'd been something else?

"You're right about one thing." She stood up and brushed her skirt. "If it hadn't been for the attack, we wouldn't be here now. But that doesn't change the fact that we are here, does it? The thing is, I'm getting close to something. I have to be or else whoever it was wouldn't continue to threaten me."

Did she honestly think he was just going to let her walk away? He stood to join her. "Where are you going? You know you can't stay at your place." He held the letter up. "Not after this. It's not secure enough."

"I'm not going to let them chase me out of my house."

Usually he loved her stubbornness, actually found it to be hot, like the way she initially turned him down. But this time when she turned it on him, he only felt frustrated. "I need you to look at this rationally."

"I am."

"No. You're not. Your place is a security nightmare."

She rolled her eyes. "It is not. It just isn't wired with the latest technology like Benedict House. Look at it this way, if they take away my house, I'll have nothing left."

"But you'll be alive." How could she not see that? "And it's not forever, it's only until we find out who's doing this and stop them."

"I'm not moving. You want to keep me safe, find a way to do it with me still in my house." And with that, she walked away. Just like nothing had ever happened, like he hadn't come up on her and found her crying because of a threat on her life.

She told him to keep her safe like she didn't think he could do it. He'd show her. She knew that after graduation, years ago, he'd worked briefly for a cyber security firm in Afghanistan. It was where he'd not only learned how to hack, but also the proper use of weapons. It was time he showed her just how well he could protect her.

* * *

Bea peeked out of her blinds later that night and let them close again with a curse. Knox had been parked in front of her place for three hours and it looked as if he planned to stay there the entire night. Seriously? She shook her head. How long did he plan to keep that up? If she ignored him, maybe he'd go away.

The best thing she could do was pretend he wasn't there. As it turned out, that was a lot easier said than done, because, thanks to the fact that before her assault they'd spent most of their time at her place, his presence was everywhere. She considered working, but she hadn't brought any files home. She couldn't watch TV because the only shows she wanted to watch were shows she'd watched with him. And she could forget about reading because in every love story she picked up, she imagined Knox in the place of the hero.

For a fleeting moment, she thought about asking him to come inside. He was already in her driveway, what were a few feet more? If she invited him in, she knew he'd sit as close to her as possible. He'd probably put his arm around her. It'd feel so good to be wrapped in his warmth.

But no, she couldn't risk it.

She was too wound up to go to bed and she wasn't in the mood to clean. She eyed the huge soaker tub in her bathroom. Now that sounded like a good idea. It had been way too long since she relaxed in the tub. At the moment, a hot and sudsy bath would feel like heaven on earth.

She started the water, poured in her favorite shower gel, and waited as the room filled with mist and the smell of lavender. Her fluffy bathrobe was in place for when she stepped out and her slippers waited beside. She hummed and swirled a finger in the water to test the temperature.

Perfect.

She pulled her hair up into a ponytail on top of her head, grabbed her eye mask, and stepped into the tub. With a sigh, she allowed herself to sink shoulder deep and enjoy the warmth of the water. Her muscles relaxed and she allowed her mind to drift. She didn't even try to stop herself from the path her mind wanted to travel.

Knox.

If she concentrated, she could feel his arms around her. His breath tickling her ear as he whispered how much he loved her. How his every touch conveyed that truth.

She smiled and he laughed.

Except it wasn't his laugh.

She told herself it was stupid, there was no one in the bathroom and no one could've got past Knox and made it into her house.

Unless they killed Knox.

Shit. Shit. Shit. Why hadn't she thought of that possibility?

She made it out of the tub with an ungraceful splash and threw her robe on. She didn't hear it until she stepped into the hallway.

Tick.

Tick.

Tick.

Her body shook with fear, her fingers so badly, she didn't think she could dial the police if she tried. *Someone was inside her house.*

Tick.

Tick.

Tick.

She made herself think rationally. She was naked except for a bathrobe. The sound was coming from her bedroom. She ran by her laundry nook, threw on some clothes, and ran out the front door.

Knox was out of the car seconds after he saw Bea fly out the front door. "Bea?"

Her eyes were filled with tears. "There's someone in my room. I thought they killed you."

She'd reached him and he put his arms around her and since she wouldn't take a step toward her house, he led her to his car. "No one's in your room, they'd have to get past me."

"There was a ticking sound." Her eyes flickered to her house. Her body shook slightly. "In my room."

"I don't doubt you heard something. I'll go check it out. Want to go with me or wait here?"

"I'm not staying here by myself."

He got out of the car, went around to open her door, and they walked together toward her house.

She tilted her head when they made it to the hallway. "It stopped."

"The ticking?"

She nodded. "There was a ticking noise coming from my bedroom when I stepped out of the tub. Someone had gotten into my house." She looked at him and could't help but remember the pain she'd felt moments prior. "And that meant . . ." she took a deep breath that made her heart hurt. "It meant . . ." She forced herself to say it. "That you were dead."

She didn't wipe away the tear that ran down her cheek at the thought.

"No one got in," he said. "No way."

"Then what was that in my bedroom?" She looked toward the room with the slightly jarred door.

Knox readied his weapon and took a step toward the door, only to be stopped by Bea's hand on his arm. "Someone is in there," she whispered.

"That's what the gun is for." He motioned with his head. "Stay behind me."

"Shouldn't we call the police?"

"They won't get here in time."

She nodded, but held on to the back of his shirt as he pushed the door open with his foot. The room was empty. Or at least it appeared that way. Just to be sure, he checked out underneath the bed. Nothing. Not even a dust bunny.

He moved toward the closet. Bea kept a tight grip on the hem of his shirt as they walked, her slight trembling made it flutter just a bit. How could anyone have got past him and into the house? He had no idea. Bea was clearly upset, though. And that was enough to make his heart beat faster.

He didn't think anyone was hiding in the closet— Bea was always complaining about how small it was— but he had to make sure. He eased the door open. It was bigger than he'd thought it would be. Someone could easily hide inside. He scanned the shoes, trying to determine if anything was out of place or didn't fit. Not seeing anything and hearing her sigh in relief behind him, he pushed aside clothes with one hand while keeping his gun aimed and ready with the other.

"I see you, Bea."

She screamed.

Knox spun around.

There was no one there.

The unknown male's laughter came from Bea's laptop. Knox approached it carefully with Bea behind him. *What the fuck?*

"Tick tock. Tick tock. As much fun as it's been watching the two of you," the voice said. "I'm going to call it a night. Pleasant dreams. I'll see you again soon."

Knox slapped the top of the computer down.

"How did he get into my laptop?" Bea asked, still shaken but not as pale. "I thought that could only happen with nanny cams."

"Unfortunately, not," he said. "I wish more than anything I could tell you it's okay and not to worry about it, but Bea, I won't lie to you. There's no way to know how long he's had access to your system. I can work on improving and upgrading your security, but it's going to take time to do it the right way."

She turned deathly pale at his remark and though he hated that he'd scared her, she had to be made aware of just how dangerous the people they were dealing with were.

"It'd be best if you didn't stay here." Surely she could see that now.

"I know." She straightened her shoulders as if preparing to fight.

"Come with me to Benedict House. You'll be safe there. I can protect you, hire security, keep you safe."

"No." She shook her head. "Absolutely not."

Though he wasn't shocked she'd turned him down, the way she shut him down—without even giving it a second thought—came as a surprise. Months ago, before they got married, when they were just talking about it, they'd joked about living in Benedict House with his two brothers.

They hadn't planned on staying in the house forever, just until they decided where they wanted to live. Much of that would depend on whether or not Bea decided to run for Congress. He wondered if she still planned on running. *Questions for another day.*

"So if you know you can't stay at your place and you won't stay at mine," he said, "where are you going to go?"

She looked pained, but there was no denying the lack of enthusiasm when she replied, "I'll stay with the reverend."

"Your *father?*" He must have heard her wrong. To say the reverend and his only daughter didn't get along was akin to saying Mount Everest was a big hill. Seriously, who called their father "the reverend"?

"Yes, my father. And don't look at me like that. We can be in the same room and be civil."

"Only if one of you is comatose." He cocked an eyebrow. "Have you forgotten Thanksgiving?"

Over Thanksgiving, Bea talked Knox into helping out at a local soup kitchen her father supported. Knox had shown up, excited to meet Bea's dad and to help give back to the community. He saw it as a way to lay a good foundation with his father-in-law. Of course, they didn't tell her dad the truth about their relationship. They agreed to introduce him as a friend in the business who wanted to volunteer.

Unfortunately, Bea had neglected to tell her father that the "friend" she was bringing was both male and a Benedict. The reverend took one look at Knox and launched into an impromptu sermon on how money was the root of all evil.

Knox did his best to ignore it; he saw no point in getting into a pissing contest with his father-in-law. Besides, he wasn't the first to think all the Benedicts cared about was money. Bea, however, took his comments personally and shot back that if he'd bother to read his Bible before he quoted it, he'd have known that the verse said it was the *love* of money that was the root of all evil.

Needless to say, the only thing the reverend liked less than his daughter showing up with a Benedict male was being corrected by his daughter over the Bible. The situation rapidly went downhill from there and finally ended with the reverend ordering them out of the soup kitchen.

And according to what Bea had said as they drove away, that was one of their better holidays. So, she'd have to forgive him if he raised an eyebrow at her statement that she'd stay with her father. In his mind, that had Bad Idea all over it.

"No," Bea said, in answer to his question. "I haven't forgotten. I'll just call and tell him that I'm having some work done on my place and need a place to crash for a little while."

"You're going to lie to your father?"

"Don't judge me. I'm doing what I can to be safe."

"All you have to do to be safe is to stay with me. It honestly hurts that you would rather stay with your father, who resents everything you stand for. He can't stand that you're a lawyer and he despises that you want to go to Washington."

"It's not like that. I would rather be with you. I just can't tell you more right now."

If she were staying with her father, she'd be under more than enough stress as it was, especially when the letter she received today was factored into the equation. As her husband, it was his job to look after her well-being and do right by her. Even if that meant he had to step out of the way.

Though it went against everything inside him, he would do it. "If that's what you think is best, you won't hear any further argument from me."

She looked up to him in shock, clearly not expecting that to be what he said. "Thank you."

"You can thank me by letting me see you moved into the reverend's house safely. And hire a security guard." She looked like she was going to argue, so he added, "I'm going against every fiber of my being by not insisting you move in with me, surely you can give me this?"

When she agreed, he knew he should see it as a victory, but it seemed a damned hollow one. Hell, she probably agreed because she was too tired to fight.

"You're staying here tonight?" she asked, not quite able to disguise the thread of hope in her voice.

Did she honestly think he was going to leave her alone? "Of course. Where else would I be?"

She gave a curt nod, but he saw the pain in her eyes. "You can sleep on the couch. But after this, you can't be here anymore. For anything. I mean it this time."

He somehow doubted with everything that had just happened that he'd sleep at all.

Later the following day, Bea watched Knox's car as it pulled away from her father's house. And then, because she was paranoid, she waited to see if anyone followed him or appeared to be watching her father's house. For five minutes, she stood by the window, waiting. Only when five minutes passed did she feel as if both of them were safe enough and moved from her spot.

It had been damn stupid of her to allow him to help her move her things, but she felt so much safer when he was at her side. She told herself it was because she was weak, but she couldn't convince herself to believe that lie. It was because she knew he loved her and would do anything to keep her safe.

She clenched her fists, willing herself not to think about love and Knox. She was doing what she was because she loved him and wanted to keep him safe, too. And that meant staying as far away from him as she could. Unfortunately, she couldn't explain that to him. Not now. Possibly not ever.

The only way to fix the mess she was in was to find out who was behind the threats and the attack. And stop them. It would be the scariest thing she'd ever done, but she'd do it to be with Knox.

She dug in her purse for the second sheet of paper that had been the envelope she'd received this morning. The sheet she'd shoved into her purse as soon as she heard Knox call her.

I shouldn't have to remind you how vulnerable your husband is.

No, they certainly didn't. Though she couldn't remember all of her attack, that one part was crystal clear. She was to stay away from Knox or else she'd find herself a widow.

She had no recourse other than to obey. She couldn't go to the police, because the threat was too vague and no one knew they were married, except the one person who was using it against her.

Her head throbbed and she suddenly felt exhausted. Not surprising, really. Panic attacks had a tendency to make her sleepy, after. A quick glance at the clock told her the reverend wouldn't be home for another few hours. She checked the locks and then cured up on her old twin bed and fell into a restless sleep.

From the looks of it, Bea needed more than a reminder about what staying away from Knox Benedict meant.

His phone vibrated and he didn't have to look to know who it was.

"Status," The Gentleman said after Tom answered.

"Benedict just left her at Daddy's house."

"She doesn't listen and follow directions well, does she?"

"I'm finding that to be the general consensus when it comes to women, sir."

Another man would have laughed. Hell, he thought it was a pretty funny joke. But The Gentleman was not another man and he didn't joke. Or at least he didn't anymore. Those who were closer to him than Tom was, claimed he would joke with Jade. But ever since the little traitor had left, The Gentleman had been more demanding and violent than ever.

"I'm not concerned with other females at the moment. Only the one not taking me serious when I tell her not to be involved with Knox Benedict." The Gentleman must have struck something with his fist. The noise came through the phone like a shot fired.

"Yes, sir. Of course."

"What are you going to do?"

Shit, he should have anticipated that question and had an answer prepared. "I was just running through my options."

"Run through them faster, but focus on the woman. I'm not ready for Knox to die."

After leaving Bea at the reverend's, Knox didn't feel like going into the office. The truth of it, if he were honest, was that he didn't feel like facing his brothers. He turned his car away from the highway that would take him to the office and headed toward the project he'd been working on privately, before Bea's attack. The one he still hadn't told her about because he wasn't sure it would ever be needed.

It was located far enough away from town to be quiet, but close enough so they could both commute to work without it feeling like a chore. There were neighbors, but no one so close that they would see them on a regular basis.

He pulled into the driveway of the historic beach-front cottage and tried to remember his joy the day he'd bought the property. He'd proposed to Bea the day before and she'd accepted with the condition they kept everything between them a secret until after the election and she'd figured out how to handle her father's ire.

He had been so in love and wanted her so badly, he didn't question why too much. All that mattered was putting the ring on the finger of the woman he loved. Love made a man do crazy things.

They had joked about living at Benedict House, but he knew as well as Bea did that he had no intention of living with his brothers forever. With Bea's love of the ocean and his own fascination with history, the modest cottage he'd found for sale could easily be restored into their own personal dream house.

At the time, he had even been able to picture children. Years down the road, of course, but they were there. Two of them. A little girl, who would look like her mother. And a boy, who would take after him. When he had bought the property, everything seemed so clear, so absolute, so possible.

Why had the attack on Bea changed all that? It was a question he had asked himself enough, but now he needed answers.

He had not seen her much since the day of the attack. On that awful day it happened, he'd been out of town, for business. He wasn't sure he would ever forgive himself that. They talked on the phone that morning, and everything had seemed perfectly normal.

He arrived back in town around noon, and hours later, while at the office, he received word about Bea. She was asleep by the time he made it to the hospital. When she woke up, she was almost agitated, and frightened to see him, though she had said that the attacker threatened Tilly as well. It had been then that she had told him to go away, that she didn't want to see him anymore, and not to call, or in any other way have contact with her.

He had been so fearful of doing her further harm, he agreed, and kept his distance. All the while thinking he was doing the right thing.

Looking back, he should have known something additional had happened. It wasn't like Bea to just act like that out of the blue. Something happened to her that he didn't know about, or something had been said to her. He wasn't sure what it was, but he intended to find out.

But first things first. He pulled out his phone and the name of the security firm Kipling had used to improve the systems after Tilly's attack.

CHAPTER 2

She frowned at the street numbers on the row of houses. She didn't think the directions sounded right when her new client gave them to her. He'd assured her, he lived on Saint Simon East, but she had been almost certain the address would be on Saint Simon West. She peered over her shoulder; for some reason she had the strangest sensation that she was being watched.

"Can I help you?'"

She jumped and almost tripped over the man standing in front of her. She thought about saying, "No," but she was late and anyone who'd been watching her for longer than three seconds could probably tell she was lost. She gave him the address she was looking for. Hopefully, he lived nearby and could point out the right place.

"Hmm." He looked around. "I think that's on the west side."

"That's what I thought, too," she said, feeling vindicated. "But when I questioned it, I was told it was definitely east."

"I don't see how," he finally said, confirming her thoughts.

She sighed and reached for her purse. "I'm going to call him one more time. Tell him I'm standing on the street and I don't see it. If you'll excuse me."

She turned around to make her call, but before she could fish her phone out her purse, a hand tightened around her throat. She threw a punch, but only hit air.

Tick.

Tick.

Tick.

She couldn't figure out where the ticking sound was coming from. Maybe it was a result of the lack of oxygen reaching her body. Maybe it the sound of her heart. Or maybe it's what you heard in the seconds before death.

"Now, now," said the voice that moments ago was agreeing with her assessment on directions. "Is this how you want to treat someone who's just giving you a warning?"

Tick.

Tick.

Tick.

"Tick. Tick. Tick. How much time do you have left?"

Still, she struggled against the arms that held her tight, catching a glimpse of a watch. Was that a monkey on the dial or was she seeing things? Who are you? She tried to ask, but his hand had effectively cut off her ability to talk. He was behind her, so she couldn't see him. She closed her eyes and tried to remember everything about him so she could tell the police later.

Oh God, there would be a later, wouldn't there?

He was dragging her into an alley and she was

defenseless to stop him. She made her body as limp as possible, hoping that would slow him down enough that someone would see him. But he was strong and carried her as if she weighed nothing at all.

"You've been snooping where you don't belong. Stay out of affairs that don't concern you and stay away from Knox or the next time, I'll kill him. And tell Tilly that she's next."

She opened her eyes just in time to see the brick wall in front of her seconds before he knocked her head against it and everything went black.

Tom's phone rang and he answered, curious as to why The Gentleman would call out of the blue. "Hello, sir."

"Tom," he replied, and then as expected, launched right into the purpose of the call. He never bothered to thank anyone for stopping whatever they were doing to talk. After all, if The Gentleman had your phone number, it was automatically assumed you'd do whatever was necessary to take his call. "I have a new facet of your assignment to tell you about."

If anyone else had used the word "facet" in describing his job, Tom would have laughed at them. But somehow it didn't sound ridiculous when The Gentleman said it. "I look forward to hearing what you have in store for me."

"Smith Brothers put out feelers for new protection agents."

Tom didn't see how that related to him unless he was being taken off of Bea's case. *Fuck. He wasn't being taken off, was he?* "Sir?"

"Knox Benedict has requested protection detail for Bea Jacobs. I took the liberty of sending over your resume and it would appear that you are the most qualified applicant."

Tom couldn't hold back a chuckle at The Gentleman's brilliance. "When do I start?"

"I'll have Smith call you to confirm."

Tom had done protective detail before and knew that working in such a capacity for Bea would not be easy. He'd have to disguise his voice to ensure she didn't recognize him. Plus, he'd have to wear a suit jacket to cover his watch. Not wearing the timepiece wasn't an option. It was a priceless, one-of-a-kind antique, but more than that, it was a souvenir he'd taken from his first kill. The watchband was the original leather, but it was the face that was so unique. The best way to describe it was an optical illusion as everyone saw something different when they looked at it. He rarely took it off. It was a bit fantastical on his part, but he thought himself invincible with it on. "Thank you, sir."

"You will ensure she feels completely safe and secure, all the while looking for the best time and place to take her out. Failure of any kind will not be tolerated."

Tom squared his shoulders. Someone was going to die. It wouldn't be him. "I understand, sir."

When Bea got back to her father's house after work the next day, he was sitting in the living room. That wasn't a good sign. She'd been hoping that while she stayed with him, they could just pretend the other person wasn't there. They had done it in the past, with varying degrees of success. Why had he decided today, of all days, to have a conversation with her?

"Where were you?" he asked. She'd barely made it into the room. "I thought you said you'd be working from home most days you were here?"

She'd told him that because she knew she'd be too scared to go into the office and she had planned to work from home most days. "I had to pick something up." She didn't mention that it was a bodyguard, or that he was parked outside right this second.

"You sure it didn't have anything to do with that Benedict guy?"

She didn't hesitate long, but it was enough for him to pick up on.

He gave a heavy sigh that she translated as, "Lord, why have You burdened me with such a daughter as this?"

"Is that all? Because I have some work to do."

"I know you're aware that everything you do reflects on me. It's true always, but even more so when you're living under my roof."

"Are you fucking kidding me?"

"Watch your language, Beatrice."

"Watch my language? Seriously? I'm twenty-nine, or have you forgotten?"

"How could I forget a daughter who turned her back on everything I taught her to go the way of the world? Who found it more important to chase the almighty dollar than to settle down and find a Godly man and serve him?" He spoke in what she called his preacher voice, which always meant trouble. "And even worse, who wants to go to Washington and that corrupt den of inequity?"

"You think I do what I do for money? I help people

every day. A lot more than if I stayed at home pushing out babies. Nothing I've ever done is enough for you and I stopped trying to make you proud a long time ago." They were true words, but deep inside, she still had that basic need for parental approval. She'd had it from her mom when she was alive and she knew her mother did her best to both provide the encouragement she never got from her dad, as well as shield her from his more hateful words. Unfortunately, since her death, she thought her dad had gotten worse.

"There has already been talk of you being seen in public with one of those Benedict boys."

She put her hands on her hips. "Now I can't be seen in public with half the population of the world?"

"Of course not," her father said like that was the most absurd thing he'd ever heard. "You just can't be alone with them."

"You're fucking ridiculous," she said. With that, she stormed out of the room."

"And watch your language," he yelled after her.

Even though the following weeks were quiet, Bea never went a few hours without thinking about the threats against her. How could she, with Tom following her everywhere? She didn't like him and he was much too quiet. Of course, that sounded ridiculous when she thought about it and she knew she'd hate it more if he chatted all the time. The truth was, she didn't like him because he was a constant reminder that someone wanted her dead.

Her resolve to stay away from Knox was tested her second night in her father's house. She woke in a sweat, gasping for air, and her hand at her throat, fighting off an attacker who wasn't there. She forced down a scream as the final shadows of the nightmare left.

No way was she going to scream in her dad's house. He was the last person she wanted to know about her nightmares. Since that was the case, she couldn't wander around the house with the television blaring and every light in the place on as well. Which is what she normally did after a nightmare.

Without thinking twice, she grabbed her phone and called the one person she wanted to talk to.

"Bea?" Knox asked, picking up on the second ring. "Are you okay? What's going on?"

Just hearing his voice calmed her. But it wasn't enough. She needed to feel his arms around her, holding her tight, while he whispered that everything would be okay. "I had a nightmare," she said softly.

"Can I come over?" he asked in a pained voice, probably because he knew what the answer would be.

She couldn't tell him no, not when she wanted him so bad. Instead she replied with, "My dad."

"Damn it, Bea. I can't stand knowing you're so upset and not be able to hold you."

She closed her eyes as if doing so would make her immune to the anguish in his voice. "Just stay on the phone and talk to me. Please." It wasn't fair of her to ask him. Not when she'd pushed him away at every opportunity. But she didn't care. She needed him.

"Like you could make me hang up," he said and she appreciated that he tried to make his voice light and carefree.

She wasn't sure how long they talked about nothing at all. She must have dozed off because she woke with a start and saw that it was after five.

"Bea?" Knox asked.

She picked up the phone. "You're still here."

"Where else would I be?"

She told herself she wouldn't call him again like that in the middle of the night.

The next time it started with her phone ringing.

She grabbed it and answered, not recognizing the number. "Hello?"

"Hello," a very business-sounding woman replied, speaking over a lot of background noise. "I need to speak with Bea Jacobs."

"This is Bea." She stuck her finger in her ear in order to hear over the noise.

"Bea, this is Barbara Eastman at the Medical University of South Carolina. Your husband was brought in about an hour ago."

Fear washed over her. "Knox? Is he okay? What happened?"

Already she was picking up her keys and on her way out of her father's house.

"We'll fill you once you arrive, but right now, he's stable."

She gave a quick prayer of thanks and drove to the hospital as quickly as she could. What the hell had happened to Knox? She conjured up one crazy scenario after another before reminding herself that he was okay. Or at least stable.

She pulled into the parking lot of the hospital and made her way to the front desk. Knox was still in the Emergency Department and she saw why the woman who called her had so much background noise. The place was swarming with activity.

She gave her name to the clerk, but was too anxious to sit and wait to be called. After what seemed like forever, but had only been five minutes according to her watch, someone appeared to walk her back.

Knox was sitting up in his hospital bed telling the staff he was fine and to let them go home. He looked up in surprise. "Bea? What are you doing here?"

The fact that he asked meant he hadn't asked for her. That realization hurt her more than she was prepared to admit. "I was getting ready to ask you the same question."

"I asked first."

She rolled her eyes, but she could handle it, because that meant he was okay. "The hospital called me. You must have me listed as your next of kin."

"Right," he said. "I had to do that when you were in the hospital so they would let me in."

I shouldn't have to remind you how vulnerable your husband is.

It was so loud in her head, it woke her up from yet another nightmare.

This time she didn't even think about doing anything other than calling him. She reached for her phone and dialed his number. The feeling that the dream was somehow a premonition wouldn't leave her alone. What if he was in the hospital right now?

"Bea?" he asked on the first ring just like last time.

"You're in danger," she said. "And it's all my fault. I'm so sorry."

"What are you talking about?"

"The man who attacked me. The one who keeps

sending me threats. He told me to stay away from you and every time I've seen you since, after you leave I'll get a reminder. You have to be careful or else you'll get hurt. Don't you see? They warned me. It's my fault."

"Stop it right there." Knox sounded angry, but she really couldn't blame him. "That does not make any of this your fault. It's the fault of the person who attacked you."

She swallowed. "I should have told you. I'm sorry."

"Don't apologize. Have you told the police?"

"No. They told me not to." And what good would it do? They hadn't been able to find the person anyway.

"Wait a minute. Is that why you kicked me out of your hospital room when you were attacked and you kept telling me to stay away from you?"

She shouldn't admit to it. In admitting that she'd kept her distance to earn the trust of a psychopath would do nothing to keep him away. Now, if he thought he could handle it, he'd be over all the time. She was too weak to turn him away and that would only serve to put him in more danger.

"You don't have to answer that," he said. "Your silence already did. But why would they want to keep us apart? It makes no sense."

"I know what he said before he told me to stay away from you."

"There's more?" he asked.

"He said, 'You need to keep away from things that aren't your concern.' He said that right before he said to stay away from you."

"He must have been warning me off the case you gave me concerning Tilly's dad."

It made perfect sense. Ban her from working a case

as well as not allowing her to be in contact with the person who gave it to her.

"You may have a point there," Knox admitted. "Does this mean you're going to stop working on the case?"

Honestly, for him to ask that made him look as if he didn't know her at all. "No way am I stopping. The only reason he wants me to stay away is probably because there's something there. I'm not giving it up. I'm going to work on it harder."

Work went better and she didn't have any panic attacks. Once or twice she wished the senior partner wasn't out of town so he could see how well she was functioning. She counted it a victory when she went the whole week without a panic attack.

She worked from home on Friday, mainly because she'd invited Knox over to look at some information she'd found on Mr. Brock. Her father was on a church retreat with several members of his congregation, which meant, if she wanted to, she could invite Knox to spend the night. She'd be lying if she didn't admit how badly she wanted him.

Lord, her father would die if he knew Knox was spending the night, but she'd yet to tell him they were married. That would go over even worse. She knew she'd tell him eventually, but she had enough going on without having to deal with him.

She found she was actually able to get a bit of work done first thing in the morning, but as the day went on, she found her thoughts wondering more and more toward Knox. By mid-morning, she gave up all pretense of working.

He told her earlier in the week that he'd see her

around one, so when her father's doorbell rang a little after eleven, she knew he was thinking the same thing she was.

"I couldn't wait another hour to see you," he said almost apologetically when she opened the door.

Truthfully, he looked so good standing there. His hands in his jean pockets, his dirty blond hair tousled slightly by the wind, and those captivating, almost golden eyes all three of the Benedict brothers had. He was the best-looking man she'd ever seen and he was hers.

"Thank God," she said, grabbing him by the collar and pulling him inside. For a fleeting second she had the thought that she should look around to make sure they weren't being watched, but she dismissed it quickly, thinking the only people watching were probably her father's nosy neighbors. The worst thing that would probably happen is they'd tell her dad. She figured she'd worry about that later.

Once she had him inside, he closed the door with his foot and took her face in his hands, pulling her close for a kiss. Her knees went weak as she pressed him to the door. They both moaned and their kiss deepened.

Desire and need she'd fought to deny for weeks rose within her, refusing to be ignored for a second longer. Knox obviously felt the same. His hands were urgent, as if he had to touch her everywhere. No, that wasn't it. He wasn't merely touching her, he was claiming her once more as his. With his lips and his hands; his kiss and his touch.

How had she thought for even a second that she could live without this? Without this man? Foolishness, she now knew. Nothing but foolishness. She would never do it again.

Some small voice in her head whispered they should move out of the foyer. It wasn't a large space, but it had two large windows and anyone walking by could see them. Especially Tom, keeping watch on the street. But Knox being in the room seemed to drown out that voice.

Knox took a step back only to whisper in her ear, "I know you want to talk about what you found concerning Mr. Brock, but I have to be honest. That man and his doings of eight years ago are the last things on my mind at the moment."

"Prove it," she whispered back, rocking her hips so they brushed his erection.

He groaned. "Keep that up and we won't ever get to Mr. Brock."

She batted her lashes, enjoying being able to tease him again. "Promises. Promises."

"Tell me before I do something crazy like strip you naked and have my way with you in the foyer. Is your father home, and if not, will he be home anytime soon?"

She leaned forward and bit his bottom lip. "He's at a church retreat. All weekend. Won't be back until Sunday night."

"He's going to be gone on a Sunday morning? Is that even legal for a minister?"

"Can we not talk about my dad?" she asked. "Because it kinda kills the mood."

"I'll never mention him again. Ever." He even held his hand up as if he were taking a pledge.

She couldn't help it, she giggled. Because as much

as she'd missed his kisses and the passion in his touch, she'd missed this, too. The playful banter. The shared smiles and laughs. The everyday giggles and the simple joy of just being together.

It wasn't until that moment that she realized how very lonely the last week had been.

"God, I missed you so much." Knox pulled her into his arms. Not for a kiss this time, but to hold her. "I missed the feel of you in my arms, the way your hair smells, how soft your skin is. I missed us."

She blinked back tears. "Me, too. And I'm not going to do it again. I don't know what we're going to do, but I can't do it without you again. I can't live like that."

A sob escaped her throat and he gathered her tighter in his arms. She sighed and put her head on his chest, hiccuping around another sob. She took a deep breath, inhaling his smell.

"Shhh," he said, stroking her hair. "You don't have to. Ever. I'm here and I'll do everything within my power to protect and keep you safe. I promise. I'll do anything except live without you."

And in that moment, in his arms, it seemed like it would be just that easy.

She sighed. Why was it that when she was in his arms, everything made sense? Or maybe it was just that she didn't care one way or the other, as long as he was holding her.

"Let's go sit down," Knox said. He kissed her on the forehead and took her hand.

"I totally killed the mood, didn't I?"

"No, of course not," he said. He stroked her cheekbone with his thumb and gave her another kiss, but on the mouth this time.

"If that's the case, why are we heading for the couch and not my bed?"

"I want to sit and talk."

She raised an eyebrow at him. "Are you serious? You want to sit and talk? Instead of going to bed?"

He still had her hand and he lifted it to his lips and pressed a kiss against it. "What I want and what we're going to do are two totally different things. Do I want you? Hell, yes. Every day in every way. Forever. But, I want to be good for you and for you to be ready. Not just rushed through in the heat of the moment."

It was hard to argue with him when he put it like that. So she decided not to even try. If he said that eventually they would end up in bed, she knew they would. Besides, he was here. That was really all that mattered. She did want talk to him about the case.

They walked to the couch and sat down next each other. He looked at the laptop and papers she had spread out on the coffee table. He picked up a paper and read it.

"You've been busy." He put the paper down.

"It's a combination of insomnia and sexual frustration." She gave him a half smile and scooted closer to him.

His fingers brushed her knee, then ever so slowly, his fingers started inching their way upward. "You won't have to worry about the sexually frustrated part after tonight. And hopefully, I'll wear you out so thoroughly, insomnia won't be a problem, either."

"All these promises."

He cocked an eyebrow at her. "You don't think I can deliver?"

"You're the one who said it's been a while. Who's

to say you'll have any stamina?" She asked with a smile.

"I know you didn't just question what I think you questioned."

God, she'd missed teasing him. "All I'm saying is that talk is cheap."

While they talked, his fingers continued to work their way upward. But his touch had been so gentle, she hadn't realized just how close they were to where she ached for him. Maybe if she held perfectly still, they'd keep moving.

"Talk is cheap, huh?" he asked. "I seem to remember you liked my talk. Especially that time we were in your office, not long after you agreed to go out with me. You were on top of the desk and I was telling you all the things I was going to do to you."

It was as if the room grew fifteen degrees hotter as she remembered the day he was talking about.

He leaned in even closer. "Do you remember how wild I made you? How you were desperate to come? And I had barely touched you?" He whispered in her ear, "What made you that hot? Was it my fingers?"

She closed her eyes and focused on the sensation of his fingers as they teased her inner thigh. In her mind, she recalled the way he'd been talking that day in the office. Before then, she'd had no idea he could talk so dirty. Nor did she know how much hearing him talk dirty would turn her on.

"You're remembering, aren't you?" he asked, and the hand that wasn't driving her mad on her thigh was slowly inching toward her breast. "Remember how badly you wanted to come and how close you were?"

"Like I could ever forget that," she said, but kept her eyes closed.

"I told you I didn't think it was a good idea with your boss in the office and right across the hall."

God, but it had been enough to get her fired, probably, if her boss had found out. And at that moment, when she'd been on top of her desk with Knox whispering all the dirty things he wanted to do in her ear, she hadn't cared one bit. She'd been so carefree then, so in love. And his hands. His hands were magic.

"What did I do, Bea?" Knox asked.

"You covered my mouth with your hand, so I wouldn't freak out the entire office."

Feeling his hand over her mouth had only turned her on more. His hands weren't rough, but they were big and strong and every touch conveyed the power he held. Even now, with those same hands barely touching her, she was well aware of his strength. For some reason, it made it all the more arousing when he was gentle.

"Did you come that day?" he asked.

She had. So hard and fast and she'd been so grateful for his hand over her mouth, because she knew without it, everyone in a five-mile radius would have known exactly what was going on in her office.

"Did you?" he asked again.

"Yes," she managed to pant out in a half moan.

"I remember," he said. "You were so beautiful when you finally came. The way your back arched and your hips lifted. The way you groaned into my hand. All for me. So beautiful."

"Yours," she repeated. "Always and only yours."

He pulled away and dropped his hands. Her eyes

fluttered open. Why had he stopped? He wasn't even looking at her and he was frowning. She followed his gaze as unease began to build in her belly. "Knox?" she asked, unable to keep the worry from her voice.

"Is that smoke?" he asked. "Or am I imagining things?"

She didn't think they were both imagining the faint swirls that seemed to be coming from the front of the house. She sniffed. "I smell it, too," she admitted as dread filled her chest.

He ran to the front door. "It's locked," he said, twisting the doorknob. He tried to flip the deadbolt to unlock it, but it didn't move. He kept trying. And it still wouldn't move. "Bea?"

She stared in horror at the door. She stood up as he ran back to her.

He looked around. "Where's another door?"

"Come on," she said, motioning for him to follow. She led down the hall, through the kitchen, to the back door. It was locked, too. He cursed and tried it himself.

"It's the craziest thing I've ever seen." She kicked the door, but it didn't budge. "I'm calling the police."

She was nervous. Knox had been very quiet. She realized as soon as she stopped talking that he wasn't at her side anymore and she heard water running from the bathroom. She jogged down the hallway to join him.

"Knox?" she asked.

He came out of the bathroom with two washcloths. They were extremely wet. "Put this over your mouth and nose," he said, handing her one of the washcloths.

He pointed to the front door and she gasped. On other side of the door unseen before now were two small canisters that were emitting some sort of smoke.

"I don't know what it is," Knox said. "It could either knock us out or kill us. Or it could blow the house up."

This wasn't happening, she told herself. There was no way someone was trying to blow up her father's house. Much less, trying to kill her and Knox.

Except she knew they were.

She covered her nose and mouth with the cloth. Was it her imagination, or was it already hard to breathe? Her heart started to race . . . was it because of fear or the gas? How were they going to get out the house?

Beside her, Knox didn't look scared at all, or worried. "Dial 911. Don't say anything when they answer. It'll take too much time." She picked up her cell phone. He shook his head. "Use the landline. Easier to trace."

She ran to the kitchen and dialed the number, then left the phone. She happened to glance out the back window and saw a black SUV, with a man standing outside. He wore sunglasses, so she couldn't tell if she knew him or not. From the way he stood, he appeared to have a gun. She wondered if they'd killed Tom.

"They've covered the front door," Knox said. "In the back as well, I see."

"Those are the only two doors," Bea said. "Should we try a window?"

"They'll be expecting that."

Of course they would. Suddenly she remembered the origins of the house. The open breezeway on the roof that added so much value, but that the reverend thought of as a security hazard. "There used to be a widow's walk. The reverend had it removed when he remodeled the house. I told him he was an idiot."

"Did he leave the stairs?"

She started to get excited. They might actually get

out of the house alive. "Yes," she said. "He had the widow's walk made into an attic. We should be able to get out that way. I know there are windows."

"The air should be better, too."

"But wouldn't whoever did this think that we would go to the attic?"

Knox shook his head. "Not unless they knew about the renovations he did. Besides, I don't know of another way to go out. These stairs?" He pointed to the main staircase.

"No. The ones at the back. Come on." She grabbed his hand and led him down the hallway to the very back of the house. "Only way to the attic."

They'd just started their way up when something crashed from the front of the house. She jumped, but forced herself to remain calm.

"What was that?" she asked.

"I don't know and I'm not sticking around to find out."

They reached the second-floor landing at the same time smoke detectors started going off.

She raced up the stairs. Her heart pounding as she realized that going back down was not an option. It was up or . . . well, she didn't want to think about it.

They raced up the stairs. More crashes sounded from downstairs and each one made her jump.

They reached the attic level and Bea had never been so happy her father was a pack rat. Once they made it inside the walk-up space, she pulled a trunk in front of the door.

"I know it won't keep them out forever, but it might buy us some time," she explained to Knox. "Can we drop these?" she asked, indicating the wet cloth she still had pressed against her nose and mouth.

"Not yet. Not until we're outside." Knox jogged to a small window on the side of the house and looked out. "Never thought I'd be so glad someone built houses so close together, but I am now."

Bea joined him in looking out the window. "We go out the window to the trees and to the neighbor's widow walk?"

"That's what I'm thinking. Otherwise it's too far to the ground."

Bea eyed the window. She wouldn't have any trouble fitting through, but Knox was a different story. He yanked the window open. "You go first."

She wanted to argue, but knew it wouldn't do any good. She climbed up onto a stool and eased herself out the window. A crash from the first floor almost made her lose her balance and fall, but she caught herself.

No sooner had she made it to the trees, when Knox emerged from the window. "The fire is on the stairs. Hurry."

She stood on a sturdy-looking tree branch and scooted as close to the neighbor's house as she could. She jumped and for a terrifying second, she feared she wasn't going to make it. But she landed with a soft thump onto the neighbor's deck and seconds later Knox followed.

They scurried across the deck and peeked over the edge. Both breathed a sigh of relief when they saw the ladder-like steps leading to the ground.

When their feet hit the ground, Knox took her in his arms and in the distance, came the sound of sirens.

CHAPTER 3

God, he'd almost lost her. He pulled her closer. Again.

He didn't care what she said, this time she was moving in with him. And if she wanted to fight him, he'd simply tag along wherever she went. Either way, she wasn't leaving his sight for the foreseeable future.

"Looks like the police finally showed up," Bea said, looking over his shoulder to where patrol cars and a fire truck came into view.

"We can talk to them later. I'm going to call Kipling and have him pick us up. We'll call Officer Adams once we're at Benedict House."

She didn't argue, but rather nodded in agreement. Now that they were more or less safe, he expected shock to set in. Already, she was looking a bit pale.

"Just be strong a few more minutes, okay?" He rubbed her arms. "Can you do that for me?"

"They blew up my dad's house," she said in a deadpan voice.

He looked around. He didn't think whoever set the fire was still around, but he didn't want to take any chances. "I know, baby. And we're going to find out who did it, but we need to get out of this neighborhood first."

She nodded. He took a step toward the next street over and stopped. Would it be safer to move or stay where they were? He hadn't spotted anyone nearby and he couldn't say the same for another street.

It didn't feel safer, with the stench of the fire so close. And to think about how close they were to being trapped inside . . .

He squared his shoulders, knowing he couldn't give into his fear. He had to be strong for Bea. He took his phone. He'd gotten them this far. He'd get them the rest of the way.

Kipling answered his phone on the first ring. "Knox, what's going on?"

"Kip, I need you to come pick me and Bea up. We're at the house beside her father's. Do you know where it's at? Let me give you the address. Ready?"

"Got it," Kipling said after the information was given.

"We need you to come now. Someone tried to blow us up. The house is on fire and there are first responders. They don't know we're here, and I don't want them knowing. I don't trust most of them. I'll call Alyssa when we get back home. Her I do trust."

Kipling cursed. "Are you okay?"

"Yes, we just need to get home. Quickly. I'm not sure where the assholes are that did this and I don't like Bea being so exposed." She shivered beside him and he feared shock was settling in.

From the other side of the phone came typing. "On my way. I'm at the downtown office, so it should only take me ten minutes to get there."

"Thank you." Knox hung up and turned to Bea. Her coloring didn't look any better. He put his arms around her. "Kipling will be here in ten minutes. Just give me ten minutes."

But standing in the yard next to a burning house, knowing you were supposed to be in that house, and not knowing where the people were who wanted you dead, made ten minutes feel like ten hours. Especially when the only thing you had to hide behind was an azalea bush.

Bea sat beside him, silent and stoic, but tears were rolling down her cheeks. So strong and yet so fragile.

Knox had his arms around her. "You know, we never went on a proper honeymoon after we got married. We should go somewhere. Where do you want to go?"

But the distraction didn't work because the tears started falling faster. He pulled her closer. "Don't cry, baby. I've got you. I'll keep you safe. And Kip is on his way. We'll get to Benedict House, take a shower, change your clothes. Just be strong for me for a little while longer."

"You know where I want to go?"

"Where? Name it and we're there."

"I want to go to Washington to see Brent and Janie."

"Of course." He knew she hadn't seen her brother and his fiancée since they'd moved to DC earlier in the year. "We'll call them tonight and see when they're free. Sound good?"

"Thank you," she whispered, leaning her head on his shoulder. As he listened to her soft sobs, he vowed he'd do whatever it took to find out who was responsible and shut them down completely. And if it was in his power, as painful as possible.

Knox kept on the lookout for anything suspicious, but he didn't see either the black SUVs or the men who'd been waiting outside the house by the time Kipling pulled up.

"Get in, quickly," he said, as Knox helped Bea into the car. "You don't need to be seen at the moment. Duck down."

Knox wasn't sure what was going on, but he knew Kipling wouldn't have said anything unless there was a good reason. He and Bea stayed low in the backseat until Kipling gave the all clear.

He didn't wait for either of them to question him, but explained. "Primary report, according to the news channel, is that Bea was inside when the explosion went off."

Knox put his hand on her knee and squeezed it. "What about me?" he asked.

"What about you?" Kipling asked.

"Do people think I'm dead, too? My car was right outside the house."

His brother was quiet.

"Kipling?" he asked again.

"I assumed you took a cab or arrived with Bea," Kipling finally said. "Your car wasn't outside. There were no reports about you."

Damn, but it was enough to make his head spin. What he said made no sense. "They stole my car?"

"It appears that way," Kipling said.

"How about the security guard, Tom?" Bea asked.

"There are reports of a man found unconscious in his car."

Knox cursed inwardly. 'Pretty sure that's him."

A few minutes later when they arrived at Benedict

House, Knox wasn't any closer to figuring out what could possibly be going on.

"I told Keaton and Tilly that you both were safe but to go out for lunch," Kipling said. "I thought you might like to decompress in silence for a few minutes."

"Thank you," Knox said. "You want to hit the shower first?" he asked Bea.

Kipling rolled his eyes. "There is more than one bathroom, you know."

"Not connected to my bedroom."

"Should I take this to mean that Lena shouldn't bother making up the guest room?"

"Yes, that's what it means." Knox stared his brother down as if daring him to say something.

But Kipling simply nodded at Bea. "Make yourself at home, Bea."

"Thank you." She looked at Knox, obviously wanting him to follow her.

He told Kipling he'd be back soon and accompanied Bea to his bedroom. "If you want to take a nap when you get out of the shower, go ahead and do so. We can hold off on talking to the police." He kissed her forehead. "I'll be downstairs with Kip."

She nodded and slipped into the bathroom. He hoped she felt better after a shower and that it would bring some color back to her face. She still looked too pale.

He waited until he heard the water running before heading back downstairs to bring his brother up to speed. He found Kipling in the library pouring two shots of bourbon, and gladly took one.

They'd both taken a sip and were getting ready to sit down when the doorbell rang.

Kipling sighed. "I'll get it. I gave Lena the day off."

Lena had been their housekeeper since they were kids and though she could have retired years ago, she refused. She was, however, still recuperating from injuries sustained during the recent attack on Tilly. Knox was surprised, but glad she'd agreed to a day off.

Knox waited in the library until he heard who was at the door.

"Officer Alyssa Adams," Kipling said. "To what do we owe the honor of your presence?"

"Knock it off, Benedict," the police officer said. "I'm no more thrilled than you are that I'm here."

"And here I thought I was your favorite." Kipling clutched his heart, but was smiling. "You injure me."

"You'll get over it," she said in a deadpan voice, but Knox didn't miss the way her eyes sparkled.

Before his brother could say anything else, Knox stepped into the foyer. "What can we do for you, Officer?"

"Mr. Knox Benedict," she said. "Just the man I came to see."

"Yes." Kipling patted his chest. "Like an arrow. Right here."

Alyssa rolled her eyes. "Officially, I'm here to question you on either the murder or attempted murder of Bea Jacobs."

Knox almost dropped his glass, it was the most ludicrous thing he'd ever heard. "What the fuck?"

Even Kipling sobered up. "You can't be serious."

Alyssa held up her hand. "I said officially." She leveled her gaze and said quietly, "It's time, Knox."

He nodded. He'd known that. It was actually past time for him to come clean with his family. "Bea's taking a shower." He wasn't going to do it without her knowing first and he wanted her by his side when the truth came out.

"Alyssa?"

Knox turned at the sound of his wife's voice and watched as she came down the stairs. Her hair was wet, so he knew she'd taken a shower. She moved gracefully, one hand on the rail, looking almost regal in her descent, even wearing yoga pants and a T-shirt.

"Welcome back from the dead, Bea," Alyssa said.

"Thanks, Alyssa," Bea said, and Knox saw that she'd gotten some of her color back. "Why do I have the feeling that I'm missing something?"

Knox put his arm around her shoulder. "We need to tell our families the truth about us. If you're okay with it, that is." After all, it had been her choice to keep it a secret. It had to be hers to let it out.

Bea took his hand and faced Kipling. "Your brother asked me to marry him four months ago. I agreed and we went to Vegas that weekend."

Knox wasn't sure he'd ever seen his older brother look so shocked. "Kip?" he finally asked.

"You're married?" he asked. "For four months and you didn't say anything?"

Bea stepped forward. "Don't get mad at him. I asked him if we could keep it secret."

"Why?" Kipling poured himself another drink.

"Mostly my father. He's not supportive and he thinks the worst of the Benedicts. I was afraid of what he'd do to Knox."

Instead of saying anything to that, he turned to Alyssa. "And you knew?"

She nodded. "I discovered it after Bea's assault."

Since Kipling appeared to be thinking everything

over, Knox took the opportunity to ask Alyssa, "Why do people think I blew up Bea's father's house?"

"Your car was found not far from the house. There were canisters of gas in the back."

"Right," Knox said. "Because the logical thing to do after blowing up a house is to abandon my car with the evidence neatly displayed."

"I'll admit, I'm not comfortable with the direction the department is taking this as a whole, especially with how they've treated this investigation and the one with Tilly. I want to get to the bottom of this."

"That's what we all want," Knox said, coming up behind Bea and putting his arms around her. "Let's go sit down. We'll tell you everything we know."

It was an hour and a half before Alyssa left and though it was a productive meeting, Knox could tell Bea was completely zapped. Once Alyssa left, he gathered her in his arms and carried her up to his bed, ignoring her protests that she was fine to walk.

He hadn't thought he was tired, but once he lay down, he discovered he was. Bea was already asleep, so he curled himself around her and joined her.

CHAPTER 4

Bea woke slowly to the sound of Knox lightly snoring. Content, she took a few minutes to simply enjoy waking up with him. *This is how it should be.*

She frowned as it hit her that had she not insisted on keeping their marriage a secret, she would have been waking up to him for a while. The loss of that time together was painful.

His eyes slowly opened and he stroked her shoulder with a soft caress. "Why the frown?"

"I was realizing that if I hadn't wanted everything between us being a secret, I could be waking up to you every morning."

"That's okay. You're going to be doing it from now on." He stretched. "What time is it?"

She peered over his shoulder to look at the clock. "Just after six in the evening."

He buried his head in the pillow. "Ugh. We should probably be social and have dinner with the family. I'm sure Keaton and Tilly are back now."

"Is Kipling really mad, do you think?"

"Mad, no." Knox sat up. "Probably more shocked than anything."

Bea got out of bed and put on the clothes she'd laid out after her shower. "How do you think Keaton will react?"

"I think he knows."

"Why?"

"Well, he knows I'm with someone. Though it'll probably come as a surprise that I'm married. We were walking a month or so ago and he guessed. Still don't know how he figured it all out. And I'm sure by now Kipling's told him the rest."

She raised an eyebrow.

"Don't tell him, but Kip is a horrible gossip. He's worse than an old woman."

She had a hard time picturing that. "He likes Alyssa, doesn't he?"

"That obvious, is it?"

"Either that or he wants to be in her pants."

Knox smiled. "Probably both. But if I know Kip, he won't do anything about it."

"Why? Because she's a police officer and not in the same social circles?"

"No. He might come off as a snob, but he's really not. You have to get to know him before he drops that mask around you. But when he does, you'll never find a better man."

"So why won't he hook up with Alyssa?"

It didn't make any sense. She didn't know Kipling that well, but she believed what Knox told her about him. As for Alyssa, it was about time she found a good man. Especially after that last one she dated.

She shivered, remembering how sick she'd been when she heard the news. Bea couldn't imagine what Alyssa had gone through when she learned that not only was the man she was dating involved in several kidnappings and possibly murder, but that he'd attempted to kill her best friend.

When Knox sat down, she knew he was going to tell her something important.

"When Kip was in college, he fell madly in love. He was a freshman, and she was a junior. He claimed it was love at first sight. He brought her home for Christmas. Apparently, she had no family. He couldn't see anything wrong with it, but we could tell something was off. She was all smiles and goo-goo eyes around Kip, but that changed when he wasn't around."

Bea raised her eyebrow. She had seen the brothers in action, and couldn't help but wonder if they had ganged up on the poor girl.

"I know what you're thinking," Knox said. "Believe me, she wasn't interested in him. It was all about the money."

"How did you know?"

"For one." Knox leaned back and crossed one leg over the any. "She was always looking under the china and silver, trying to find the name."

Bea wrinkled her nose. "That's just tacky."

"Right?" Knox asked. "But Kip didn't see anything wrong with it. He shrugged it off, and said it was because she didn't have much growing up."

"What happened next?"

"They went back to school in January. Everything was quiet for a while. Then I think she started asking for money. Just little at first. For rent. Or some bill she couldn't pay. Eventually he started telling her no, or at least he did when the requests became outrageous. She told him if he loved her, he would give her the money."

"Nothing good ever comes from a sentence that starts *If you love me, you would*."

"Exactly. I think Kip started to realize that, so he broke it off with her. She didn't take it well."

"What happened?"

"She talked trash to everyone about him. Just junk mostly. He tried to take it all in stride, ignore her. He never told anyone how much, but we could all tell it was getting to him."

Knowing what she did of Kipling, Bea was willing to bet that he didn't want to do anything or take any action.

"Dad finally called Kip into his office one day. Derrick was there and he and Dad discussed filing a libel suit. Derrick ended up sending her a letter and everything stopped after that."

"But he never looked at women the same, did he?"

"Can you blame him?"

"No, but surely he knows not all women are like that."

"I think his head knows that, but going through that experience changed him. He rarely dates the same woman twice for fear of getting his heart broken." He stood up. "I'm going to shower. Are you up for a family dinner when I get out?"

"Sure," she said. She needed to call her father again. She'd called him and left a message as soon as she'd arrived at Benedict House, but he had yet to call her back.

She tried to reason why he wouldn't have called. He was at a retreat, so it was possible he didn't have his phone with him. If that were the case, he might not have heard that his house no longer existed. Or he could be driving back and she knew he had a very strict "no phone while behind the wheel" policy.

It was sad she came up with so many reasons why her dad hadn't called, when the cold hard facts were he just didn't care. Would he express any concern for her? So far she hadn't told him about the threats she'd received. Would that move him at all? She squeezed her eyes shut, not wanting to give into the tears that seemed so close to the surface lately.

She didn't know why her father's silence surprised her so much. He'd always been closed off emotionally. He'd always been that way and he was never going to change. She needed to admit it to herself.

She put her phone away and decided to change for dinner. Maybe she'd call him later. Maybe not. If she was going to run in the next election, which was in two years, she had to get busy. Lately, she had to admit, running for Congress didn't have the same appeal it once did. She'd been thinking about seeing if Keaton and Tilly could use her for pro bono work at the Benedict Charity division they recently started. She couldn't help but believe she could get more accomplished without the red tape she knew she'd find in Washington.

When she entered the dining room with Knox fifteen minutes later, the rest of the family had already gathered. Keaton and Tilly were back. She gave Tilly a big smile.

"Hey, Tilly," she said as Knox pulled out her seat.

The younger woman's eyes danced with mischief. "You know, if you wanted to get married first, you could have just said so. You didn't have to go all secret ceremony."

"You sly dog." Keaton punched his brother on the shoulder. "Were you two already married that day I realized you were dating someone?"

But Knox wasn't ready to give up all his secrets. "I might have been."

Keaton just laughed and shook his head. "Dig in. Lena made pot roast before taking the day off."

They all ate in silence for a few minutes. Silence. That struck Bea as odd. Shouldn't there be reporters calling and knocking on doors and such? Any time a Benedict made the news, the estate would normally be swarming with the press.

"I'm surprised it's so quiet," Bea said to no one in particular. "I'd have thought the press would be trying to take over."

Kipling loaded up his plate with mashed potatoes. "They probably would be if they could get past the security guards. Speaking of which, Tom's been released by the medics."

Bea stopped eating. "He's okay then?" She hated that he'd been hurt while watching her.

"Yes, I am," Tom said, appearing in the doorway.

Kipling cocked an eyebrow at him. "I thought you were supposed to resting?"

Tom looked at bit paler than normal. "Yes, sir, and I will. I just wanted to come by and apologize to Ms. Bea and Mr. Knox for not keeping them safe. I feel horrible."

Bea smiled at him. "Tom, seriously. You were knocked out. It's certainly not your fault."

"Beg your pardon, ma'am, I still feel responsible."

"Did you see anything at all suspicious?" Knox asked.

"No, sir." Tom shook his head. "They came up behind me. I didn't see a thing."

Knox started to say something else, but Bea interrupted him. "It's okay, Tom. Go take the rest of the night off. You look like you're about to fall asleep on your feet."

No one said anything until he left.

"I'm so sorry to hear about your father's house," Tilly said. "Let me know if I can do anything for you."

"Actually, you know what? You can help me with something. I believe the attacks on me and Knox are somehow related to your father." Bea looked over at Knox, who just nodded for her to keep going. "You wouldn't happen to have any old paperwork or anything I could take a look at, do you? I think your father was set up."

It was a long shot, but on the off chance Tilly had something, she had to ask.

Tilly's eyes grew wide with excitement. "I do have some stuff. Keaton and I were going through some boxes my mom had in storage. There were a few with some old things of Dad's. Mostly legal stuff. It'd be wonderful for you to look over them since you'll be able to understand them. I keep trying, but I'm not getting very far. I can bring them here."

"Yes, that would be wonderful!"

"They're at my apartment." Tilly looked at Keaton. "Can we go pick them up tonight?"

"Sure," Keaton said. He looked to Bea. "Do you want to come pick up the boxes with us?"

Before she could formulate a response, Knox

answered for her. "No," he said sharply. "She's not going anywhere." To her, he said, "Someone tried to blow you up today. You're safe here. I really don't want you out in public at the moment."

She supposed she should be irritated that not only did Knox answer for her, but he basically just told her she wasn't to leave the house. Yet somehow, she couldn't feel that way. His words made her feel protected and safe. And really, she didn't want to leave the house. She felt as if she were residing in a bubble, one she had no intention of leaving anytime soon.

"I'll stay here," she told Tilly and Keaton.

"We'll leave right after dinner," Keaton said. "We shouldn't be gone long."

True to his word, they left as soon as they finished and returned less than an hour later. Knox directed them to put the boxes in the library.

He stood beside Bea as Keaton brought in two banker's boxes. Tilly followed behind.

"I haven't had a chance to go through them really good yet," she said. "Chances are they're nothing. Because otherwise, wouldn't someone have already gone through them?"

"Not if they didn't know they existed." Bea didn't know why, but she couldn't shake the feeling that Tilly might have what she needed to prove that Mr. Brock was somehow related to the threats on her and Knox.

Maybe. Just maybe they'd find a clue in one of the boxes.

"I'm going to take Tilly out of here," Keaton said, putting an arm around her. "She's been through enough lately and I don't want her upset by what you find or don't find in those boxes."

Tilly spun around and put her hands on her hips. "I can handle what's in those boxes just fine."

Keaton took her hand and led her from the room. "We'll talk about it upstairs."

Bea raised her eyebrow at Knox.

"Keaton told me earlier today that Tilly had nightmares for weeks following the shooting incident. He's trying to protect her." He went over to the first box and opened it. "You want to do this tonight or wait until morning?"

"There's no way I'll be able to sleep knowing all this is down here." Bea eyed the boxes. "Besides, I took that nap earlier."

"True, but you did have a trying day. We both did."

"You don't have to stay up with me, if you don't want to," she said, knowing full well he wasn't about to leave her alone to go through the boxes. "You can go on to bed if you want."

"Not going to happen." He pointed to the other box. "You want to start on that box while I take this one?"

"Definitely. It'll go faster that way."

Bea opened the box closest to her and got down on her knees next to it so she could examine the contents better. It looked as if someone had emptied a filing cabinet into the box. As far as she could tell, everything was in unlabeled file folders.

She took out the one in what appeared to be the front of the box and opened it. After reading the first few papers, she flipped through the rest in the folder. Nothing she was finding made sense.

"This isn't right," she said.

Knox looked up from his file. "What's wrong?"

"When did Mr. Brock die?"

"Umm, seven years ago, I think. I'm not exactly sure."

"But it was before your parents died, right?"

"Definitely before."

"This folder contains newspaper clippings about the plane crash your parents died in." She sighed in frustration and slapped the folder down on top off the box. "This can't be Mr. Brock's stuff, it looks like it could be Tilly's mother's."

"Maybe his stuff is farther back or mixed in," Knox said.

He was probably right, and she told herself what she was looking for was there, she just needed to look closer. She put the newspaper clippings down and was getting ready to go on to the next folder when a handwritten note that looked to be a journal entry fell out from inside the stack of newspapers.

She frowned as she read it.

Mr. and Mrs. Benedict left for the Charleston airport together on the morning of April 10. This upset him for some reason and he let his gentlemanly facade down. He got agitated and said Mrs. Benedict was supposed to be staying at home to take care of her sons. He then left to make a phone call. When he returned, his face had lost all color and he wouldn't speak to anyone. He left and didn't come back to the office for a week. Rumors say he spent most of that time drunk.

She flipped it over, but there was nothing there. "Knox?" she asked and held up the note. "Do you recognize this handwriting?"

He squinted and looked at it. "It might be Mama Ann's."

"Mama Ann? Do I know her?"

"I don't think so. She was Tilly's mom."

"Was?"

He grimaced as he replied, "Breast cancer."

He didn't have to say anything else. Those two words said it all. She would have to go and talk with Tilly later to tell her how sorry she was about her mother. Yet the fact remained, she had no idea why notes about the Benedict plane crash would be in a box with her late husband's papers.

"Here." She handed him the note. "Read it all."

He took the paper and read over it, the frown never left his face. "I wonder who *he* is?"

"Was your mother not to go with your father on that trip?"

Knox narrowed his eyes as if thinking. "I can't remember. Obviously what I remember most about that trip is the crash itself and not so much what preceded it."

"How long after your parents took off did the plane crash?"

Knox stood up and walked over to where she was working. He got the top and placed on the box. He didn't look angry, just sad. "I can't remember. It was one of those things I tried not to think about."

"We need to see if Kip knows. The fact that your parents are somehow involved makes me think someone's after the entire family."

His face grew grim as he pondered her words. He sat down beside her and took the lid off the box. "It's here somewhere," he decided. "We just have to find it."

She put her hand on his upper arm in a silent show of support.

"Maybe files got put in backward." He pulled the last

folder in the box. A smile crept across his face as he read. "This is more like it."

"What?"

"Copies of Mr. Brock's datebook."

Encouraged, she reached for the next to the last folder and opened it to find copies of e-mails. The first few appeared to be nothing other than Mr. Brock asking for monthly reports and following up with several European executives. All in all, not the most entertaining or helpful. She couldn't for the life of her figure out why anyone felt them important enough to save.

She looked at the box, sitting there, stuffed with papers, and not too far away sat the box Knox had been going through previously. It would take days to completely go through the boxes. But she didn't know how long she had until another attack was made.

With renewed determination, she turned to the next piece of paper in her stack and was stopped short by what she saw. It wasn't an e-mail at all, but rather a handwritten note. She read through it quickly.

It was addressed to Ann, and much of it were the typical things a husband and wife would discuss. However, the next to the last paragraph had a different tone:

I know you enjoy spending time at the Benedicts'. I can't go into details here, but I ask that you be careful while you're there. I've overhead some alarming information this week. We'll talk when I get home.

Bea shuffled through the rest of the papers, desperately wanting to find another handwritten note, but only finding work e-mails.

"Are you serious?" she asked no one in particular. "You give me handwritten notes about an unknown man getting drunk and you don't tell me why Ann has to be careful at Benedict House?"

"What?" Knox looked up from what he was doing.

She passed him the note. "Next to last paragraph."

He read it quickly. "Is that all?"

"All I've found so far." She waved toward the boxes. "Talk about your needle in a haystack."

"We have to approach this as if every paper was put in the box for a reason. This might all be tied together."

Bea snorted. "I have a feeling the reason most of the papers were put into the box was to hide what's really important. Why else would you have the personal note in the middle of spreadsheets?"

"What type of spreadsheets?" Knox looked up in interest.

"I don't know. Monthly reports about something. That's what the e-mail paper clipped to them says." She picked one up to show him and frowned. "This can't be right. The e-mail and spreadsheet have different dates." She looked at two more. "They all do."

"Let me see." He held his hand out.

She handed him one. "You have the e-mail from Mr. Brock and then a spreadsheet almost three years later."

She looked at the box and the way it was packed. Something was off. You didn't haphazardly put together documents.

"I think it was done that way on purpose," she said. "So that anyone looking quickly would think what I did and just think they're old reports."

"They aren't reports." Knox said, picking up another

set of mismatched papers. "They're an itemization of items paid."

"Do they mean anything to you?"

"Not without context. Whoever kept the list used a code so anyone looking wouldn't see the payee." He slid a sheet to her. "See the company named Finition Noire?"

"Yes."

"It has a star beside it, yet Office Tango doesn't. I know we used to contract with Office Tango, but I've never heard of Finition Noire."

"So the star means it's a code? Finition Noire? Black Finish?"

He gave a hum of agreement. "And it looks like someone paid them a lot of money." His finger trailed up to find the date. "Around the time my parents were killed," he finished in a whisper.

Tom waited impatiently for The Gentleman to call him back, fuming the entire time. It was times like this he needed to be able to call the man instead of requesting a call through a third person. It was a ridiculous system and would lead to trouble one day. He had half a mind to tell him himself, but of course when he called, moments later, he only had one thing on his mind.

"They have paperwork, boss," Tom said. "Brock's wife had it in storage."

Mumbled curses filled the line. "How much do they know? And who knows it?"

"Right now it's Bea and Knox, but I'm sure they'll tell the others. Probably tell that policewoman, too." He took a deep breath before telling him the rest. "They have the company name."

This time, there were no curses, only a dangerous silence and then, "I need to destroy them all at once."

"Yes, boss."

"Shut up and let me think."

Tom didn't say anything more. Finally The Gentleman spoke. "I need to plan the takedown. While I do, make sure Bea doesn't forget about us."

CHAPTER 5

She was sitting on the beach with Knox. He'd said something funny to make her laugh when suddenly, she couldn't breathe anymore.

Tick.

Tick.

Tick.

He was back.

Her hands flew to her neck, frantically trying to pry his fingers away. Expecting flesh, she was startled when she felt leather.

Tick.

Tick.

Tick.

A watch! His watch was what made the ticking sound. She had to see it. Somehow she knew that if she could see the watch, she'd know who he was.

Desperate now, she flailed. Twisting. Turning. Kicking.

"Bea. Bea." The only noise was the sound of Knox,

gently saying her name. "You had a nightmare. It's okay. I'm here."

She blinked several times and took a deep breath. And another. She felt her neck, but there was nothing there and only Knox was in the room. She glanced around in momentary confusion. She'd had a dream and there was something important she needed to remember.

"Are you okay?" Knox asked, his forehead lined with worry. He pressed a kiss to her forehead and the dream disappeared completely.

It felt so good to be in his arms. She burrowed deeper into them. "I am now."

He kissed her again. His lips lingering just a bit longer as he stroked her upper arm. "Do you want to talk about it?"

"No."

"Are you sure you're okay? You frightened me." He ran his hands over her shoulders in a soothing motion that also warmed her body.

She closed her eyes and nodded while leaning into his touch. "I'm much more okay when you touch me."

"In that case." His hands drifted from her shoulders downward to her waist. He slowly teased the thin material of her pajama shirt up so he was stroking bare skin. His hands inched their way up slowly and came to rest on her breasts. He flicked her nipple.

"Still okay?" he asked, placing his hands in a spot where she knew he could feel her heart race.

"As long as you don't stop." She leaned into his hands, wanting more of his touch. She tilted her head, exposing her neck for him, and willing him to touch her there to erase the memories of the dream.

"Oh trust me, I don't plan to stop for a long, long time." He lowered his head, just a bit and nibbled. She moaned. "And maybe not even then."

She ran her hands over the expanse of his back, delighting in the way his muscles rippled underneath her touch. So hard. How was it possible for him to be so gentle when he'd toned his body so much? "I could touch you forever."

She bet she could. As it was, she never got tired of the feel of his skin, his smell, or any part of his body, actually.

"Let's not stop now, then." He pulled away and though she knew what was coming, her eyes never left him as he slowly pulled his shirt over his head and let hit drop to the floor.

He was gorgeous. Every rock-hard, lickable inch. She had to have her hands on him and she wasted no time sitting up and resting her palms against the hard planes of his chest. He sucked in a breath.

"There's not a force on heaven or earth that can make me stop right now." She moved her hands up to his shoulders and doing so brought her face closer to his chest. She leaned forward and licked him.

"Damn, Bea," he said in a partial moan.

"You like?" she asked.

"I assume that's a rhetorical question?" He took her hand and pressed against his growing erection. "Just in case it wasn't, here's the answer."

She loved the way she was able to arouse him. Loved that she could move him with just a touch or kiss. It was only fair—after all, he did the same to her.

Since he was the one who had moved her hand down, she thought it only proper that she left it there.

She dropped the other hand to drift toward his waist. She slipped her hand under the elastic and he hissed as her fingers brushed his length.

"I don't have to ask if you like that," she said.

She tried to scoot down, wanting to taste him, but he stopped her. "Not right now."

"But I want to taste you."

"Later," he promised in a growl. "Right now I need to be inside you too badly for you to have your mouth on me."

Since she was about insane with the need to have him inside her as well, she wasn't going to argue that point. She sat back up, and drew her shirt over her head.

He caressed her and each stroke, lick, and kiss heightened her desire for him.

His fingers danced along the edge of her waistband. "Why are you still wearing pants?"

"Because I want you to take them off."

Her words unleashed something within him. He nearly growled as he pushed her back on the bed and grabbed the waist of her pants, stopping only long enough to undo them before jerking them down with one hard motion. He tossed them aside, not looking to see where they landed.

He moved closer, pushing her knees apart, and fitting himself in between them. He rubbed his hand along her slit. The simple motion had her groaning in need.

"So ready for me," he said, feeling her wetness. "Good thing, I don't think I can wait another minute."

She lifted her hips. "Then don't."

He took himself in hand and lined himself up with her. She closed her eyes but he stopped her. "Watch."

She looked down where he just brushed her entrance.

"Watch," he repeated again.

She didn't feel as if she could look away even if she wanted to, as he slowly pushed inside her. She sucked in a breath; it had been so long, and he was so big. He went slowly—she knew it was his attempt to allow her to adjust to his size—but never stopped. He kept moving inward, pressing on, deeper and deeper inside her, until he was all the way in.

"Jesus, Bea," he said in a strained voice. His forehead was dotted with sweat, a sure sign he was holding on to his control by mere thread.

She waited for him to move, knowing he needed to by the way his muscles strained. Yet he remained still.

"You said you could look at me forever," he murmured. "I could stay inside you forever. Just like this. The feel of you tight and hot around me, the way you accept me deep inside your body. And you make me just want to go deeper and deeper until there's no us because we are one."

Then he started to move slowly. So slowly, she thought she'd go mad with the feel of it.

"And then I think no." He continued his leisurely pace. "This is what I could do forever. This slow move-in-and-out of your body. Barely doing anything, knowing the entire time all we both want is for me to move faster, but denying ourselves for the moment. Knowing it's coming, but not rushing to get there. Making us both wait."

He leaned forward, pressing her farther into the mattress. She loved how his weight pushed against her, but she wanted him even deeper. She shifted her hips, angling them upward to allow him better access and when he didn't move, she hooked her legs around his waist and pulled him close that way.

He slipped in another inch and she held on to him tightly, letting him pull out only the slightest bit before she pressed her heels against his backside. He lifted up on his arms and looked down on her.

"Know what else I like?" he asked.

She shook her head, not sure she had the ability to speak.

He grinned and then flipped them over so she was on top.

"I like watching you ride me. See how you get yourself off on my cock." He put a hand on either side of her waist. "Ride me, Bea. Use me however you wish."

She felt powerful astride him and the change in position had shifted him inside her. But still it wasn't enough. She wanted more. She rose up slightly and rocked her hips. Pleased with the hiss he gave in response, she switched to gyrating her hips.

They worked together in unison. He would thrust upward right as she would move her hips down. Each of them striving for the other's pleasure. For several long minutes the room was quiet except for the sound of their bodies moving against each other and their shallow breaths. His hands traveled all of her body, caressing, teasing, loving. She lowered herself and kissed him deeply. Still he moved within her, his thrusts never stopping.

As her release approached, she moved faster, rode him harder. He was just as desperate, almost frantic in the way he pounded into her, like he couldn't get deep enough. They moved together as if this was the first and only time they would ever be together. She banished the thought as soon as it popped into her head inside, choosing instead to focus on him. He was magnificent in his pleasure, in the way he loved her.

She bent low for another kiss and this time he lifted a hand to hold her head in place as he plundered her mouth. In that moment she knew she'd do whatever it took to keep him safe. He was everything to her and she couldn't imagine a life without him.

She told herself to stop, that she was being morbid. Even so, when he pushed inside her with one last hard thrust, emotion swept over her so intense, she couldn't stop the tears that rolled down her cheeks.

Breathing heavily, Knox pulled out and gathered her to his chest. "Are you okay? Did I hurt you?" His voice was heavy with concern.

She gave him a tearful smile that she wasn't sure alleviated his concern. "No," she said, lifting a hand up to his face and cupping the side of his cheek. "You're so perfect. So good. I love you so much."

He gave a sigh of contentment and pulled her to lay down beside him. In his arms, after what they just shared, she felt as if everything was right in her world. So much so, she was almost afraid to breathe, for fear that motion would disrupt the perfection of the moment.

She snuggled into his embrace. Took a deep breath and inhaled the maleness of him, while finding comfort and safety in his arms. "Can we stay here forever?" She knew it wasn't possible, but when she was in his arms, she could pretend the outside world didn't exist. More importantly, there wasn't anyone wanting to kill her.

* * *

Knox stood by Bea's side the next morning when she called Alyssa and put the phone on speaker. He and Bea had stayed up late into the night making copies of the papers from the box. He felt as if they were making progress, he only wished the process would move quicker.

Alyssa was intrigued when she called her. "You have information that suggests the Benedicts' plane crash wasn't an accident?"

"That's correct. We also believe it's somehow connected to the threats I've received. We made copies of everything if you'd like to come by and pick them up."

"Of course," she replied. "I'll be by later this evening."

Bea told her that she'd see her soon and then hung up. All Knox could think about was how to tell his brothers his suspicions.

"What's the frown for?" Bea asked, coming up behind him and wrapping her arms around him.

He sighed and reached up to take her hands. "Trying to figure out the best way to tell Kip and Keaton that Mom and Dad might have been murdered."

"You tell them the truth. Straight up. Lay out the facts."

He brought her hand to his lips and kissed it. "They're probably having breakfast now. Want to go down with me?"

"Sure, let me slip some clothes on."

She tried to take a step back, but he wouldn't release her hands. "I can't tell you how good it felt to have you in my arms all night. To love you again." He turned around so they were facing each other. "How did you sleep?"

"Better than I have since before the attack."

His lips curled up into a smile. "I guess that means we should make love every night from now on."

"I guess it does," she said with a smile of her own.

He contemplated kissing her again, but this time on the lips. However, he knew if he did, there was no guarantee they'd make it downstairs before his brothers left for the day. So he let her go with a sigh and a softly spoken, "Soon."

Fifteen minutes later, they made it to the dining room, though the air between them hummed with anticipation. Knox was disappointed to only find Keaton and Tilly seated at the table.

"Where's Kip?" Knox asked, sitting down and pouring a cup of coffee he passed to Bea.

"He left before seven this morning," Keaton said. "I'm not sure why. I didn't talk to him. I was still in our room when he left."

"What's up?" Tilly asked.

Lena walked into the dining room with a plate of pancakes for both Knox and Bea. "Work for this family for fifty years, you'd think they'd have the decency to tell me when they got married. I'm only giving you breakfast so I can make sure you have enough strength to make babies."

"Good morning, Lena. Thank you for breakfast," he said, knowing she was only half kidding.

"Lots of babies," Lena repeated. "And soon. Good morning, Ms. Bea. You take good care of my boy."

"I will," Bea said with a soft smile. "Thank you."

The tiny woman gave them both a plate and then stood back appraising the two couples at the table. "You two boys have found some mighty fine women. No doubt your mama and daddy would be very happy."

Keaton took Tilly's hand. "I know they would be."

"Now we just have to find a woman for Mr. Kip." Lena finished with a nod of her head. "Lord help us all, but that one's enough to send me to an early grave. No telling what kind of woman would make that boy settle down. No telling at all."

"Speaking of settling down," Keaton said with a sly grin. "I know Knox wasn't making any babies last night. I woke up at one thirty and someone was running the copy machine."

Knox met his brother's grin with one of his own. Little punk didn't know everything.

Lena gave a grunt of disgust and turned to leave, but Knox held out his hand to stop her. "Wait, Lena. You should hear this, too. I wanted to tell everyone together, but I'm not sure when that would happen."

"Does this mean the boxes I brought over were helpful?" Tilly asked, the hope in her voice obvious.

"Yes," Knox said. "They might turn out to be extremely helpful." He saw the hope flash in Tilly's eyes, and hastily added, "Unfortunately, we haven't found anything to exonerate your father."

"What did you find then?" Keaton asked.

Knox reached under the table and took Bea's hand, giving it a squeeze before answering. "We found information we believe suggests that Mom and Dad's plane crash was not an accident."

Keaton's fork dropped and clanked on his plate.

Tilly's hand flew to her mouth. Lena fell into the closest chair.

"What was in those boxes?" Keaton asked no one in particular.

"I don't understand," Tilly said. "Those boxes were Dad's papers and he died long before Mr. and Mrs. Benedict."

Bea straightened up in her chair. "Someone, your mom if I had to guess, had gone through and added notes, moved things around so the important information would be easy to overlook. That sort of thing. Like she was afraid of someone."

"Last night, we made copies of everything and I called Alyssa this morning. She's stopping by sometime today. I'd really like for everyone to be here, so we need to find Kip."

"I'm here," Kipling said, walking into the room. "What did I miss?"

Late that afternoon, Jade looked at the huge house in front of her with unease. It had never been her intention to come to Benedict House, but she didn't know where else to go. Bea hadn't shown up at her law office the last few days and she wasn't at her apartment. If she wasn't here, she wasn't sure what she was going to do.

The day before, she'd seen a newspaper that said Knox Benedict had tried to kill her, but that didn't make any sense at all. Especially since she knew it had to be The Gentleman who did it.

The day before there had been security guards all over the place, but there weren't any today. Probably because there weren't any reporters hanging around.

She hadn't seen or heard the news in twelve hours. More than likely, the police no longer thought it was Knox who blew up that minister's house.

She felt winded just from walking to Benedict House. She was getting weak and that just meant she was in more danger than before.

The problem was finding a place to sleep that wouldn't be discovered by The Gentleman or his minions. As it was, she slept very lightly, waking up every few hours and moving to a different location for a few more hours of restless sleep.

When she paired that with the meager amount of food she ate, she knew she wouldn't survive much longer. Bea had to be at Benedict House. Jade wasn't naïve enough to think the Benedicts would take her in for free and while she didn't have a lot of material possessions, she had knowledge.

Didn't they say knowledge was power?

Hell, forget power. She'd trade her knowledge for a hot meal and a place she could sleep for more than three hours.

She didn't want to ring the doorbell. She looked like yesterday's thrown-out garbage. No way would they let her in. But if she waited outside or, even better, could find Bea when she was alone in a room, maybe she could get in that way.

Jade scurried to the side of the house she'd been in almost two months ago when she met the younger Benedict brother. There had been a rock she'd found to step on that let her glimpse the kitchen.

Ah yes, there it was.

She stepped onto it and rose to her toes.

"You there! Freeze! Police!"

Damn it. Damn it. Damn it all to hell. She recognized the female police officer who was always hanging around.

Jade lifted her hands and turned around. The female officer had her gun aimed at her. She tried to tell herself it was nothing, standing in a strange yard with gun pointed at her. It didn't work. It was scary as hell. Though not, some part of her reasoned, as bad as it would be if Tom held her at gunpoint. Odds were, the officer wouldn't shoot her.

"Who are you and what are you doing spying on the Benedicts?" the officer asked.

Jade didn't think she could convincingly pass herself off as a reporter, so she settled on the truth. "I'm looking for Bea. I'm one of her clients."

"Haven't you heard of a phone?" The officer was still on guard, but at least she'd lowered her weapon.

Jade stopped herself from rolling her eyes. "Do I look like I have a phone?"

"You look like you're trying to pull off a breaking and entering."

"I'm not. I just want to talk to Bea."

The officer relaxed a touch, probably sensing how weak Jade was. "Then you're in luck, because she's expecting me." She mentioned with her hands. "Come on."

If the officer thought she was calling Jade's bluff, she was in for a surprise. Even so, the woman kept her hand around her upper arm. Like she was going to run when she knew she'd have a gun pointed at her within seconds. Three months ago, she'd have bet money she could have given this cop the slip. Not now, though. Not with being as weak as she was.

Jade had been in historic homes before. Heck, her

room^{at} The Gentleman's place was nice enough. But part of her couldn't help but be amazed at the structure that was Benedict House.

She didn't know she was being obvious until the policewoman whispered, "Gorgeous, isn't it?"

Jade stiffened. "If you like uppity snooty homes."

The other woman laughed. "It's more than the house that always strikes me. It's the history. Do you know the original house was built here before the Revolutionary War? I mean, I know that's nothing compared to places in Europe, but it's old for America."

"Are you into history?"

"A little. How can you live in Charleston and not be?" She flushed as if she'd revealed something she hadn't planned on and rang the doorbell at a set of massive wooden doors they'd made it to.

Jade thought it must be nice to be able to think about something other than where your next meal was coming from and if you'd be able to find a safe place to sleep that night. She almost told the police officer what she'd been thinking, but before she could, the door was opened by a petite woman she recognized as being involved in the standoff she'd witnessed.

"Good evening, Officer Alyssa," the tiny woman, who must be the housekeeper, said. "Come on in. They're inside the library waiting for you." She looked Jade up and down, and Jade braced herself for a sharp comment or look of disgust, but neither came. Instead she smiled pleasantly. "Will your guest be joining you? Or would she like to wait for you in the kitchen with me? I have some leftover pot roast."

At the mention of pot roast, Jade's stomach growled

loudly. Alyssa looked torn, recognizing perhaps, how hungry Jade was.

Finally, she said, "She can come by the kitchen in a few minutes. She has to speak with Bea first."

The housekeeper nodded and led them down a light and airy hallway. At the end was another set of double doors. She pushed them open and motioned for Jade and Alyssa to walk through.

Alyssa went first and Jade tagged along, expecting to see only Bea, but looked up to find five sets of eyes on her.

Damn. She was screwed.

CHAPTER 6

Bea stood up at the sight of Jade walking in with Alyssa. The young woman looked worse than she had last·time she saw her. Not only that, but she looked downright scared at the moment. Her eyes were big as she took in the vast room and the people in it. Though she had been thin the last time she saw her, she seemed to have lost more weight. Or maybe it was the look of utter exhaustion she had.

"Jade," Bea finally said. "I didn't expect to see you here."

Actually, now that she thought about it, she couldn't think of a reason why Jade would be with a police officer. Bea glanced over to Alyssa and raised her eyebrow.

"She said she was your client," Alyssa said.

"She is," Bea confirmed. "But that doesn't explain why she's here."

"I pulled up and noticed a movement on the side of the house. I walked over to investigate and I saw her, standing and trying to look into a window. She said she was your client so I brought her in here to confirm that."

"Her name is not Jade," Keaton said. "It's Kaja. This is the woman who showed me the secret passage." He reached down to take Tilly's hand. "She helped save you."

"It is?" Alyssa said.

She might have said something else, but Bea wasn't paying any attention. Her focus was on Tilly and her expression of pure shock and anger.

Keaton noticed it at the same time. "Tilly? What is it? You look like you've seen a ghost."

When Tilly finally spoke, her voice was edged with steel. "That's because I don't know her as Bea's client or as the mystery woman who showed you the secret passage. Were you the person who pulled the fire alarm at the homeless shelter?"

Jade didn't hesitate before answering, "Yes."

"Did you know that as a result, a woman was kidnapped and has never been seen since?" Tilly asked, her normally warm voice now icy cold.

Jade's reply was softer this time, but she still answered, "Yes." She looked up and no one could miss the brief flash of fire in her eyes. "Yes, that is all I have to say. I'm not here to explain myself to you. I came to talk to my lawyer."

Kipling stood and walked to stand by Jade and Alyssa. "I'm Kipling Benedict and since you're on my property and in my house, you're going to answer a few questions."

Jade stood poised like a rabbit, ready to run away at the slightest provocation. Kipling obviously sensed it, too.

"I suggest you drop the idea of running away. This will go much better if you answer my questions."

His stare and tone had been known to frighten grown men, but Jade didn't seem to mind the questions. She gave a nod in agreement.

"What's your name?" Kipling started with.

She licked her lips. "Kaja Jade."

"Kaja Jade what?"

"Kaja Jade Mann," she replied, but she had hesitated before saying it.

"I don't believe you," he said.

Jade simply shrugged as if to say *not my problem.*

"What were you doing at the side of my house?"

"I told you, I'm a client of Bea's. I came to see her."

"Why do you need an attorney?" Kipling asked. "And why her?"

"That's enough." Bea stood up and shot Jade a glance. "You don't have to answer anything you don't want to right now."

"The hell she doesn't. She was snooping outside my house and has been in contact with members of my family."

"She's my client and our relationship is privileged," Bea said.

"How long has she been your client?"

Bea refused to confirm one way to the other. Kipling was a smart man, he knew how attorney-client privilege went. She wasn't about to say anything about Jade, how long she'd been her lawyer, or her case. Especially with a Charleston police officer not ten feet away. She crossed her arms and gave him her best icy glare. It always worked in court.

Bea cocked an eyebrow. "Circumstantial."

"Let's not forget," Kipling added, "she admitted that

she was the person who pulled the fire alarm at the shelter that Keaton and Tilly were visiting. An alarm that might have been used to cover up the kidnapping of a woman who has never been found."

Knox jumped up. "Watch it, Kip. What are you inferring about my wife?"

Knox and Kipling stood nearly toe to toe. So far, no one was taking a swing.

Kipling took a deep breath. "I'm only saying, I understand the privileged relationship she has with this girl, and no, maybe she can't tell me everything, but that doesn't mean I have to willingly allow her to stay in my house."

Bea started to say something, but Jade cut her off. "No, he's right. I shouldn't be here, it's not safe for you guys around me. I'll leave. Right now. It's just . . . can I. . . ." She closed her eyes and said in a rush, "Can I stop by the kitchen and eat? I won't stay, but please . . . I'm so hungry."

Her sentence ended in a sob and there were tears running down her cheeks.

Good Lord, how long had it been since she last ate? Bea looked at Alyssa, but the officer appeared as shocked as everyone else.

Bea rushed to Jade's side. "Come on, let's go into the kitchen. We'll find you something to eat." She put her arm around Jade and turned to walk out of the room. Before she left, she shot Knox a look. *Take care of your brother.*

Knox watched as his wife half walked, half carried the thin young woman from the library. He didn't miss the look she shot him as she left. Jade was her client and she'd made her choice to protect her. He wasn't sure that was the smartest thing to do, especially considering everything Kipling had brought up. But while what his brother mentioned made sense, there wasn't anything concrete in what he said.

Or as Bea would say, "Circumstantial evidence and hearsay." Besides, that woman didn't look strong enough to hurt a flea.

"She's homeless and starving," he told his older brother. "Seriously, what did you think was going to happen? She was going to take us all down? Did you even look at her?"

"It's not her I'm necessarily worried about. It's the entourage of violence and attacks that seem to follow her." Kipling looked over to Keaton who was in deep discussion with Tilly. "Didn't you say she was standing outside watching when Elise had the gun on Tilly?"

"She was, but Elise had nothing to do with the clubs or the attacks there and Jade helped me get inside. She wasn't in on it." Keaton frowned. "She looked so different. At that time, she looked like she could kick major ass."

Alyssa stepped forward. "She's been on the streets since then, I'd be willing to bet. That's a hard life."

"I can't believe your Kaja and my Jade are the same person. How is that even possible?" Tilly asked. "When I saw her, she was dressed completely in black and had blue streaks in her hair. You see her as almost a superhero and Bea knows her as a street urchin. I have to say, Knox, I'm going to have to stand with Kip on this one. We don't have a clue who she really is."

"And we won't know unless she decides to tell us," Alyssa said. "Should I leave and come back later to pick up the files you called about?"

"No," Knox said. "No, I'll go get them. I'd meant to bring them in here earlier and got sidetracked. I'll just be a minute."

He left the library and walked to the office he and Bea had taken over with the Brock case. Once inside, he was making sure he had everything when a muffled sob stopped him cold.

He didn't think it was Bea, Jade had been the one crying as they left the library, but he had to make certain. The kitchen was across the hall from the office. As quietly as he could, he tiptoed out into the hall, making sure to avoid the third floorboard from the right of the office because it always creaked when someone stepped on it.

Bea and Jade were sitting in the breakfast nook with their backs to him. Bea must have found the pot roast and, not for the first time, he was glad Lena always made enough to feed an army. From the looks of it, Jade had quite a lot to eat.

At the moment, though, the young woman had her head buried in her hands. Bea set a glass of tea down and put her arm around Jade's bony shoulders.

"I know what it's like to have a difficult relationship with your guardian," Bea said. "Though my situation isn't as complex or as violent as I think yours is, I know that pain."

Jade had stopped crying and was watching her.

"Have you decided what you can tell me?"

Jade shook her head.

Bea smiled. "How about you eat while I talk, okay?"

Jade didn't answer verbally but rather, she picked up her fork and took a huge bite.

"My mother died when I was young. I grew up hearing whispers that she died of a broken heart, that she really didn't love my father and that she was still in love with her first husband who died. I had a half brother, but his time was split between our house and his father's family. Why Mom married the reverend, I've always wondered. If it wasn't for the fact that he's so damn righteous, I'd think she got pregnant before they got married."

Knox thought he heard Jade snort.

Bea continued, "The reverend never made it a secret that he wanted a boy. Unfortunately, since my mother died, he was stuck with me and he never let an opportunity pass that would allow him to tell me that as a female I was lesser than a male. He saw me as weak and unworthy. And I was a horrible disappointment for going to law school. Law isn't an acceptable profession in his mind for a woman. All we're good for is pushing out babies and cooking. I wanted more and didn't see anything wrong with the path I took. I still don't."

Knox's heart ached for his wife. He'd had no idea the circumstances of her childhood. Why had she never told him?

"To this day," Bea said. "I think the only reason I'm who I am today is because of my mother's parents. I stayed with them a lot and one day, when I was ten, I told them I wasn't going back to the reverend's house. He didn't care."

Jade had finished her dinner and was watching Bea.

"I always wondered," Bea mused. "How a man who

had dedicated his life to the One who is known for love, could live with so much hate inside him."

Knox knew his parents hadn't been perfect, but he never doubted their love for each other or their children.

"How old were you when you went to live with your guardian?" Bea asked and it looked like Jade was going to answer when Tom walked in front the entrance near the dining room.

"Just wanted to let you know I was back from dinner," Tom said, and stopped short at the scene before him. Knox was almost certain the guard snarled before schooling his expression.

"I don't remember," Jade said, and he didn't think it was his imagination that she looked paler than before.

"Thanks, Tom," Bea said, and turned to Jade. "That's okay. Let's get you to a bedroom so you can get a good night's sleep. We'll talk in the morning over pancakes."

"But Kipling said . . ."

Bea smiled. "His bark is worse than his bite. Don't worry about him. You need sleep."

He looked down the hallway, he needed to head back to the library before someone came looking for him and gave away the fact that he'd been listening. By the time he heard a chair scrape across the floor in the kitchen, he had already grabbed the files and was on his way down the hall.

"Here's what we have," Knox told Alyssa, handing her the copies he and Bea had made the night before. "Bea attached some notes to a few of the pages. I'm interested to get your take on the matter. I wonder if we're too biased to look at it objectively."

"What's your take on Jade?" Kipling asked.

Knox scratched his head. "I hear what you and Tilly

are saying, but I trust Bea, too. She's a good judge of character and I don't see her taking on a case, especially one that has to be pro bono, if she didn't believe in what she was fighting for."

Kipling raised an eyebrow. "What exactly is she fighting for?"

He gave his brother a smug grin. Bastard thought he had him. "I don't know. She didn't tell me and I didn't ask. Goes back to that trust thing."

"Smooth." Kipling nodded. "Very smooth, bro."

"I think we need to give the poor girl a break," Knox said. "She's been living on the streets and before that she was in a homeless shelter. I think it's safe to say she's not a trained ninja sent to take us out."

"Might want to hold off on that call."

Knox turned to see Bea striding into the library. Alone.

"If she is a trained ninja," Knox said, "I hope to hell you didn't leave her alone in the kitchen. Poor Lena has been through enough lately."

"She's not a ninja," Bea said, walking up to Knox and hooking her arm around his. "And I didn't leave her alone. She's sleeping in one of the guestrooms."

"In this house?" Kipling asked.

"Yes, in this house. Did you think I sent her to the neighbors?" Bea put her free hand on her hip as if daring him to say something. "She was so tired, she was falling asleep while eating. Since she's been on the streets, she's only allowed herself to sleep in one spot for two or three hours. I'm surprised she was still functioning the way she's been living."

"Why is that?" Knox asked.

"You and I aren't the only ones with someone after

us," Bea said. "I'm working on getting a place for her to stay."

Neither one of them moved or said anything else. It was Alyssa who finally broke the silence. "I'll be on my way," she said. "I'll let you know what we find, one way or another."

CHAPTER 7

"How long do you think she'll sleep?" Knox asked Bea as they went through more files.

Bea checked her watch. So far she'd been out at least four hours. "I really don't know. With her stomach full and knowing she's safe? I wouldn't be shocked if she slept until sometime tomorrow afternoon."

He put down the paper he was reading. "Earlier, you told Kip you were working on a place for her to stay?"

"I was thinking about letting her use Brent's house. I mean he's not going to be using it anytime soon." Not only that, but Brent had a top-of-the-line security system in place.

"Seriously?"

"What?"

"You're going to let a near perfect stranger, whose past is shady at best, criminal at worst, stay in your brother's restored multimillion dollar historical home?"

"Now you're starting to sound like your brother." Anger and grief both raged through her body. It was a very peculiar feeling to say the least, especially when paired with the kinship she felt toward Jade. "I thought you would understand. You know, since you're the so-called saint."

Knox looked away and sighed. She knew it had been a low blow. Knox didn't like that nickname, given to him by the local newspapers because he was the Benedict brother who was never caught at nightclubs at all hours of the night or who sported a new girlfriend every other day.

"I'm sorry," she said. "I shouldn't have said that."

He nodded.

"It's just . . . I look at her and I see her pain." She knew she wouldn't be able to explain it the right way or to convey to him exactly how she felt. "Her biological parents are both dead and she's been living with a guardian who's involved in criminal affairs. She hasn't told me what yet. She said she could provide evidence to use against him, but I have to work a deal so she's pardoned. As you can probably imagine, that's hard to do when I don't know who her guardian is or what crimes he's committed."

"You're trying to gain her trust," he said.

He was finally getting it. "Yes, that's part of it. But she's all alone and I feel that. I lived that. Not to the extreme like she has. I was never out on the streets. But I know what it's like to feel as if it's you against the world."

"I told Kip I trusted you and here I am second-guessing you. I'm the one who should be apologizing, not you."

"I'll take full responsibility for her actions. That's how much I trust her."

He gently stroked her cheek. "Then that's good

enough for me and you won't hear another word from me questioning you."

"It's okay to question me," she said. "If I'm ever doing anything you don't understand, I want you to question me. Just don't shut me out. I hate that."

Knox framed her face with his hands and she saw the truth in his eyes when he whispered, "Never," and then sealed his promise with a kiss. Her heart was still light as she watched him walk to the desk and sat down.

She remembered how her father had shut her out. He'd never talk, he'd turn almost statue-like. So much so that it felt like she was talking to a stone. She was never sure which she hated more: his silence or his words that only told of how much life would be better if she'd only been a boy.

Somewhere in the back of her mind, she took note of the fact that her father still hadn't called about the house. She had called him again, and again got his voice mail. Worry that something was horribly wrong began to work its way into her thoughts.

Knox must have sensed her melancholy, because he got up from the desk he was working and silently crossed the room to her. He held out his hand and she allowed herself to be pulled up and into his embrace.

For several long minutes, he just held her. She blinked back tears because he felt so good and strong and she was positive he could shield her from anything.

He softly stroked her hair and his voice was rough when he whispered, "I will never shut you out. Ever. If you want to talk, I'll listen. If you just want me to hold you, I'll hold you. I could never be a stone around you, Bea. How could I when it's you who makes me feel alive?"

He made her feel alive, too. More than that, he made life feel alive. She almost giggled at how silly that sounded, but it was all true. She pulled back and looked in his solid and trustworthy gaze. "I love you, Knox Benedict."

He planted a chaste kiss on her lips. "And I love you, Beatrice Benedict."

She laughed and punched him in the chest. "Don't ever call me Beatrice. I hate that name."

His eyes danced with mischief. "I think it has a nice ring to it. 'Please rise for the Honorable Beatrice Benedict.'"

"I don't want to be a judge, I'm not even sure I want to run for Congress anymore." It was the first time she'd said it out loud and, she had to admit, it felt good.

"You're not?" Knox asked.

"I'm beginning to think I could get more done working with Keaton and Tilly. Think about how the three of us could help Jade. It makes more sense than trying to do something in Washington."

He answered her with a kiss. One that was most definitely not chaste. Bea moaned and stepped further into his embrace. She wanted his hands on her again. Like the night before, she wanted to feel him above her, and under her, and in her. She wanted him to remind her that they were both alive and in love.

But as much as she wanted, she knew nothing of the sort would happen in an open office on the first floor of the family home he shared with two other brothers, an almost sister-in-law, and a sleeping young woman filled with equal parts secrets and danger. He pulled back and groaned.

"I haven't kissed you enough today," he said.

"It's been a busy day."

"It should never be that busy."

"How true." She gave him quick kiss. "I'm going to call Brent. Want me to tell him we're coming for a visit?"

"Yes. Ask if Friday afternoon is good."

"Please." She waved her hand. "I'm not asking anything. I'll him we'll see him Friday."

tell

Knox watched his wife as she prepared for bed a short time later. He wasn't sure what it was that made a woman going through her nighttime rituals so hot.

She was brushing her hair and caught him staring. She met his gaze the mirror, gave him a sultry smile, and kept brushing. He stood and made his way slowly to her, never once breaking eye contact.

He stood behind her and reached for the hairbrush, which she put wordlessly in his hand. She closed her eyes as he resumed brushing her hair. Its color had always fascinated him. To call it red would be too simplistic because dozens of colors glimmered under the light. And he wasn't sure how exactly she got it to be so soft, but he loved dragging his fingers through it.

He placed the brush down and gently slid the fingers of both hands into her hair and began to massage her scalp. He'd discovered early in their relationship that she simply adored having her scalp massaged. Such an easy thing to bring her pleasure.

Under his hands, he felt the remaining tension leave her body and within seconds, she made appreciative groans deep in her throat. Still, he kept his fingers moving, willing any stress or concern out of her body. At least for tonight.

He stopped before he relaxed her so much, she fell asleep. He'd made that mistake before. On their third date, they'd gone boating. When they returned to the dock, her hair was all tangled and the way she brushed it made him flinch. He'd finally taken the brush from her and told her to let him do it so she'd have some hair left.

He recalled her soft sighs of pleasure and he'd been thrilled she reacted so strongly to his touch. He'd finished and looked forward to finding out if other parts of her body reacted the same way. But as soon as he put the brush down, he'd heard her soft snores.

He smiled at the memory and brushed her hair over her right shoulder, exposing her neck to him. He bent down and whispered against her skin, "Feel good?"

Her eyes didn't open and her voice was a bit hoarse when she replied, "So good."

She wore a silver gown with tiny straps and he couldn't resist the urge to tug one down and kiss the top of her shoulder.

She hummed in appreciation and he kissed his way across her back, delighting in how her skin pebbled up as he did so.

"Still good?" he asked.

Her reply was a lazy nod.

"Open your eyes," he said.

This time the eyes that met his were dark with lust and need. He placed a hand on either of her shoulders. "I want you. I want to have you in that bed under me. Right now. But I know it's been a long day, so if you don't want the same thing, tell me."

She rose to her feet with the elegance of a queen and turned to face him. With slow, teasing moves, she lowered the gown strap he hadn't touched and in one smooth move, whipped the gown over her head and let it flutter to the floor. She took his breath away. She wore nothing under the gown. Just Bea. Pure glorious, Bea.

"God, you're beautiful," he said.

She was unashamed before him, but then again, it had always been that way between them. They were two parts to a better, more complete whole and as such, embarrassment had no foothold.

She turned again, this time to walk toward the bed, looking over her shoulder only once to ensure he was following.

Like he'd go anywhere else.

She climbed onto the bed and rose to her knees and when he stood before her, she slipped her hands under his shirt and pulled it over his head. With both hands, she palmed his chest, but when she reached for his waistband, he stopped her.

"Not yet," he said.

"Not yet?" She cocked an eyebrow at him.

"I wanted tonight to be about you." His heart still ached from what he overheard her telling Jade. He couldn't fix that, but he could give her this.

"In that case, what I want is to take your pants off."

He batted her hands away again. "That's not what I meant."

"Just one little kiss?" She licked her lips. "Please?"

Damn, like there was any man alive who could turn that down. "You're impossible . . . have I told you that before?"

"Only on days that end in *y*." She reached again for his waistband and this time, he didn't stop her.

He closed his eyes and sucked in a breath as she

lowered his pants and set him free. She ran her hands up his thighs and he cracked one eye open, only to see her licking her lips again.

"Jesus, Bea," he croaked out.

"Just one kiss, right?" she said.

He nodded.

"Okay, then I pick a French kiss."

Before he could say anything, she pulled him toward her and took his entire cock inside her mouth, swirling her tongue around his length.

"Holy mother of God." He grabbed onto her hair, afraid he'd fall otherwise.

She pulled back, a deliciously satisfied grin on her face. "There you go. One little kiss."

"You, Mrs. Benedict, are evil."

"In that case, I'll never do it again." She moved on the bed, onto her back in the middle.

"Well," he said, coming to rest beside her. "I don't know if I'd go that far."

She twirled a piece of his hair around her finger. "No?"

"Not at all. In fact, I liked it so much, I think it's only fair I repay you. With one exception."

She parted her legs as he moved to slide between them. "Oh?"

"Yes." He grabbed her hips so she couldn't move. "I'm not stopping at one kiss."

"Cheater!"

He chuckled. "How is that cheating? I never said I was only going to give one kiss. If I recall, my exact words were, 'I want tonight to be about you.'"

He was pleased to see she didn't try to argue with him, instead deciding to fist her hands into the sheets.

"That's more like it," he said.

But before he could even pay her back a little, a high-pitched siren wailed from somewhere inside the house, causing them both to jump up.

He felt Bea tense and tremble. He pulled her close and murmured, "Stay with me, Bea. I've got you."

She gave her head a slight shake and whispered, "What is that?"

"Security alarm. I remember the noise from when they were testing the damn thing."

Bea froze and went deathly pale again. "Someone broke in?"

He cursed at himself for not thinking before he answered. "It means something tripped the alarm. But I promise you this, no one is going to hurt you." He gave her a gentle kiss, pleased to see her tremors had stopped. "I do suggest getting dressed, though. I'm sure the police will be here soon."

They dressed without speaking, both letting out a sigh of relief when the siren stopped. Even then, his ears still rang. He kept a close eye on Bea, while trying to act like he wasn't doing so. She'd regained some of her color back, but she was trembling every so often.

Footsteps down the hall alerted them to the fact that the house's other inhabitants were up and about. He stood at the door and waited for Bea, unwilling and unable to let her out of his sight for any length of time.

She walked to him and he hated the look of defeat he saw in her expression. He pulled her close to his chest. "Nothing and I mean nothing is going to hurt you. Especially here. Not on my watch."

She pulled back and ran her thumb over his cheekbone. "Oh, Knox. You silly man. You think I'm worried about me?"

He just looked at her.

"I'm worried they're coming after you."

He held her tighter. "God, Bea. I love you so much. I swear nothing's going to get to me, hurt me, or take me away from you. I'd like to see them try."

She gave a deep restorative sigh and nodded. "Let's go see what's happening." It was such a change from how she'd been directly following the attack. His feelings were torn. Part of him was humbled that she wanted to protect him so much, but mostly he was angry at the assholes who put her in such a position. Though he had to admit, it made him feel better to know that she trusted in his ability to keep her safe than she did in the assholes' ability to harm them.

They walked together to the large office on the first floor where the security hub was located. Keaton and Tilly stood nearby, watching and listening to Kipling talk on the phone.

His back was to them. "Yes, you can cancel the police. Correct, no need to have them come by." He hung up the phone and looked directly at Bea. His look was so pissed, Knox felt as if he should jump between his wife and his brother.

Knox took a step forward.

Kipling held up his hand. "Stand down, Knox."

"What's the look at Bea for, then?" he asked, not ready to stand down just yet.

"According to the monitoring center, the alarm was tripped from the inside," Kipling explained. "Where's that damn security guard? Any other time, he'd be breathing down our necks."

"What?" Knox asked. "How?"

"The secret passage we had fitted with an alarm after what happened to Tilly." Kipling looked around. "I think only one other person outside the family knows about that passage. Where is she?"

"Probably scared to death of seeing you and getting the third degree again." Bea looked just as furious as Kipling. "And if she tripped the alarm, I'm sure she had good reasons."

"Yeah," Tilly said. "Just like she had good reasons at the homeless shelter."

"You have to admit, Bea," Keaton chimed in. "It's starting to sound a bit off."

"*Starting* to? A *bit* off?" Kipling shook his head and motioned for Bea. "Go get your *client* and bring her here."

"She's gone," Tom said, breathing heavy as he entered the office. He looked a mess, shirt untucked and tie askew.

"What do you mean gone?" Bea asked.

"I was walking through the house, making sure everything was locked up, before I turned in for the night. I decided to make sure that office with the papers you've been going through was secure. I stepped into the hallway and saw her coming out. I told her to stop, but instead of listening, she takes off running. She was too fast and had too much of a head start. I couldn't catch her."

Only silence met his statement.

"You couldn't catch her?" Kipling voiced the question they all had. Or at least Knox knew he had the same question. "Are you that incompetent? Seriously, she looks malnourished and can't weigh over ninety pounds. Earlier, she was so exhausted, she was practically asleep standing."

"Beg your pardon, sir," Tom said. "She's a snake, that one."

Knox couldn't help but notice that while his words and tone were calm and even, Tom's eyes held nothing but rage.

"Also," Tom continued. "I know her. I worked in the public school system a few years ago and she was expelled for stealing. Bad apple, that one. It's my recommendation that you not let her in the house again or at least let me handle it if she shows back up."

"Told you," Tilly said with a self-satisfied nod of her head.

"Thank you," Kipling said with a sigh. "Hopefully, that's all the excitement for one night. I propose we all go back to bed."

Bea had a strange look on her face, but she took the hand Knox offered and followed him up the stairs.

He knew something was wrong the minute they stepped into the bedroom. It took only a second for him to realize it was the breeze coming through the window, which he thought was strange since they hadn't opened it. It wasn't until Bea ran to the middle of the room and picked up a rock, that he realized someone had busted the window.

"I'd like for Kipling to try and explain how Jade did this." She dropped the rock immediately and shook her hand. "Ow! It cut me!"

She held her hand up and he saw her palm was covered in red. He could see the shock and panic start to settle in her eyes and he knew he had to do something.

"Come to the bathroom." He took her hand and led

her to the connecting bathroom. He turned the water on and started washing her hands. "It's actually quite juvenile if you think about it. Throwing a rock through the window? Seriously, are they going to toilet-paper the house next?"

But Bea wasn't laughing. "They did it to let us know they're watching and they know exactly where we are. You shouldn't look at this like it was something done by a person who lacks sophistication."

"I should report it."

"Not tonight," Bea all but begged. "Please not tonight. I can't handle one more thing."

He didn't think that was the smartest thing to do. If there were evidence, the police needed to go ahead and get busy on following leads. But he suspected Bea was almost at her breaking point, and he didn't have to heart to subject her to another round of police questions tonight.

Against his better judgement, he left her in the bathroom to clean up while he tidied up the room as best he could. He hung a sheet over the window, figuring it was better than nothing and by the time Bea came out of the bathroom, the bedroom was as neat and glass-free as he could make it.

He settled Bea in his lap on the bed. They were both too wound up to sleep, but neither one of them was in the mood to pick up where they left off when the alarm sounded.

"I know we're playing into their hands, but I just can't tonight." She pulled back to look at him. "I mean, at least Tom's here, right? Just because he couldn't keep Jade from leaving doesn't mean he can't protect us?"

"I wouldn't have him here if I didn't think he could."

After a while her body relaxed. He kissed her forehead.

"I was thinking," he said. "What do you think about heading to DC earlier than Friday? We can get a hotel if it's too soon for Brent and Janie and they're not ready for us."

She pulled back. "I'd like that, but are you okay spending even more time with Brent?"

"Yes, of course. I think we just got off on the wrong foot. We need to tell him we're married, too. It's only fair since my family knows. Yours should know, too."

Except for her dickwad father who still hadn't called.

She yawned. Maybe now, she'd be able to get some sleep.

"Sounds good," she muttered, eyelids drooping.

"Go to sleep," he whispered. "I'm here and I'll keep you safe."

Jade stood in the shadows, watching as the lights went back out in the massive house. Holy shit, she'd just about peed her pants when the alarm went off as she let herself out of the secret passage.

She'd hated to leave without saying good-bye, but she had no choice with Tom nearby. She shivered at the memory of being so close to him. Bea hadn't seen it, but Jade saw the murderous look he had when he recognized her.

She wished the Benedicts had liked her. Then maybe she could have been honest about Tom. Of course, she was used to people not liking her. She expected people not to like her. And Kipling made no secret as to what he thought of her.

She'd thought Keaton might be different. He'd

seemed friendly enough to begin with. But he'd probably heard an earful from his girlfriend. Not that Jade
could fault Tilly. The woman had every right to dislike
and not trust her.

Then there was Knox. She had a feeling he only put
up with her and stood up for her because he didn't want
to piss off his wife. If it wasn't for Bea, she had a feeling he'd act the exact same as Kipling.

She didn't know what she'd been thinking coming
in the first place. It had been a bad idea from the get-go.
Though the food had been really good. She rubbed her
stomach. If she closed her eyes, she could still remember the heady scent of the pot roast.

As she'd waited for the house to go to sleep, she realized she still hadn't told Bea about The Gentleman.
She'd wanted to hold off until Bea was certain she
could work out a deal to pardon her. And that had left
Jade in a quandary.

She thought about the clue she'd ended up leaving.
Please let Bea find it or anyone other than Tom. With
a heavy heart, she said good-bye to the Benedict house,
turned, and walked away.

CHAPTER 8

Bea woke up in Knox's arms. She felt achy. It was entirely possible she hadn't moved at all since she went to sleep, but she was loath to move out of the comfort of Knox's embrace.

"Good morning," Knox said.

She smiled and lifted her head, but her smile died on her lips when she saw the dark circles under his eyes. "Good morning. Did you sleep at all?"

"I don't think so," he said. "I may have dozed a time or two."

"I'm sorry, was it because I was in your lap?"

"No." He kissed her forehead. "No, not at all. I was just thinking."

"You're going to be tired later today."

"I'm going to work from home."

Work. Ugh. She needed to call her boss. Actually, she decided, what she really needed was to take a leave of absence. At least until this threat was dealt with. Even then, she might not go back, especially if she decided to work with Keaton and Tilly.

Any major decision, though, needed to wait until after breakfast. She wasn't going to commit to anything until she had a full stomach.

"What time is it?" she asked.

"Just after eight thirty. Ready for some breakfast?"

Her stomach rumbled an answer and they both laughed.

"I'll take that as a yes," he said with a smile.

They dressed quickly. Bea purposely kept her eyes from the covered window and the red stain Knox hadn't quite been able to get out last night. She'd let Knox and Kipling deal with that.

They ate in silence for a few minutes, each of them thinking their own thoughts. The house seemed too quiet to Bea and too big. Suddenly, she was glad Knox had booked tickets to DC for later in the day. She wanted nothing more than to get away from Charleston, if only for a few days. Surely if she stayed in town, she'd go crazy. Plus, she wanted to talk to her brother and Janie. They'd had their own issues similar to what she was going through.

It wasn't until she was at the airport that she found the handwritten note stuffed inside her purse. And she didn't have chance to read it until they were seated and waiting for takeoff.

Bea,
I'm sorry I had to take off without saying good-bye. Maybe one day, I'll be able to explain. I really hope I can. If not, thank you for being so kind to me. If I ever had a sister, I'd want her to be like you.

Please be careful around Tom. Watch him. He's not what he seems. If I know him, I'm sure he'll make up some lies about me. Believe them if you want. Heaven knows I'm no saint. But no matter what, if you discard everything else I say, believe me about him. Also, you may want to put those boxes you and Knox have been going through where he can't find them.

Just saying.

My name is Kaja Jade, but Mann isn't my last name. I'm sorry I can't give it to you yet, but if I have any hope of surviving, I have to go where no one knows me from Adam.

As you have probably guessed, my guardian is no gentleman. My mother died before I was five and he took me in. I don't remember much about my mother, but I remember she loved me and she could sing like an angel.

All my best,
Jade

She passed it silently to Knox and blinked back the tears that filled her eyes unbidden.

Brent and Janie waited for them inside the airport terminal. Though she knew she'd missed her brother, it wasn't until he took her in his arms and softly whispered, "What can we do to help?" that she truly realized how much she'd missed not having him in the same city.

She pulled back only to find that Janie had tears in her eyes as well. Bea gave her almost sister-in-law a hug and introduced her to Knox. Knox greeted her warmly and Bea watched to see how her brother would act toward him.

Brent had not been happy when he learned that she was dating a Benedict. Of course, by the time he'd found out, they were days away from getting married. She'd told Brent a thing or two that day.

But now, Brent shook Knox's hand, patted him on the shoulder, and welcomed him to Washington. It was more than Bea had hoped for and she couldn't help but think his relationship with Janie had changed him for the better.

Not that Brent had been in bad shape before he found the love of his life. Not in the least. He'd always been one of the good guys. He'd just had a very clear idea of the type of man who he wanted to date his only sister. Unfortunately, Knox, with his family's reputation of wealthy playboys, hadn't fit into his idea of a suitable mate.

"We're glad you guys are here," Brent said, leading them outside to the waiting car. They all piled in and Bea sat back for the traffic-filled drive to Brent and Janie's penthouse. By silent agreement, they kept the conversation light. There would be enough time in the days to come to discuss the more unpleasant topics. For tonight, they would all just enjoy each other's company.

"Probably should have taken the Metro," Brent admitted after he dodged the third reckless cab.

Bea didn't want to say, but she didn't think she'd feel comfortable in the Metro. She couldn't help but think about being in an enclosed subway while the faceless man who haunted her dreams slowly approached. She shivered just thinking about it. No thank you. She'd deal with traffic.

She resisted the urge to look over her shoulder, telling herself there was no way they were being followed. No one other than the Benedicts even knew they had left for DC today. She cringed. If you didn't count the pilot and the airport staff . . .

She made herself stop, knowing she'd go crazy if she thought about it too much.

"Hey." Knox reached out and placed a hand on her knee. "What's going through that beautiful head of yours that made you frown all of a sudden?"

"We're safe here, right?" she asked quietly, not wanting Brent and Janie to hear. "I mean, no one knows we're here, followed us on the plane or anything?"

He frowned and picked up her hand. "I won't lie to you. I respect you too much for that. Is it possible? Yes, of course. Do I think it's probable? No."

She swallowed the fear at his admittance that it was possible. He'd told her the truth and that was what she wanted. Not a lie that would give her a false sense of security.

"And let me tell you this," he said, leaning close so his breath tickled her skin. "I know of three people in this car alone who would move heaven and earth to keep you safe. And I, for one, would go up against the devil himself to ensure you stay that way."

She lifted her head for a kiss.

"Hey," her brother said from the front seat. "This is a government car. Knock that out."

Janie snorted. "You're a fine one to talk."

Brent winked at her.

Twenty minutes later, they walked into the penthouse Brent and Janie called home. Bea had been afraid it'd be too contemporary for her taste; she knew from helping Brent decorate his home in Charleston how much he liked traditional decor. But she was pleasantly surprised when they stepped into the sleek modern space how well the decorator had managed to blend the rich antiques in and make it all work.

"Thanks," he said when she told him that. "I'd love to take credit for it, but it was all Janie." He pulled her close and whispered something in her ear that had her blushing and pushing him away.

"You did a great job," Knox said.

"Thanks." Janie's face had regained its normal color. "I enjoy decorating, but it's just a hobby."

"Well, if you ever decide to give up police work, I'd be willing to bet you could turn it into a second career. You're really good," Bea said in agreement with her husband.

"Come on," Brent said. "Let me show you around the place."

Knox and Bea followed Brent for a quick tour, while Janie disappeared into the kitchen. They ended the tour in the guest bedroom they would be staying in.

Brent had already placed their bags in the room earlier and after he showed them the bedroom, he got a knowing grin on his face.

"I didn't tell you earlier," Brent said. "But Janie and I have a dinner to go to tonight. It's for work, so I really can't get out of it. And I'd invite you to go, but it'll be boring as hell and I don't want to put you through that."

"You're not going to be here?" Bea asked. "Our first night in DC?"

"I'm afraid not," Brent said. "I'll leave the car in case

you want to go out. However, I think you're going to probably prefer to stay in. Am I right?"

He slid his hands into his pockets, and rocked back on his heels. It only took one look at him for her to see what he was doing. Sure, he probably had a work dinner, but she bet he could get out of it if he wanted to. No, what he was doing was giving her and Knox some time to be alone.

She looked to the side and caught Knox's eye. He winked. Bea would be willing to bet he knew what was happening as well.

"Yes, I think we will stay in," she said, receiving a confirmation nod from Knox.

"I believe Janie has put something together for you for dinner tonight. All you'll have to do is reheat it." He looked at his watch and then back at them. "I need to get ready, you two make yourself comfortable."

He closed the door on his way out. When she heard his footsteps echo in the hall, she turned to Knox. "Did what I think just happen really happen?"

"You mean that your brother all but told us to have wild monkey sex since he and Janie would be out of the penthouse?"

"I wasn't going with those exact words, but yes." Although now that he'd used those words, the image of her and Knox hanging from a chandelier wouldn't leave her mind.

The thing was, as much as she wanted to hop into bed with Knox, she was counting down the seconds until they could talk about Jade's note and Tom.

They walked out to the hallway, and ran into Janie. She was all smiles as she pointed toward the kitchen.

"I made lasagna, all you have to do is reheat. There's some salad stuff in refrigerator and bread on the countertop. We will be back late. Probably after midnight."

With that, Janie took off toward the bedroom and moments later, she left with Brent. Bea turned to Knox expectantly and he held out his hand.

"Tell me," he said. "What have you figured out?"

She took his hand, pleading with her eyes for him to believe her. "Jade isn't the enemy everyone thinks she is and I'm pretty sure Tom was lying in the office earlier."

CHAPTER 9

Knox didn't look as surprised as she thought he would. "What makes you think he was lying?"

"His body language. The way he stood and the way his eyes shifted. I see it all the time in court."

"Why would Tom lie about that?"

She cringed. "That's the part I'm trying to figure out. And when you add in that letter from Jade . . ."

"You believe Jade."

He spoke it as fact and with no judgement in his voice. She nodded. She did believe Jade. She knew most people wouldn't, but she did. She told herself she wasn't being played by a sob story. She could always see through those. No, something in her gut told her that Jade was trustworthy.

She took Knox's hand. "I do. I can't fully explain why, but I do."

He placed his other hand on top of hers. "Then I do, too."

* * *

The next day, she was still basking in the fact that Knox sided with her about Jade. It felt so good to have that support.

"So tell me," Janie asked while they were all eating lunch. "How you two met."

They were in the penthouse's dining room. Bea had been admiring the view from the huge floor-to-ceiling windows that overlooked the city. She looked up at Janie in surprise. "What?"

"Come on," Janie said. "I love to hear how-we-met stories. I don't know yours."

Bea looked over to Brent, he just shrugged. "I don't know how you met, either," he said.

Bea gave Knox a smile. "I had a client who brought suit against Benedict Industries."

Janie looked at her with wide eyes. Brent actually dropped his fork.

"What?" her brother asked.

"It's true," Knox said, obviously enjoying the shocked faces. "She walked into the board room that day and I almost forgot my name."

"You did not." Bea rolled her eyes. "I remember you being almost a complete jerk."

"That was a defense mechanism."

"It was a good one. Almost too good."

Knox made her laugh by winking at her. "I had it all under control."

Brent chuckled. "You're right," he said to Janie. "Hearing how-we-met stories is kind of fun."

"See?" Janie said. She took a bite of her salad and swallowed before talking again. "What happened next? Obviously, you guys somehow met up again."

"Actually, it kind of was like fate," Bea admitted. "The next couple weeks we kept running into each other. The first time it was at a coffee shop, I was walking in as he was walking out. That time, he just lifted his cup, saluted, and walked out the door."

"Just for the record," Knox added. "I had a meeting starting less than fifteen minutes that day. If I didn't have anything planned, I would've stayed and talked."

"Or so he says," Janie said.

"Right?" Bea asked. "I didn't believe that the first time he told me, either."

"I mean, if he didn't so much as say hello when he was sitting right next to you, why would you think he'd speak at a coffee shop?" Janie turned to Knox. "Where did you see each other next?"

"It was at that little art gallery," he said and Bea finished with, "The one closest to Benedict House."

"I know that one," Janie said.

"And then—" Knox tried to take over, but Bea wasn't going to let him skip over the art gallery.

"I was looking at a landscape and suddenly I looked to my side and Knox was there. He said something like, he felt that if he didn't ask if he could get me a drink, the Fates would sigh, shake their heads, and give up. He said he couldn't stand the thought of not seeing me, so he had to do it correctly this time."

"Oh my God." Janie lifted her hand to her chest. "That is so romantic. So you let him get you a drink?"

"No," Bea said. "Because right at that moment, my date came up with a drink for me."

Brent whistled. "Brutal, man."

"Had he heard you?" Janie asked.

"Yes, he had," Bea said, because she knew Knox

wouldn't offer that information. "And while he was none too pleased, I thought it was romantic, too." She gave her husband a smile before continuing. "By that time I knew who he was. So while I couldn't leave my date—"

"Yeah, you could have," Knox said.

"But, the next afternoon, I went by his office, his brothers weren't in. I made sure before I went inside. I told the admin I was an attorney and had to speak to him urgently. She sent me right to his office, no questions asked."

"When I looked up and saw Bea standing there," Knox said. "My first instinct was to fire that admin."

Bea reached over and took his hand. "But he changed his mind when I asked him if I could buy him a drink."

"And I told her, there was no way I was letting her buy the drinks." He lifted her hand to his mouth and gave it a kiss. "Three weeks later, I asked her to marry me."

"That fast?" Brent asked and then, not waiting for either of them to answer, asked Bea, "So, that day I stopped by your office and you two were inside with the door closed. . . ."

"Yes," Bea confirmed. "Already married."

"Damn," Brent said.

"I didn't see any reason not to propose," Knox said. "I mean, you find what you want, you go for it, and when you get it, you don't let go, right?"

"Makes sense to me." Brent leaned back in his chair, all the while looking at his fiancée with knowing eyes. "Janie and I weren't quite that quick, but we weren't far behind you, either."

"What was it about my brother that first caught your attention?" Bea asked. She knew they had met in a bar where Janie was working undercover, but not very many of the details.

Janie's eyes danced with delight. "For sure it was the way he chased off the drunk who was hitting on me with just a few words and a lifted eyebrow."

"Smooth," Knox said.

"And we were pretty much together from that day on," Brent said.

"He keeps saying he's going to take me to Greece," Janie said.

"As soon as you marry me."

Janie twisted her ring. "We do need to set a date, don't we?"

"We? Woman, I told you to tell me when and where and I'd show up."

"Next May," Janie said.

"Really?" Brent sat up.

"Really." Janie looked to Bea. "Could I bother you to come back to DC to help me look for dresses in a month or two?"

"Of course. And you have to know it won't be a bother at all."

"The one thing I still don't get, though," Brent said, looking to Knox, "is why the secrecy? Why didn't you tell anyone you were married?"

"That was me," Bea confessed.

"Why?" Janie asked.

"It was my dad." She closed her eyes briefly at the thought of her father and told herself she was not going to cry. "He absolutely hated that I became a lawyer.

And when I told him I was going to run for Congress, he almost shut me out. I knew if I told him I married a Benedict, he'd ruin me."

"He would do that?" Janie asked.

"And not think twice about it," Brent added. "I'm sorry Bea. I wish I had known."

Bea shrugged. "Like I said, it seems so petty now. Especially in light of everything that's been happening."

She knew Brent and Janie understood. It hadn't been that long ago that they had been through their own personal hell. It was, however, comforting to see that they had come through it, not only safe, but also stronger. And, from all appearances, more in love than ever.

"Going through something like that," Brent said, "like what you're going through now, certainly does put things into perspective."

"I hate that you're going through this," Janie said. "I remember all too well what it was like and I don't wish that on my worst enemy."

Brent grew serious. "It goes without saying, but I'll say it anyway. If there's anything at all we can do. Anything at all. Let us know."

She didn't miss the way he looked at Janie. Bea remembered the fear he had when she'd been kidnapped. He had been beyond devastated, not sure he would ever see her again. And even then, had said he wasn't sure how he could live without her.

She hated that her and Knox's current circumstances brought back those scary feelings back to the couple. She also knew, they were happy to provide support for them. It was a situation that not many people could understand, not having lived through it themselves.

"That's enough about that," Janie said. "Tell me

about your wedding. Where did you get married and all that fun stuff."

This, she could talk about. She smiled, remembering that weekend. Looking over to Knox, and seeing his smile, she could tell he remembered it well, too. Though she mostly remembered tangled sheets and long kisses filled with passion, those weren't the memories she was going to share.

"You're going to laugh," she said.

Janie smiled. "Excellent, we all need to laugh."

"Knox flew me to Vegas."

Janie put her wineglass down. "Shut up."

"I did," Knox said. "In the honeymoon suite and everything."

"It was fun," Bea said. "One of the wildest and craziest things I've ever done."

"It's good for you to do wild and crazy things," Brent said. "You haven't done enough of those."

It was true. In her life, first being sheltered so much by her parents and then as she got older, being so dedicated to school and then law school, she had no time for wild and crazy. Then a smooth-talking, good-looking man from a family with a reputation for being a bunch of playboys swept her off her feet. She could honestly say life had not been boring for a second after that.

She looked at Knox in gratitude. "Falling in love with Knox was definitely the coolest thing I'd ever done."

CHAPTER 10

The Gentleman was getting restless. He got up from the bed, pulled on his pants and shirt and looked at the stupid bitch who was still in his bed. He shoved her. "Get out."

That's what he got for bringing them into his room. If he'd just gone to her room like he normally did, he could just leave and not have to deal with the aftermath. But when the urge hit him, he didn't feel like going to her place, so he'd had Louis fetch her and bring her to him.

Louis, that was a loyal employee. Nothing like that worthless Jade. Of course, it helped that he paid for Louis's daughter's very expensive medical bills. Power. That's what it was. He had power over Louis, therefore the man would do whatever he asked.

That had been his mistake with Jade. He'd treated her like a daughter. He'd given her everything and she'd repaid him by leaving. He'd been soft when it came to Jade. He'd never make that mistake again.

He picked the phone by the bed up and punched two numbers.

"Hello, sir," Louis said. "How can I assist you?"

"I need my bed cleared and sheets changed."

"Yes, sir. Shall I take the woman back to her place?"

"Yes, and she's refusing to get out of bed. Why don't you and your friends have fun with her once you drop her off."

The naked woman scampered out of bed so fast, she tripped and fell to the ground with a sob.

"Thank you, sir."

The Gentleman hung up. "Too late. You should have listened the first time. I'm not even sure I want you after Louis and his friends have had you. I'll probably let them keep you."

She just looked at him with those wet, red eyes. She couldn't talk because he'd gagged her, but she was making noises behind the cloth in her mouth. He reached down and grabbed her hair.

"That is assuming they still want you when they finish. If they don't, I have a few gator friends who love worthless whores. If you don't want to meet them, I suggest you show Louis and his friends a good time."

He chuckled and shoved her down. Louis could be a mean SOB, he'd seen him in action. The piece of trash at his feet likely wouldn't live past tonight. That was okay, The Gentleman was bored of her. He needed someone with more spunk, more fight, more passion.

He knew just who he wanted.

He left the bedroom and went into his office to boot up his computer. The camera he'd installed at her place hadn't been triggered in weeks. She thought she was safe since she took up with the Benedicts. The truth was, she'd only made the game more interesting.

He picked up his phone and called Tom.

"Hello, sir," he said, answering on the first ring.

"Status," The Gentleman replied.

"The happy couple has left DC, sir, on a private jet. Flight plan has it arriving in Charleston within the hour."

"They're back earlier than I'd been told they would." That pissed him off. Tom had told him they were going to be in DC through the weekend. He'd planned to have Tom drop off a special gift to be waiting upon their return. Now he couldn't have it in place.

"It was a last-minute decision, sir," Tom sounded stressed. Good. "They only decided this morning."

He looked at his watch. "And why am I only finding out about it now? When I call you?" He felt his blood pound through his veins. He was so tired of incompetence. "Do I need to make an example out of you?"

He'd already roughed Tom up for Jade's last mistake before she took off and he'd had to make sure the others knew that type of behavior would not be accepted.

"No, sir," Tom said. "You don't have to do that."

"And why not?" It might be good to hear the man beg.

"I didn't call you because I was following up on an important tip."

He was trying to bargain. That was cute. It wouldn't work, but he wouldn't let on to that just yet. "What tip would be so important, it took precedence over telling me about Bea's movements?"

"I think I know where Jade is."

The Gentleman stood speechless. He tightened his grip on the phone.

"Tell me," he finally managed to croak out.

Bea laid her head on Knox's shoulder as the car pulled up to Benedict House. "Part of me wishes we could have stayed in Washington. Being home is a constant reminder that someone out there wants me gone."

Knox squeezed her knee as the car came to a stop. "No matter what, we're in this together and you don't have to face anything by yourself."

He pulled their luggage out and they started walking up to the house. There wasn't a sense of coming home when she looked at Benedict House. It was a nice enough place to stay and she didn't mind, but she wouldn't want to live there permanently.

They had discussed where they would live once they told everyone they were married and she officially ran for office. At the moment, though, it felt like there were a million things in the way of finding their own space. And she wasn't stupid, Benedict House had top-of-the-line security and she wasn't about to let go of that.

Everyone must have gone into the offices today because the house was silent as they entered. Just as well, she wasn't in the mood to be very sociable. She mentally ran through what she needed to do while they ate lunch: call Alyssa to follow up on the case, try to find Jade, and get back to work on Mr. Brock's files.

The doorbell rang, disturbing the silence. Knox moved to get up, but Lena told him to sit down.

"Finish eating," she said. "There's not anything at that door more important than you eating a good lunch. I'll get the door."

"Thank you," he said with a smile, and sat back down.

Lena disappeared down the hall and though Bea could hear voices from the foyer, she couldn't make out what they were. When Alyssa entered the kitchen seconds later, she assumed the policewoman had stopped by to talk to tell her there'd been a break in the case.

But as soon as she saw Alyssa's face, she knew it had to be much more.

"It's Jade, isn't it?" she asked.

Alyssa shook her head. "No. I'm sorry. There's no good way to tell you this."

Knox stood up and moved to stand behind her, placing his hands on her shoulders. Dread filled Bea's belly.

"The fire crew found human remains in your father's house," Alyssa said calmly.

Bea wrinkled her forehead. "I don't understand. Was it one of the assailants?"

"The body was burned too badly for visual identification. We had to use dental records to identify the body."

"Oh." That made sense. She still didn't fully understand what Alyssa was trying to say.

"When was the last time you spoke to your father?" Alyssa asked.

"The day before the church retreat. I've tried to call him a few times, but . . .

The truth hit her then. Why he hadn't called or answered his phone. And most important, why Alyssa was there.

There was a horrible ringing in her ears and Alyssa might have said something else, but Bea couldn't hear what it was. Knox squeezed her shoulders. There was a high-pitched wail and she wondered what it was and why nobody was stopping it.

Knox lifted her up and sat down with her in his lap and she realized the noise was coming from her. Even then, it took a few minutes for her to stop.

"Oh, my God," she said. "That's why he hasn't called. They killed him, didn't they?"

She looked up to find that her outburst had drawn the rest of the family to the kitchen. They all stood around like they didn't know what to do or what to make of her.

"I'm sorry," Alyssa spoke softer than before. "The dental records were a match."

She'd thought all those awful mean things about him not calling and it wasn't because he was an ass or hated her, it was because he was dead.

God, she was the world's worst daughter. But she knew the real grief was coming from what they would never share now that he was gone.

"Was he killed before . . ." She closed her eyes. She couldn't say it. Couldn't think or entertain the possibility that he'd been alive somewhere in the house while she and Knox were there.

"Don't," Knox whispered in her hair, obviously picking up on her thought process. "Don't think like that. Don't do that to yourself."

But she had to know. She looked over to Alyssa with pleading eyes. Alyssa would tell her, she had to tell her.

Alyssa shook her head. "We don't know."

Bea took a deep breath, blinking through the tears that once again threatened to fall. "We never got along. Never. I used to say that we were so different, there was no conceivable way we were related. That doesn't mean I wanted him dead."

"Of course you didn't," Knox said. "No one thinks that."

But as the reality sunk in and her tears began to fall in earnest, she couldn't help but feel that if she were a better daughter, he'd still be alive.

Tom was expecting the call. "Sir?"

The Gentleman wasted no time. "Why was a body found at the Jacobs's house?"

"The revered came home unexpectedly to pick up a few things he needed for his weekend trip and saw us making preparations for the fire. I took care of him."

"How?"

"Made him send a message to the church members going on the trip, saying he had to deal with an emergency out of state and they would have to reschedule the conference. Then I shot him and hid his body in the basement."

The Gentleman didn't say anything for a long moment. "Good thinking on your feet."

Tom felt his body relax. "Thank you."

Two days later, she eyed a pile of mail on Knox's dresser that had been gathering there since they got back from DC. She didn't want to deal with that at the moment. Probably it was all Knox's mail anyway; she doubted anyone would send her mail at Benedict House.

Knox walked into the bedroom. "A lady from your dad's church just called to talk with you about your dad's service. I told her you'd call back this afternoon."

"Thank you."

Knox picked up the mail. "What do you have to do as far as a service for your dad, anyway?"

"I'll get together with some of the ladies from the church. If he wasn't who he was, I'd just do something small, you know? Family only, private service." She sighed. "But I can't do that. Well, I could, but I'm not."

Knox frowned at a letter and put it to the side, while continuing to go through the reminder of the stack. "That doesn't mean you have to make it a huge production. You can have a simple service."

"That's my plan. And I want to delegate as much as possible. Some of those ladies would jump at the chance to organize his service."

Knox smiled. "You could always say you were too distraught to plan anything."

"Right. Like they'd believe that."

He finished going through the mail, setting it all aside and picking up the one envelope he'd separated out earlier. From where she sat, she could see it had been addressed by hand.

"I don't even want to know if that's what I think it is." She shivered, remembering the letter she'd received at the office by courier. But even as she said it, she knew it probably wasn't. Why would they have sent something to Knox when they'd always sent things to her?

Knox pulled out a piece of paper and Bea didn't say anything as he looked over the single page. He dropped onto the bed. "What the fuck is this? Someone's idea of a joke? Because I'm not laughing."

It didn't sound like it was a threat, but whatever it was, he was certainly pissed.

"What is it?" she asked.

He shoved the paper at her. "A sick joke."

At first glance it looked like a normal birth certificate. She didn't see what caused Knox's reaction until she looked closer. The name was listed as Baby Girl Benedict. The mother was listed as Jane Doe, but it was the father who caught her eye.

"Is this your dad?" she asked, not wanting to believe it, but unable to see another option.

"Supposedly. It has to be a fake. There's no way Dad had an affair and got some woman pregnant. The very thought is preposterous."

Bea ran her finger over the paper. "Raised seal. Those are incredibly difficult to counterfeit. Don't you think you should at least entertain the possibility that it could be real?"

He scrubbed his fingers through his hair. "Yeah, I suppose anything's possible."

"Maybe we should show it to Keaton and Kipling. They might remember things. Kipling's older. Maybe he heard your parents arguing or heard rumors of an affair or something."

He thought for a few minutes before finally saying, "Okay. You're right. We'll talk to them when they get home."

They finished unpacking and then they each went about doing his or her own thing. Knox made a few phone calls and Bea touched base with the church. The remains of her father had been released and the ladies of the church had taken over planning the service. By the time she finished talking with them, she heard Keaton, Tilly, and Kipling return for lunch.

She went to meet Knox in the downstairs office. He looked up from his computer and silently took the birth certificate and joined her.

"Hey, guys, you're home." Keaton was just sitting down with Tilly at his side. "I wasn't expecting you until later tonight."

"We decided since we were up we might as well head home," Bea said. She looked over to Knox, who still looked angry.

"Something going on?" Kipling asked, obviously picking up on his younger brother's mood.

Knox took a deep breath. "I was going to wait until after we ate, but let's go and get it out of the way. When we got home there was a birth certificate mailed to me. It looks to be that of a girl born to a Jane Doe and Dad."

This was obviously news Kipling had never heard, as indicated by the shock written all over his face when Knox gave him the paperwork.

Keaton, on the other hand, coughed around the bite he'd taken. "You have the birth certificate?"

"What you mean *the* birth certificate?" Knox asked.

"I'm talking about the birth certificate of the supposed child that Dad had with his mistress," Keaton said.

"You know about her?" Knox asked.

"How did you hear about her?" Kipling said at the same time.

"We should've told you," Tilly whispered in a voice loud enough that everyone could hear.

Bea was struck silent. Not only did Keaton know, apparently Tilly did as well. She glanced over at Knox. He was just as shocked as she was.

"Tell me what you know," Knox said.

"Early in the summer, when Elise was here, she tried to blackmail me into marrying her." Keaton took Tilly's hand. "She said she had evidence that pointed to Dad having a mistress who got pregnant. According to her, he wanted her to have an abortion, but she refused and ran off. When the girl was four, the mistress resurfaced. According to Elise, she wanted money. When Dad refused to give, she threatened him."

Keaton paused. "Here's the part that explains why I didn't bring it up to you. When he found out the little girl was alive, he arranged for both the mistress and the girl to die in a car accident."

No one said anything for several long seconds, until Kipling broke the silence.

"Horse shit," he said. "There's no way Dad would have killed anyone."

"I know," Keaton said. "I thought the same thing and figured if Elise made up that stuff about Dad killing off people, she probably made up the daughter, too. But now you say you have a birth certificate?"

"Why all the sad faces," Lena said, coming into the dining room with a huge salad.

Lena!

Bea looked at Knox, who nodded and then cleared his throat to get Kipling's attention. Kipling caught his raised eyebrow and gave a curt nod.

"Lena," Kipling said. "Will you have a seat for a few minutes?"

Lena placed the salad in the middle of the table. "I have to go get the bread and if this is about me retiring, I already told you it's not happening."

"It's not that," Kipling assured her. "Though I do wish you'd take a vacation."

"And just what would I do on vacation? Sit around? No thank you. I'm very happy right here."

"We actually wanted to talk to you about Dad," Knox said.

"Oh." Lena hadn't been expecting that and dropped into a nearby chair. "Well, I'll do my best to help in any way I can."

"There's not a delicate way to ask this," Kipling said. "So forgive me for being blunt. Are you aware of my father having a mistress?"

Lena's face turned pink and she clamped her lips tightly.

"Lena?" Knox asked.

"I don't want to speak ill of the dead," Lena said. "It's not right."

"Holy shit!" Keaton said. "He did. Did Mom know?"

Kipling glared at his youngest brother and slid the birth certificate in front of her. "We're trying to see if this could possibly be real."

Lena took her glasses out of her front shirt pocket and picked up the paper. She read it with a frown on her face and when she finished, she put the birth certificate down, folded her glasses, and put them back in her pocket. No one said anything.

Lena finally took a deep breath. "No matter what, your daddy was a good man. He loved you boys and your mama and don't let anyone tell you any different. He was a good, good man, but he wasn't perfect. He had his issues, just like we all do. And his biggest issue was that he loved women. All kinds of women. Didn't matter. And he wasn't always as discreet as he thought he was."

Kipling sank back into his seat, next to Keaton, who had been shocked into silence. Bea reached out and took Knox's hand. Hearing about his father's infidelity couldn't be easy. He ran thumb across her skin and gave her hand a squeeze. She closed her eyes for a moment and said a silent prayer that she and Knox never came to such a point in their marriage.

"Your mama knew how and who he was," Lena continued, her eyes open, but clearly she was looking back in time. "Every time he'd say he was going to change and he was sorry and every time he go right back doing the same thing. Your mama was a saint, she'd always forgive him and welcome him back with open arms. I used to think she was plum crazy, but she loved him too much. You ask me, that was her issue, not knowing how to put her foot down to that man."

Lena tapped the birth certificate. "So, no, it doesn't surprise me that one of his affairs led to a pregnancy. The real shock is, why hasn't she been nosing around trying to get money? I recall one time, one of his women called Mrs. Helen up and asked for hush money. Your mama said words I didn't know she knew and to this day, I haven't heard some of them again." She tilted her head. "I don't understand at all why either this woman or this child hasn't rung the doorbell, looking for a handout."

Keaton cleared his throat. "Elise knew about this mistress and her child. She suggested Dad had them both killed." Under his breath, he added, "That would certainly explain why we haven't heard from either one of them."

"That crazy girl said your daddy had them killed?" Lena looked at Keaton as if he'd grown another head. "That's just her crazy talking. Your daddy was many things and not all of them were good, but the one thing he was not was a killer. If those two died, it wasn't by his hand."

"Do we know for a fact that they're dead?" Kipling asked.

Knox picked up the birth certificate. "Hell, I haven't got used to knowing I had a sister and now you're going to tell me she's dead."

"That's one of the reasons I didn't bring it up," Keaton said. "One, I wasn't sure she existed. Two, why bring it up if she's dead?"

Kipling leaned forward. "Because you don't keep secrets like that from your family. You knew we had a sister and didn't bother telling anyone. And you," he said, pointing at Knox, "you went off and got married and didn't tell anyone. Are there any other secrets anyone would like to get off their chest today?"

Knox was still examining the birth certificate. "I wonder if Mom knew he had a daughter with another woman?"

"Mrs. Helen knew just about everything that happened in this house." Lena wiped her eyes. "I imagine she knew."

"If she knew everything that went on in the house," Knox said. "Then she knew about the mistress and the baby. She would have also have known if he killed them and no matter how in love she was, I don't see her standing by and letting someone die."

"Mrs. Helen would have put a stop to any plan where someone died," Lena said. "I remember now that I think about it, they used to have the worst fights. Not very often, because Mrs. Helen would take a lot. I don't mean your daddy was hitting her. I mean it took a lot to get her going, but once she did? Hang on tight."

"I remember them arguing," Kipling said. "It wasn't very often and I think they tried to hide it. Or at least not to do it in front of us."

"I don't remember it at all." Keaton frowned.

Bea had opened her mouth to ask Knox if he remembered anything, when her phone rang. She didn't recognize the number, she decided to answer on the off chance it was Jade.

"Hello," she said, but no one answered. She'd almost disconnected she heard a sound that made her body freeze.

Tick.

Tick.

Tick.

That damn watch.

Tick.

Tick.

Tick.

Then came the voice she remembered in her nightmares.

"Bea, Bea, Bea," he said in a mock scolding tone of voice. "What am I going to do with you and your inability to listen and follow directions. You know, some men are turned on by stubborn women. I'm not one of them. I like to break them."

She tried to speak, but found the words wouldn't form.

On the other end of the phone came an evil laugh. "Oh, yes. I'll love to watch you break. In fact, I think I've changed my mind. I no longer want you dead. Oh no. You'll be so much more fun alive."

Her mouth opened but no words came out.

Knox jerked the phone away from her. "Listen here, you asshole—"

Even with Knox holding the phone, she could still hear the man on the other end interrupt. "If it isn't Saint Benedict himself," he said, followed by a chuckle. "Do you hear the ticking in the background, Knox? Each person only has so many ticks to tick in their life. I wonder how many you have left?" He chuckled again and then disconnected.

Knox cursed and threw the phone on the table, but his demeanor changed when he looked over and saw Bea. Ignoring the worried expressions of his family, he pulled her to him as close as the dining chair would allow.

"He can't get you, Bea," he murmured to her. "I won't let him."

"Don't you see?" she asked. "He already has."

"I'm going to find him and then I'll kill him."

Kipling banged his fist on the table. "And I'll help."

"Count me in," Keaton said, and Tilly nodded in agreement.

"We need to find out what information he wants to stay buried so badly." Knox continued to stroke her back while he talked. "I still think it has something to do with Tilly's dad."

Later that night, she was acutely aware of the way Knox watched her as she prepared for bed. She slipped her nightgown over her head, and as always, she marveled at how her body responded to him even when he wasn't touching her.

His current expression told her he knew exactly how he made her body feel. He moved closer and reached for the strap of her gown.

She swatted his hand away. "No, we are not going to do anything tonight."

"You still aren't caught up in that fact that my brothers are here, are you?" he asked. "Because I don't think I need to remind you we did the same thing in DC with your brother and Janie right down the hall."

"That's different."

"How?" he asked. "Because it was your brother and not mine?"

It sounded stupid, even to her own ears. "Yes." She took a deep breath and tried to figure out how to explain her thought process without hurting his feelings. "I'm more comfortable with Brent, I don't know your brothers all that well."

He seemed to weigh her words and she swore she could picture his brain churning though various replies. Finally, he spoke. "Okay. We won't do anything sexual while in Benedict House."

He gave in way too easily, but she replied with a simple, "Thank you."

His overly enthusiastic smile clued her in that she'd probably just been had.

"However," he added, and she knew she was right. "That does not mean that I won't get you to the point where you'll be begging me to take you."

"Is that right?" she asked, wondering how he could do something like that without touching her.

She didn't have to wonder for long. Almost as soon as they made it to bed, he rolled her way.

"Do you know what I'm thinking about?" he asked.

She pulled the covers up to her chin. "If I had to guess, I'd say sex."

"Yes, well, that's a given," he said. "But specifically what kind of sex and with whom am I having it?"

"Since you're asking me these questions, I'll have to say you're having it with me. Because if you're in bed with me and thinking about having sex with another woman, I'll cut your dick off."

"Remind me to keep you away from the knives in the kitchen."

"Was I right?" she asked.

"Yes, of course you were. Do you honestly think I even remotely consider other women when I have you as my wife?"

She touched his cheek. "You better not."

He turned his face and kissed the palm of her hand. Then he sighed and tugged her so she rested on his chest. She snuggled into his embrace. She always felt so protected in his arms. When she was in his arms, she couldn't imagine anywhere else she'd rather be.

She ran a hand down one of his arms, her fingertips brushing over the muscles. And, because she couldn't help it, she lowered her head and placed a soft kiss on his shoulder.

"You feel so good in my arms," he whispered. "Just like you were made for them."

"You know in Greek mythology, it was said that humans originally had four arms, four legs, and a head with two faces."

"No way," he said.

"You think I can make this up?" She lifted her upper body, just a bit, so she could see his face. She continued when he shook his head. "Anyway, Zeus feared they were too strong, so he split them. After that, humans had one pair of legs, one pair of arms, and one face. They would roam the earth, looking for their other half, their soul mate."

"Where do you learn all this this stuff?"

"Brent's dad was Greek, and Brent spent a lot of his summers in Greece with his grandparents. I went with him one summer." She frowned, remembering when she'd come home. She'd gone on and on about Greece, the people she met there, how wonderful the food was. Later that night, she overhead her dad telling her mom that she wasn't to go back to Greece.

She didn't want to talk about Greece or her dad. What she wanted, she realized, in stark opposition to what she'd said previously, was Knox. She wanted to feel his passion when he took her in his arms. She wanted to feel his love in his lips as they traveled over her body. She wanted him to make everything disappear as he took her thoroughly and for those few precious moments all she had room in her head for was him.

She was fairly certain he wouldn't have a problem with her changing her mind. Even so, she decided not to tell him, but to show him.

She peppered kisses across his shoulder, first one and then the other. She let her hands drift downward and brushed the expanse of his chest. He groaned and pulled back.

"You need to stop," he said.

She placed a kiss on his chest. "Do you want me to stop?"

"Hell, no," he said through clenched teeth as she kissed his chest again. "But you said you didn't want to do anything."

"I changed my mind." She spoke without moving

out of place. "I've decided I don't care if your brothers are in the house." She hooked her fingers around the waistline of the shorts he'd worn to bed. "Hey, what's this? I thought you slept naked?"

"I do. It's just since you said nothing was going to happen tonight, I thought it would be for the best if I slipped some shorts on."

"You're not opposed to me taking them off?"

"Are you serious with that question?" He cocked an eyebrow at her and she had to laugh.

"You may have changed your mind, or decided you weren't in the mood," she said, working on tugging his shorts down.

"Put it this way," he said. "The day I'm not in the mood to have sex with you is the day I'm dead."

"In that case." She didn't want to talk about him being dead, she'd much rather attend to the business at hand. With one move, she had his shorts down his legs and with a quick shake, they were off.

"Jesus, Bea."

She grinned because she knew she'd caught him off guard. She kept her eyes on his while she teased his inner thighs with her hands. "Remember that night I gave you one kiss?"

"Yes," he ground out in half a moan.

"Tonight, I'm not stopping with one." And without giving him time to think or react, she leaned over and took his entire length in her mouth.

His hips bucked off the bed and he muttered something she couldn't quite make out.

She lifted her head. "Was that a 'please stop'?"

"That was a 'please for the love of all things holy and a few that aren't, don't stop'."

"Since you put it that way," she said, and took him in her mouth again.

He placed his hand on her head, not to guide or to force, but to gently rub her scalp the way he knew she liked. She hummed, to show much she liked what he was doing, and his hand tightened in her hair in response to how it made her mouth move around him. He cursed under his breath.

She kept on licking and tasting, wanting to give him as much pleasure as she could. He let her continue for a few minutes, but eventually tugged her hair.

"Stop, Bea."

"Why?"

"Because I don't want to come in your mouth." He was almost panting and the muscles of his thighs tightened beneath her fingers.

She thought about keeping her mouth on him and letting him finish, but decided she wouldn't. She gave his length one last kiss and then climbed his body. "One day soon, I'm going to take you all the way back in my mouth and swallow every drop you're able to give me."

"Deal," he said. "But right now, I want to bury myself in you as deep as possible. So deep. And I want to stay there and bring you more pleasure than you've ever known. So deep and for so long, when I'm not in you, you feel like part of you is missing." While he'd been talking, his hands had been busy, stroking her breasts, a fingertip circling her nipple. He slipped a hand between her legs. "You want me."

"Always," she whispered with a shiver.

He rolled over so that they were on their sides, facing each other. He wrapped the fingers of one hand around the top of her upper thigh and hitched it up so her leg wrapped around his waist.

She felt so open and exposed and she kept waiting for him to move, anticipating that delicious feel when he first entered her. But he kept still.

She gyrated her hips, desperate and needy for some friction and still he wouldn't move.

"Knox," she whined.

He closed his eyes and smiled. "Can you feel it? The anticipation? It's so sweet, isn't it? At times, it's almost as if you can feel it before it happens, can't you?"

Yes, she could feel it now, but she knew it was just a shadow of what the real thing would feel like. An echo of it. "Please."

He moved closer and she could feel the heat of his body at her entrance, but he stopped seconds away from touching her. "So, so sweet," he repeated.

"Knox," she begged again. "Please."

"And she was so needy," he said. "Tell me what you need."

She rocked her hips in frustration. "You."

"Ah, yes," he said and ever so slowly, pushed his way into her.

She sucked her breath in through clenched teeth. Always the feel of him the first time he entered her was so sweet in its fullness and the way he stretched her.

"Somehow," he said, "as good as I think it's going to be, and as wonderful as I remember it being, it never comes close to the real thing."

He was fully inside her now and though she yearned for him to move, he suppressed her once again by remaining still.

"You're driving me mad," she said.

"Consider it payback," he said. "For every day, all day. The way you look, the way you walk, everything about you. It leaves me burning with desire. So yes, this is payback."

She grabbed onto his biceps. He was straining with the will not to move and she was glad he was experiencing the same consuming desire she was. She knew all she had to do was move her hips, but she knew that wasn't what he wanted, so she remained still. Content for the moment to let him have his way.

When he started to move, his thrusts were slow and easy, and the entire time, he whispered. He whispered about how much he loved her, how beautiful she was, and how good she felt. And though she often didn't feel it, in his arms she felt beautiful.

He loved her with his body, taking time to ensure she felt everything he did. The feel of him within her, paired with the words he whispered, made her feel weightless and warm. But most of all, she felt loved and adored.

He started to move faster and she responded in kind, hitting his backside with the heel of the foot around his waist. He gave a grunt each time she did so and she did her best to draw him closer.

"Yes," he said, thrusting deeper.

She kicked harder and in response he moved faster. She wished they could hold on to this moment forever. That they could somehow live in this timeless moment, where nothing could get to them, or separate them, or drive them apart. Where it was just him and her, and the universe was content with leaving them alone.

But as perfect as the moment was, it couldn't last forever. Her hips moved in time with his, and before too long, her climax was upon her. She shook with the aftershocks as Knox roared through his own release.

As they laid in the darkness, the only sound being the catching of their breaths, she thought this moment was pretty perfect, too.

"I love you, Bea," Knox said.

She kissed him briefly. "I love you, too."

If only this moment could last forever. This quiet stillness. This peace. She wasn't ready to return to reality, so she decided to close her eyes and pretend just a little bit longer.

Jade approached the house from the beach. Looking over her shoulder the entire time, to make sure she hadn't been followed. It had been a stroke of luck that as she went through the office in Benedict House, looking for a stamp, that she found the information about this house.

Apparently, Knox planned to surprise his bride one day. Until he did, Jade was going to use it. She had purposely waited almost a week before traveling to it, on the off chance she was being followed. Now that she felt as if she was in the clear, it was time to make herself at home.

She frowned when she saw the house. It was more rundown than she had anticipated. Still, however, it looked to be structurally sound. And it was a much bigger space than one person needed.

She'd been afraid to take a key for fear one of the Benedicts would find it missing, put two and two together, and figure out she was the one who took it. She didn't need a key, though, and as long as there wasn't an alarm, she was golden.

She moved swiftly from the beach to the back deck and peered into a window with a broken shutter. There didn't appear to be any electricity going to the house as far as she could tell. That was good. No electricity meant no alarm. Not that she would have used electricity even if the house had it. No use tipping off anyone to the fact that someone was in the house when it should be empty.

Fortunately for her, the days were still long enough that she'd have daylight well into the evening. For once, it appeared fate was smiling upon her.

She looked over her shoulder again, just to make sure the beach was still empty. Knox had done an excellent job in ensuring the location of his house was private. There were only a few houses nearby and they were far enough away that they couldn't see her at the moment.

When she had scoped the place out earlier, she had noted some kids playing in the streets. That could be a problem because kids remembered everything, especially somebody like her, pulling out of place in such high-class neighborhood.

She didn't see the kids now, and in fact there was nobody on the beach. She shrugged her backpack off her shoulder, and pulled out her lock-picking kit. In less than two minutes, she was through the door.

Once inside, it was obvious the house needed more work than what was apparent from the outside. Which was perfect for her, because that meant it was less likely for somebody to come by and find her hiding place. She wasn't sure how long it would be until Knox and Bea moved into this place or until they started doing renovations. Either way she figured she had enough time to concoct a good plan.

Maybe now she would be able to sleep some and she could always fish in the ocean. So if you combined the food with the sleep, she might actually be able to come up with something to do to get away from The Gentleman for good.

She went through each room of the house, and finally decided to make her spot upstairs. From the upstairs windows she could see a large span of beach, which would tip her off if someone was coming.

She found a few blankets stuffed away in a closet. After pulling them out and shaking the dust off, she decided they would do good enough. The sun was going down and she pulled out her last peanut butter sandwich, telling herself she would fish tomorrow. Her stomach rumbled its approval.

From the outside came the sound of kids playing in the ocean. She peeked from behind the window and saw they were far enough away that they probably couldn't see her. She wished she had a pair of binoculars; maybe she should try to find some tomorrow. Surely she could lift a pair from somewhere.

But now, for the first time in a week, she laid her head down and fell asleep, telling herself she could sleep all night.

The next morning, Knox worked from home downstairs. Bea had wanted to go into her office, but he had told her that was not a good idea. His reply couldn't have come as a surprise. She simply agreed and was currently in their bedroom on a conference call.

"Knock, knock," Keaton said from the doorway.

"Good morning."

Keaton stood, leaning against the doorframe with a knowing look on his face. "Missed you and Bea at breakfast this morning."

"We had a late night and decided to sleep in."

"Ah, yes, sleeping in." He gave his brother an exaggerated wink. "If that's what you want to call it."

"We were sleeping in."

"Only because certain activities kept you up all night."

"True, but listen," Knox said. "Don't tease about that around Bea. She was a bit shy and worried, especially with so many people in the house."

"I would never tease Bea. There's no fun teasing her, all my joy is derived from teasing you."

"Thanks," Knox said. "I think. Did you need anything or did you come by simply to annoy me?"

Keaton reached to his rear pocket and pulled out a sheet of paper. "Out of all the things Elise had, this was the only one of them that appeared to be real."

He passed the paper across the desk. Knox's took it and his eyes grew wide as he took in what he'd been handed. "A death certificate?"

"Yes." Keaton wasn't teasing anymore. "Our supposed sister."

"I think it's fairly certain at this point to say we had a sister." Knox pointed to the death certificate. "Now, whether she's still alive is another question all together. Along with what are we to make of all this data and shit."

"Tilly said she thought it was all connected somehow."

"Bea and I think the same. Somehow and some-where there's a thread that connects Tilly's dad to this missing sister and the threats on me and Bea."

"Still getting those?" Keaton asked.

"She got a phone call last night. Some jerk and a watch. It almost sent her into a panic attack."

"She still gets those?" Keaton asked.

"Yes, but thankfully not as frequently or intense as they've been in the past."

"Is she seeing someone?" At Knox's raised eyebrow, he added, "I meant a professional. A therapist or some-thing. Tilly went to one after her ordeal. If you like, I can get the phone number."

"Sure, give it to me," Knox said. "I'm not sure she'll go, but I think it'd be a good idea to at least have the number."

"I'll look it up and give to you later today." Keaton looked at his watch. "Got to go. I'm late meeting Tilly."

Knox told his brother good-bye, right as Bea came in.

"What are you looking at?" she asked after giving him a quick kiss.

"This death certificate," he said. "I can't put my fin-ger on what, but something's off."

Bea looked over it. "Something's definitely odd."

Knox sighed and went back to his desk. "Maybe we're looking at all of this wrong."

"That's it," she said, so softly at first he thought he imagined it. But then she looked up at him and smiled. "It's a fake."

"It is?" He pushed back from the desk and went to where she stood.

"Look at this." She pointed to the number in the upper right corner. "It's four numbers."

"And that's not right?"

She shook her head. "No, and because of that, it's not valid. It's a fake. Now look at this." She handed him a paper she'd printed from Mr. Brock's HR file. "What do you see?" Bea asked.

He put the list down and pointed. "Tilly's dad had his issues with the company at almost the exact same time the death certificate was issued. That can't be a coincidence."

"I don't think so, either. Unfortunately, it only brings up more questions instead of answering them. I mean, do we really think that Tilly's dad was somehow involved in the death of your sister?"

"Maybe that was why he had to be kicked out of the company. He knew too much." But as soon as he thought it, he dismissed it. "But then again, it didn't seem like Dad. I can't see him treating his good friend like that. Not any more than he could see Mr. Brock stealing from them, I guess. But when everything had come to light back then, the evidence had been so solid against Mr. Brock, Dad really didn't have a choice but to fire him." Knox remembered that time. His father had been depressed. His mother almost hysterical.

Bea reached for his hand and gave it a gentle squeeze.

"I remember thinking about Keaton and what he was going to do without Tilly. Even back then they were close," Knox said.

"Answer this for me. Was Mr. Brock the kind of man who would have screwed over his employer that way? And not just his employer, but his best friend as well?"

"No," he answered. "It didn't make sense. There's something we're missing."

He had to find it, before it was too late.

* * *

The morning of Bea's father's service, she woke up to rain. It was appropriate for such a type of service, but that didn't make her feel any better. If anything, it only made her realize what a complete failure she was as a daughter, which was bad enough. But that was made worse because she knew she'd never be able to mend that relationship.

At least Knox didn't try to make her feel better. He simply did what he could to help her, without making much in the way of conversation. Instead, he was as supportive as he could be just by being there and being by her side. There had been some talk among the brothers about her not going to the service, but she'd put her foot down. In the end, they compromised by hiring additional security and putting a good number of them to work outside, with plenty of guards inside as well.

The service was supposed to start at eleven and she spent the time leading up to it feeling like a robot. She functioned, but she tried not to feel or think, frankly not to do much of anything. By the time they drove off for the church, she was ready for the whole thing to be over. All the Benedicts went with her, including Tilly and Lena. She tried to tell him it wasn't necessary, but they would have none of that and insisted they go along with her.

Brent and Janie met her at the church, having just flown in about an hour before. They were only going to be able to stay for a little bit, but Brent was the only living blood relative she had and she didn't care how long he stayed as long as he was there. He hugged her at the church and when she sat down, Knox on one side and Brent on the other, she felt so protected and safe.

It was strange to be in her father's church without her father being there. She kept expecting to look up at the front and see him standing at the pulpit. And though she wouldn't have thought it before, it hurt her that she should never seem there again.

While members of his church knew of some of the difficulties between her and her father, they didn't know the extent of it or the details. She wanted it to remain that way. By the time the service started, she was willing to bet every member of the congregation had come up to her to speak to her about the loss of her father.

A neighboring minister and friend of her father's had offered to do his service. She knew him by name, but they had never spoken before. Throughout the service, she kept looking at the urn that held her father's ashes and trying to convince herself that he was really in there and wouldn't be coming back. Her mind searched for an earlier time in their life, when she got along with her father. When they didn't argue about everything. She was saddened as she couldn't remember one. Not a single one.

The ladies of the church who planned the service had asked her if she wanted to say a few words. She told them no, that she thought it would be more meaningful for those he'd lived to serve to say a few words. It might be bad of her not to say anything, but it was the truth.

She sat in the front row of the church and she knew the weight of numerous eyes on her back wasn't a figment of her imagination. They were probably wondering who she thought she was sitting there when there was no love lost between her and her father. When she walked in, she'd wondered if the church would be filled. She should have known it would be.

People from all over the city, from the well-to-do to a few members of the shelter he'd help support. They all came to pay their respects to the man they knew and admired. She was pretty certain none of them knew the real man. Take for instance the flowers. To her father they were a colossal waste of time and money, yet flowers lined the front of the altar. From potted plants to huge sprays of roses. All sent to show their love and respect for a man who didn't appreciate the gesture in life and, if he could speak from beyond the grave, would no doubt tell them not to waste their money on flowers.

Bea couldn't help but calculate an estimate of how much had been spent on "a bunch of weeds that were just going to die anyway." She started with the big sprays and in doing so, noted a large arrangement of dark-colored roses that had she didn't remember seeing when she'd looked at them earlier. In fact, now that she was seated, she was certain they hadn't been there before. Add in that strange color—they looked black, but surely that couldn't be right—and the whole thing had a creepy vibe to it.

"How are you holding up?" Knox slid a hand down to her kneecap, and whispered in her ear.

"I feel like I'm going to throw up." And now that she'd noticed them, she couldn't get that spray of roses out of her head. "Do those flowers there on the end look strange to you?"

"I hadn't noticed them, but now that you brought it to my attention, I have to agree. Very strange and rather ominous."

The minister shot a nasty look their way and she decided they hadn't been as quiet as she'd thought they had been. She cut her head to the right for a quick glimpse at Knox, but he was staring at the flowers she'd pointed out. His hand drifted toward his back pocket, where she knew his phone was. He stopped, though, and gave her a quick nod as if to say they would deal with it after the service.

Finally, after what seemed like hours, but in fact had probably only been about forty-five minutes, the minister had them all stand for one last prayer. There wouldn't be a graveside service since there was no body to bury. Due to the condition of his body, Bea had elected to have his remains cremated. His ashes would be stored at the church.

Of course, even after the service was over, people still came up to her. She didn't know half of them, but they knew who she was, and that was all that mattered. So for the next half hour she played host and grieving daughter, even though she felt like neither.

It was well past noon by the time everyone had left, other than the Benedicts and a few members of the church. She took the moment of quiet to walk over to the odd-colored roses that had captured her attention during the service. She read the card that was attached to the ribbon. The glass of water she held dropped and shattered on the floor.

Knox was the first one to her side. She held up a trembling finger and pointed to the flowers. There in bright crisp font was a message.

REJOICE IN THE TRUTH. YOU WILL BE REUNITED SOON.

Anyone from the church would have read it as a message meant to bring comfort and hope, but she knew better. Whoever had ordered the flowers and requested that message hadn't done it as a means to provide comfort. Oh no. She knew exactly what it was. A thinly veiled threat and a warning. Whoever was after her hadn't given up, they were simply biding their time.

Bea and Knox were digging through another file box when the doorbell rang. Knox got up to check the security camera before answering the door.

"It's Alyssa," he said.

Bea stood up and brushed her pants off. "I wonder if she has new information?"

They let her in and went to go sit in the living room. Bea thought Alyssa looked tired. She had bags in her eyes and appeared altogether harried. The police officer didn't sit on the couch, but rather collapsed into it.

"Would you like some coffee?" Bea asked.

"I probably should," Alyssa said. "But I think at this point it would have no effect on me. Except make me crash when the caffeine wore off."

"That bad?" Bea raised an eyebrow.

"Another girl disappeared last night." Alyssa sighed. "It's been a while since we've had one. I guess I thought maybe it would stop. It is never going to."

"Was this one from the same club?" Bea asked. She remembered reading that most of the missing girls had worked at one particular club. Those that hadn't worked there still had some sort of connection to it.

"Yes," Alyssa said. "I'm about ready to put that place out of business. Surely if I requested a health inspection, they could find a reason to shut it down." She looked around. "Is anybody else here today?"

"No, just us," Knox said. "Everyone else went out

to eat. Bea and I stayed here so we could look through some old files."

And because he didn't want her to leave the house. But Bea didn't say that. It was obvious that Alyssa could read between the lines and see the truth, though.

"There are a few things I want to talk about," Alyssa said.

"If it isn't Officer Adams."

They all turned around to see Kipling walk into the room. He gave Alyssa a look of frank assessment, and a hint of something else. Interesting, Bea thought.

"Mr. Benedict," Alyssa said. "I'm glad you're here."

Kipling snorted. "I'm sure."

"No, truly. This concerns you as well."

"I thought you went out to eat?" Knox asked.

"I did, but I wanted to stop by the office and I'd left a few things here," Kipling said. "I came by to pick them up and was going to sneak in the back. Then I saw we had company."

"Either way," Alyssa continued, "I'm glad you're here. Like I said, this concerns you as well."

"Have you found something?" he asked.

"Actually," Alyssa said, "it was something you found. We just happened to put two and two together with the information we had. We had some files of information we had found in our earlier investigation. Based on the information we had from previous investigations, added to the new information you sent us, we have reason to believe that your parents' plane crash was not an accident."

The silence that encompassed the room was deafening.

Kipling dropped into a nearby chair with a curse. "Are you serious?"

"Yes, that's why I wanted to come by in person and talk to you. This is very sensitive. And confidential. We aren't going public with it and we're going to investigate it quietly. We ask your cooperation do the same. I don't mind if you tell Keaton and Tilly, but other than that, please don't let this go further than this room."

"What information did you find that may make you reopen the case?" Knox asked.

"It was several things, but the most important where in the spreadsheets we found attached to the documents you provided. They show money sent to an offshore account. We were able to trace the account and it led to a dummy account for a well-known hitman."

"I can't remember," Knox said. "Were the spreadsheets from before or after Mr. Brock was fired?"

"I believe," Bea said, "that the e-mails were before he was fired, but the spreadsheets were after."

"Which begs the question," Kipling said. "Who had those spreadsheets?"

"The obvious answer is Tilly's mom." Bea couldn't imagine why she held on to them, though. Especially if she knew what they were. "And we can't ask her, she died of cancer six years ago."

"If you've traced money to the hitman," Knox asked Alyssa. "Who transferred the money in the first place?"

"That would be the confidential part." Alyssa looked unsurprised that he had asked.

"Which means you do have somebody in mind." Bea wondered how difficult that information would be to get.

"I can't comment on it since it's an open investigation."

Kipling sat forward with his hands on his knees. "I get the feeling that you're jerking us around."

"I would do no such thing."

"I think it's pretty shitty for you to come in here and tell us our parents didn't die in an accident, that instead they were murdered and, yes, you have an idea of who did it, but oh, that's confidential, and I can't tell you."

"I didn't have to tell you anything."

"Why did you?"

"Forgive me if I thought you'd want to know that your parents had been murdered." Alyssa stood up. "I'll make sure not to give you any more information. Technically, I shouldn't have given you what I did."

"Sit down."

"I can't give you any additional information than what I already have."

"We know this person?"

"What part of *I can't give you any additional information* do you have trouble understanding?"

"I just think—"

"Kipling," Knox interrupted. "Leave it be and leave her alone. She gave us all the information she could and we should be thankful for that."

"Thank you," Alyssa said. "But I really do have to be going."

Bea stood up. "Thank you for coming by."

"I'll let you know if anything comes up that I can talk about." Alyssa said her good-byes. "I know the way out, no need to show me to the door."

No one said anything until they were sure she had

gone. When her car had disappeared down the drive-way, Kipling stood up.

"Okay, here's what we're going to do. Bea, you finish looking through the file box, to see if you can find anything pertinent. Knox, have you searched the dark web yet?"

Knox shook his head. "But I think it's time I do."

"I agree," Kipling said. "Bea, you're good with the files? Knox will search the dark web. And I'll dig around the attic to see if I can find something in those boxes of Dad's we have up there."

They all agreed and decided to check back with each other at noon.

Bea waited until Kipling left before talking to Knox. She put a hand on his shoulder. "Be careful. The dark web is nothing to mess around with."

She knew he was an adult and that he knew what he was doing, but she couldn't help but be worried. Knox reached down and kissed her on the forehead.

"I've been doing this for years. Trust me on this. If there is information out there, I'll find it."

"Who do you think it is?" she asked. He had a determined look on his face that made her wonder if he knew more than he was letting on.

"The person that killed Mom and Dad?" At her nod, he continued, "I'm not sure. From what I gathered, he's still alive. Knowing that, I think it's possible, everything is related. And I wonder if they're in Charleston. Were they close to Dad? If so, it might be somebody we know."

She hadn't thought of that—the potential that it was somebody the family was close with. "That's scary to think about." Especially if that person was responsible for the threats against her.

"Don't worry," Knox said. "We're getting close. I can feel it. We're going to find this SOB and bring him down."

Knox left Bea in the living room going through the box of Mr. Brock's papers. On his way to the downstairs office, he passed a pile of mail Lena had brought in, waiting in the kitchen. He went through each piece to make sure there wasn't a threat against Bea. If there was, he would make sure she was prepared before she saw it.

There was nothing addressed to her except for a legal envelope from a law firm. He tilted his head. A family law practice. Curious, he opened it. He pulled out the papers inside, and as he read them, the mail he'd been holding fell to the ground.

What the fuck?

What the actual fuck?

She was going to file for divorce?

What the fuck? he repeated in his head.

From the address on the envelope, the papers had gone to her apartment first. Then, since she had forwarded her mail to Benedict House, it had been rerouted here. His hands shook in anger and he stormed out of the kitchen.

"What is this?" he asked, throwing the papers down on top of the box she was working in.

She picked them up and read them. "Where did you get these?"

"They were in the mail was delivered today."

"You went into my mail?"

"That's the question you have? Did I go through your

mail? Hell, yes, I went through your mail. I wanted to make sure that asshole hadn't contacted you again. And there wasn't any mail from him, but there were a pack of divorce papers. Care to explain that?" His voice was calm, but his eyes blazed in anger.

She put the divorce papers to the side. "I talked to this firm right after my accident. At the time, I thought it best to get a divorce or to at least appear as if I were filing for divorce."

"I can't believe you went through the trouble of having someone to draw up divorce papers. Were you planning on filing them?"

She was hurt he could even think that. "I hadn't planned on it. All I thought was that if I went through the motions, the men who were watching me might drop their guard. At least enough for me to get some peace and a good night's sleep."

"Did it ever occur to you to ask me or to talk to me about any of this? To maybe, I don't know, let me in on your plan?"

"No, because then it wouldn't appear real."

Knox ran his fingers through his hair the way he did when he was agitated. She hadn't expected him to take it well, but that didn't make the reality any easier.

He turned to walk out of the room.

"Where are you going?" she asked.

"I need some air."

No. It didn't make it any easier at all.

Tom picked up his binoculars again to watch the young woman as she walked up the beach. He wished she'd turn around or that he was positioned better to see her face. He'd been following Jade for the last two hours, wanting to nail down her routine so he could come up with the perfect plan to take her down.

He knew for a fact he had to be one hundred percent perfect before he put in a call to The Gentleman. It had been unspoken, but he knew he had only one more chance to get this right. One more screwup and he was done. He'd told the Benedicts he was taking his mom to the doctor. They had loved that, he thought with a chuckle.

Jade was much skinnier than he remembered her being. He supposed that's what living on the streets would do to her. He wouldn't say he was sorry, because he wasn't. She'd caused him pain and suffering, it was only fair she suffered as well. Poetic justice and all that. Of course, no one would be writing poetry over what he planned to do to her. Or if they did, they were fucked up more than he was.

He needed to get closer. She was currently carrying a fishing pole. Obviously, she was on the hunt for dinner. He needed to position himself in a way that he could see her when she walked back to the house. And he needed cover, so that he could hide and she wouldn't see him. All he needed was one look, one second of recognition, and that would be all she wrote.

He wasn't sure how many fish she planned to catch. He wouldn't think someone of her size would eat very many, but you never knew. For all he knew, she had some way to keep them cold and would fish for several days. On the other hand, she might only be catching what she would eat today. What he had to do was plan for the worst. Or in this case, the shortest.

He walked back, away from the beach. Good thing there weren't very many people around. He probably would have a hard time explaining what he was doing. Much better that no one saw him. Now he had to keep it that way.

Taking care to be as unnoticeable as possible, he hurried away from his spot by the tree. He walked down the street as if he belonged there. He'd learned that when someone had an air of confidence around them, they didn't seem to draw as many questioning stares. Not that there was anyone nearby to question him. And that was the way he wanted to keep it.

The driveway leading up to the house where the woman who might be Jade was staying was overgrown. It seemed perfect for somebody who was staying in a place they shouldn't be. His heart beat faster as it became more and more likely this was Jade.

He found a dune in the house's side yard, far enough away to provide cover, while still being close enough to for assurances of who he was dealing with. And its size made it perfect for him to hide behind without being seen.

He got into position and prepared to wait. He was surprised at how quickly she caught a fish. He was even more surprised when she started packing up. Apparently, she was only after one fish today. He patted himself on the back for his hunting skills.

Now she just had to turn around. He wasn't sure he took a breath as he waited. When she did, his heart jumped to his throat. It was Jade, and she looked horrible. From the looks of it, she thought her location was very secure and as such, she didn't have plans to move along anytime soon.

All of that suited his purpose just fine. His blood pulsed with the excitement of finally being able to tell

The Gentleman where Jade was and how run down she looked. He knew not to count his chickens before they hatched, but couldn't help but imagine The Gentleman's delight and appreciation. He'd made a mistake not taking her in when he first found her. He wouldn't be making it the second time.

Should he just grab her now and take her in? Or call The Gentleman and allow him the pleasure of doing so? Choices, choices, choices. And this time, all of them good. It was a wonderful position to be in.

His phone rang. Not the one signaling The Gentleman, but the one he didn't want to answer, but did, knowing that it would be what The Gentleman wanted.

"Hello?" he said. Even as he answered he knew he wouldn't be grabbing Jade until tomorrow. Looked like today was her lucky day. He'd make sure she didn't have another one.

CHAPTER 11

Bea hung the phone up with a sigh. Her senior partner had agreed for her to take a leave of absence, but he asked that she prepare a summation of the cases he was working on. She didn't mind and it was certainly a reasonable request, but it meant that she had to go by the office to get her paperwork and that was going to be a hassle.

Knox, even in his upset stage, wouldn't want her to go. And while she could send someone to pick it up, it would be so much quicker and easier if she did it herself. She wasn't stupid, she wasn't about to go by herself, but she was going to go. She'd take Tom. Jade's warning rang in the back of her head, but she discarded it. Besides, it was just a quick trip to her office and back.

A quick glance down the hall showed Knox was still in the office. He'd been in there ever since he walked out on her earlier. Obviously, he was on the phone because the door was closed. Normally, she'd be upset that he'd closed the door, in what she saw as a way to shut her out. This time, however, she was thrilled as it allowed her to do things she'd have trouble being truthful about if he'd had it open.

She sent Tom a text quickly, grabbed her purse, and went to wait outside, hoping if anyone saw her they'd just think she was walking around the yard. With her back to the house, she made show of bending down to smell a few flowers.

As she waited for Tom to get the car and to come by, she thought again about the divorce papers. Yes, she probably should have brought them up sooner, but in all honesty, she'd forgotten about them and, really, what was the big deal? She'd explained everything to Knox. He was the one being unreasonable.

But as she thought about it more, she realized how upset she'd be if the situation was reversed. She could see that finding them had been a shock. She'd give him that much. And she also knew he was reasonable and she fully expected that after he got over the shock and processed what she'd said, that he'd see her side.

Knox wasn't a man who held on to his anger for any length of time. She wondered who he was on the phone with and if he'd found anything with his search? She also wanted to know if he still thought it was a possibility someone had killed Tilly's mom. Tilly and Keaton had arrived home not long ago, so they should be at dinner. Although, she didn't think dinner was the best time to discuss that with Tilly

Tom got into the dark sedan and headed toward Benedict House. Bea had sent a text asking if he'd accompany her to her law office. And just like that, the mouse walked into the trap.

Because the text asking to take her to the office came in so fast, he didn't have time to alert The Gentleman. Not if wanted time to run by her office before she actually made it there. And he did, imagining her face when she walked inside. He would make that call as soon as Bea stepped inside the office. The time had come to deal with her permanently.

Since he'd told The Gentleman how close he was to finding Jade, it seemed she'd become his focus. Tom had a feeling that would change once he heard that Tom had Bea. After she'd been dealt with he'd tell The Gentleman he knew where Jade was. He smiled at the thought. It was about time things went his way.

Bea plastered on a fake smile when Tom pulled up. She slipped into the backseat, buckled her seatbelt, and told him she was ready. He didn't say much, but seemed to stare at her through the rearview mirror. She told herself it wasn't creepy, that he was just checking to make sure they didn't have a tail. She remembered Jade's warning not to trust him. She put her hand on door handle and briefly thought about jumping out at the next stop sign, but talked herself out of it. He was just taking her to her office, after all.

She got out her cell phone, and contemplated texting Knox. Just let him know where she was and when she expected to be back. Then she decided she didn't want to hear about how she shouldn't have left the house. She shoved the phone back into her purse.

The ride to the office took longer than it normally did. She'd forgotten there was some sort of festival happening in town so there were more tourists than normal. She drummed her fingers against the arm rest and checked the time. All the while feeling as if Tom was watching her.

Creepy.

Oh, well. What was done was done, and she couldn't stop it now. She'd get to the office, grab the paperwork, and make it back to Benedict House with no one being any wiser.

Finally, they pulled up to the office and she hopped out of the car.

"I'll be just a few minutes inside," she said. "Wait here and make sure nobody shows up?"

Tom nodded.

Just as well, she wasn't paying him for his conversational skills.

She unlocked the door to the office and couldn't stop the habit of looking over her shoulder. Of course no one was there. Just Tom waiting in the car. Honestly, he was scary and intimidating enough to keep any bad guys far, far away.

She smiled to herself as she walked down the hall. It felt good to get out of the house. Stuck inside Benedict House for what seemed like weeks, she hadn't yet grown accustomed to the feeling of cabin fever. She wished she'd thought ahead of time and arranged to have lunch with girlfriends or something.

No, best that she didn't. She was pushing it enough coming to the office, no need to tempt fate.

Her office door was closed and locked, just the way she'd left it. She was actually surprised. For some reason, she'd expected someone to have broken into it. Taking a deep breath, she unlocked the door and stepped on a sheet on paper when she opened it.

She bent down to pick it up with trembling fingers. The entire time hoping against all hope it wasn't another threat or taunt. It was flipped over so she couldn't see anything that was on it.

Right as she picked it up, the floor creaked from somewhere near the lobby.

Her heart pounded. The office should be empty. It was the weekend, she was the only person who should be inside right now. She flipped the paper over. There was only one word printed on the paper. But that one word was enough to freeze her in fear.

Checkmate.

The office was filled with the sound of blood pounding in her head, Over and over.

Tick.

Tick.

Tick.

Only, it wasn't her head. It was in the office. Panic seized her body and fear wrapped its sharp tentacles around her heart. And in that moment, she knew she was going to die.

I'm so sorry, Knox.

Sorry she left Benedict House without telling him. Sorry for the pain her death would cause him. Sorry because she wasn't sure he knew how much she loved him.

Footsteps sounded out in the hall and she made a vow that even though she knew she wouldn't make it out of this alive, she wasn't going to go down without a fight. She wasn't going to go easy. She would fight as long as she was able to pull air into her lungs.

She scanned her office, looking for something that

could be used as a weapon. Her eyes fell on a metal pen she'd been given as a gift by one of her clients for Christmas a few years ago. At the time, she thought a pen to be a ridiculous gift. Why spend so much money on a pen when you could pick one up anywhere for almost pennies? But as she picked the pen up and tested its weight in her hand, she gave silent thanks to the client who gave her what she had originally thought was useless.

She turned and waited for her tormentor to appear in the doorway.

CHAPTER 12

Knox was going to kill someone.

He was going to start with every last man who worked at the security firm Kipling had on retainer, then he was going to move on to anyone at Benedict House that let Bea leave the house.

He picked the phone up and called Tom for the third time. The line had been busy both times before and he swore under his breath when it was again.

"Kip!" he yelled down the hall, knowing his older brother was hanging out in the kitchen, trying to avoid him. "Give me the cell phone number for the owner of that damn firm."

Kipling appeared in the doorway. "Is Tom's number not working?"

"Tom's not answering his damn cell phone," Knox told him. "I'm going to lay down the law when I see him again. He is always to be reachable via phone."

"You think he took Bea somewhere?" Kipling asked. "Or that she told him not to answer his phone?"

Knox stopped and took a deep breath. He needed to

get his shit together, calm down, and think about this reasonably. "At this point," he told his brother, "I have to assume anything is a possibly."

Kipling nodded, dug into his desk, and pulled out the number to the firm and passed it to Knox.

Knox pounded the digits into his phone and gave a sigh of relief when the line rang instead of giving a busy signal.

"Smith," the voice on the other end said.

"This is Knox Benedict. I believe one of the guards I hired from your firm, Tom Anderson, took my wife somewhere about an hour ago and now he's not answering his phone. Do you have another number or some other way to get in contact with him?"

There was a pause, too long of one in Knox's mind. "Hello?" he asked.

"Are you sure it was Tom, sir?" the guy finally asked.

"Yes, I'm sure." Knox cut his eyes to Kipling to let his brother know what he thought of the firm he'd hired.

"There's no good way to tell you this, sir," the guy on the other end of the phone said. "But we show this contract as cancelled as of a week ago."

Bea slipped the pen in the pocket of her pants. She didn't have to wait long for the person to appear in the doorway. Though it really didn't make sense when he did.

Her relief at recognizing Tom lasted for mere seconds. Just long enough for her to process that the smile he gave her wasn't friendly, but evil. Even then she didn't panic. Not until he casually lifted his left hand as if checking the time and she noticed he was wearing the watch that invaded her dreams. Her chest grew so tight, she couldn't breathe. Spots swam before her eyes and she curled her fists so her nails dug into her palms. She couldn't just give up. She couldn't.

"Your time is up. You have a very bad habit of not following directions," he said in the voice that tormented her sleep.

"You." It was the only word she could get out. The only word she found could encompass all the pain from remembering how he'd hurt her, the fear from how he tormented her, and the despair of what he was going to do now.

"You finally remember me," he said.

She saw no point in answering. It was obvious she did, her only regret was that she didn't pick up on it sooner. She lifted her chin higher and looked down her nose at him. Now that she saw him up close it was obvious who he was. She could have smacked herself for not noticing before.

"How did you get a job at the security firm?" she asked. She really didn't care, but she thought it was in her best interest to get him to talk. Had Knox realized she'd left Benedict House yet? Even if he had, would he write off her absence or would he come looking for her?

He would come. He had to come. It was a tiny sliver of hope, but at the moment, it was all she had.

Then just as quickly as she decided that he would come to her, she understood why Tom hadn't made a move toward her. He didn't want her dead. Yet. For the moment, he needed her alive so he could use her to draw Knox.

She forced a smile to her lips. "He won't come, you know."

The guard snorted. "He'll show."

"Don't be so sure." Somehow she knew the next few

minutes would be instrumental in whether she walked out of the office or not. "We had a huge fight. Believe it or not, it was over divorce papers."

That statement took the know-it-all grin off his face and for a brief second a look of disbelief took its place. "Divorce papers?"

"Yes," she replied. "As it turns out, I can follow directions. I was in the process of divorcing him. Except he found the papers this morning and it didn't go over all that well."

He was getting ready to say something when a buzz from his back got his attention. He pulled out his phone and smiled as he read the display. "He must not have been that angry. He just left Benedict House and from the GPS we put on his car, it appears he's headed straight here."

He waved his gun toward the chair in front of her desk. "Sit down."

She hesitated. If she said no, it would force his hand. Would he shoot her and maybe people nearby would call the cops at the sound of gunfire? Or should she sit down and think of a way to warn Knox?

"I said: Sit. Down." Obviously, Tom had grown weary of her taking so long to decide. He aimed the gun at her feet and shot.

Bea yelped as the wooden floor exploded beneath her. Any hope of the sound of gunshots drawing someone's attention shattered along with the wooden planks. He'd used a silencer.

He grinned at her horror. "Now."

She stumbled on shaky legs to the chair and sat down.

"Very nice." He walked toward her, brought a thin

rope from out of his pocket and tied her arms to the chair. "Now we sit and wait."

She wiggled her hands. He'd tied them behind her and while he'd done it tightly, she'd managed to shove the pen up her sleeve before he did so. If she wiggled the right way, she could reach it.

Now was when she should ask him all her questions. Her face must have given her away because he stood at her desk and said, "I've been given permission to shoot you if you get too chatty."

She shut her mouth. Maybe she could learn just as much by listening to him. The fact that he'd said he'd been given permission told her that there was more people involved than just him. It also told her that he wasn't in charge.

"I've enjoyed being close to you." He walked and stood to where he was right by her side. He wasn't touching her, but he was definitely in her personal space. "In fact, I might not kill you. I may save you for my boss. I'm not totally sure what he'd do with you, but I have a pretty good idea." The guy seemed to get off by talking to her. She couldn't decide if it was a good thing to know what these guys had in store for her or if she'd be better off not knowing.

She shifted her hands, picking at the knot with the pen, and willed Knox to drive slowly. If she had enough time, she thought she might be able to untie it.

"He's been extremely hard on his women lately. Though from what I've heard, it's not any better if you survive a night in his bed. He'll just pass you along to the guards or some other employee. They're even worse than he is."

No, she definitely didn't want to hear this. She kept listening for the sound of a car pulling up. The driveway and parking lot were covered in gravel. If Knox drove across either, she would hear. Of course, so would Tom.

The guard got up and walked to the window. While his back was to her, she worked her hands as hard as she could on the rope binding her wrists together. At the merest suggestion in his body language that he was getting ready to turn around, she stopped and held her hands still.

She estimated she needed another ten minutes and she'd have the knot released. How long had it been since he'd told her Knox was on the way? It didn't take that long to drive from Benedict House to her office. Of course, there was the festival. Even still, she anticipated hearing his car any second. There was no way she'd have the knot undone by the time he arrived.

Tom's phone buzzed again. He turned his back to her when he answered.

"No" he said to whoever was on the other end while her hands and fingers worked frantically to loosen the knot more.

"The streets were crowded, though," he said. Apparently, she wasn't the only one who thought it was taking entirely too long for Knox to show up. She decided to take that as a good sign. She had to—the other option was to look at it to mean he'd left Benedict House with no intention of coming by her office and she couldn't bear to think that.

"You want me to what?" he asked, right as she heard the sound of a car driving over gravel. Of course, he heard it, too, and turned back to the window. Bea would have given anything to be able to look out the window, but from her chair, she only saw sky.

Instead of dwelling on it, she used the time she had while his back was turned to work on the rope some more.

"He's here," he finally said as a car door slammed from outside and Tom ended the call.

He turned around and she stopped moving her hands. *Almost.* If he'd only kept talking a little bit more.

"Looks like you were right after all," he said. "Your husband didn't come. Only his older brother."

Kipling came and not Knox? That didn't make any sense.

"Doesn't matter to me," the guy kept talking. "One dead Benedict is as good as another."

"Tom," Kipling said from the front of the building. "Come on out and bring Bea. Game's up. The police are on their way."

Tom laughed. "No, thanks. We'll stay right where we are."

"Help, Kip!" Bea shouted. "He has a gun."

"Shut up." Tom stomped over to her and slapped her face. Tears sprang to her eyes and her cheek throbbed. "Stupid bitch."

"Bea, I'm coming." Kipling said.

Tom stood his ground. "Step one foot in here and I'll shoot her. I swear to God."

Tom had turned to face the door and with his back to her, she hurried to finish untying her hands. She got them free and focused on not giving away her accomplishment.

"I've called the police," Kipling said from the front of the building. "They're on their way."

Tom turned back to the doorway. "Doesn't matter. You'll be dead."

She heard Kipling's footsteps as he made his way through the office. He wasn't headed straight to hers like she thought he would. From the way it sounded, he was taking his time and stomping through every room on the way to her back office.

Suddenly, Knox appeared in her peripheral vision and her heart soared with the knowledge that he'd shown up and the hope that she might just make it out of the office alive. She fixed her fingers and wrist, trying to get the blood flowing again.

Tom saw her move. "What are you doing?"

She decided to play dumb.

"Nothing, obviously," she said. "I'm tied to a chair."

He took a step toward her. "Don't get smart with me." He raised a hand, like he was going to strike her again and she cringed as she waited for the blow to fall.

"Don't fucking touch her." Knox appeared in the doorway, holding a pointed gun at Tom's head.

She gulped at the sight of him holding a gun. It looked so out of place in his hands. She'd always seen him as a businessman, someone who sat behind a desk. To see him with a weapon didn't make any sense, but the ease with which he carried it seemed to indicate he'd held a gun or two.

Tom didn't appear to be all that impressed. His weapon wasn't pointed at either her or Knox, but he hadn't discarded it, either.

"So you have a gun," Tom said. "Big deal. I can still shoot her and even if you shoot me, which I don't think you will, she'll still be dead."

"Wrong, asshole." Kipling appeared from the adjoining office, holding another gun.

Knox didn't look at her, all his attention was focused on Tom. "You make one move toward her or if you lift your gun . . . hell, if I think you're breathing too heavy, I shoot. Understood?"

Tom seemed to weigh his options. Part of her wanted him to do something to give either brother a reason to shoot him. But she wasn't sure either Knox or Kipling had ever killed someone and she knew that could leave a lasting imprint. For that reason and that reason only, she hoped this incident ended without bloodshed. If it were anyone else holding the gun at Tom, she'd want them to blow him into a thousand different pieces.

Tom lowered his gun and she sighed in relief, thankful no one was going to die. Kipling and Knox exchanged a look, and Kipling nodded. The slight drop in alertness from both brothers didn't go unnoticed by Tom. Moving faster than she'd imagined a person of his size could move, he lifted his gun and took aim at her.

"No!" Knox yelled, but she was already out of harm's way. In one move, she fell from the chair onto the floor, not wanting to think about how close she'd been to not getting herself untied.

She covered her head as the sound of gunfire ran out. Something hard and heavy fell on her, knocking her flat to the ground. She tried to move, but the body on her was too heavy.

"Knox," she called out, but there was no answer.

Working up strength she didn't know she had, she pushed herself upward, causing the body on top of her to roll off her and onto the ground. Tom, she noted with some relief.

She looked around frantically and saw Knox on the floor. He wasn't moving and there was a growing red circle on his left shoulder.

"Knox!" she yelled. She tried to stand up, but the fall from the chair must have injured her leg because it wouldn't hold her weight. She crawled to him.

"Knox," she whispered, placing a hand on his chest and bursting into tears when his breathing moved it. His eyes weren't open, but he was breathing, which meant he wasn't dead.

"Hang in there. I'll call for help." Already she heard sirens approaching. She glanced to her left and saw Kipling on the floor. He groaned and pulled his knees up as if getting up. Satisfied he was okay, she turned her attention back to her husband.

Knox's eyes fluttered open. "Bea?" he asked softly, causing her to cry more.

She stroked his cheek, knowing she had to touch him and reaching for a spot that wasn't injured. "Yes. Yes. It's me and we're okay. Help is on the way. You just be still and hang in there."

All at once, his eyes grew murderously cold and a deadly rage settled over his expression. "Knox?" she whispered.

He roared while reaching for her at the same time. She tried to get out of his way, but he grabbed her by the neck and somehow with his injured arm, pulled her so her face pressed against his chest.

Above her, a gunshot rang out and something behind her fell to the floor.

"Got him," Knox whispered and then promptly passed out, dropping the gun he held in his right hand.

She looked over her shoulder and found Tom, crumpled on the flood with a gunshot to his chest. But it was the knife he held that captured her attention.

The realization of how close he'd been to stabbing her in the back made her shiver and as the tremors took over her body, she wondered if they'd ever stop.

The Gentleman turned the television off with a curse and slammed the remote control on the table in front of him. How did Tom get killed by the Benedicts?

Unfortunately, this was the next in a long line of fuck-ups. It seemed lately that everything he tried to do, every plan he put in place, someone fucked up.

Maybe that was the problem. Maybe he'd grown too complacent with his delegation. Trusted too many people to do the job and to do it correctly. Back when he was the only person running the operation, he didn't have these issues.

He stood and walked to the window. It was raining. Many people didn't like the rain. He didn't mind it. To him it was like the rain washed away all the old and paved the way for something new. That's what he needed to do. He needed to cut the operation down, trim it, prune it. Get rid of the dead weight.

Hadn't he learned early on that the only person who was one hundred percent trustworthy was himself? And hadn't he often preached that if you wanted something done right, you had to do it yourself?

He'd trusted Jade and she'd run off.

He'd trusted Tom and he'd got himself killed.

No more. From this point onward, he was not only the one making the plans and calling the shots, he was also the one who executed everything. He felt his heart grow lighter the more and more he thought about it.

Perfect. This would be perfect.

Cut out the middleman. They were useless anyway.

He would need time to reorganize, assess, and plan. That was no problem, he could lay low for however long he needed to. He chuckled. It might actually work to his benefit to play it that way. The Benedicts would likely grow complacent. They'd forget he was out there. Which would make their demise all the better.

He couldn't wait.

CHAPTER 13

Knox woke up in phases, it seemed to him. First, he became aware of the sounds. A steady *beep, beep, beep* he assumed was his heart. Then came the whispers, and he realized they hadn't noticed yet that he was awake. He strained, trying to make out the voices, to tell who they were, but they were much too soft. Somewhere nearby someone was pushing a cart. A metal cart down a hard-surfaced floor.

He had no idea where he was. A quick mental check of his body revealed a left shoulder that hurt like nobody's business. Had he somehow hurt his shoulder? He couldn't remember.

He searched his brain for some hint as to where he was and what had happened to him. Thought back to the last thing he remembered. The only thing he recalled was a gun and Bea.

Bea!

He struggled to sit up, but found he couldn't. His eyes flew open in his desperate attempt to find his wife.

"Bea!" he tried to yell, but it came out more like a

whisper. He looked around the room, but didn't see the one face he needed to see above all the others.

Oh God, had he been too late?

He remembered now how his shoulder got hurt. Tom had shot him. He'd kill him. A red seething rage overcame him as he recalled the man standing behind Bea with a knife. Then he remembered the look of shock on her face when he pulled her toward him to get out of the way so he could shoot the guard.

He didn't have the time to explain what he was doing, he'd just reacted on instinct. Just seconds prior, he was certain he only had the energy to breathe. Seeing Tom's intent to kill Bea proved him wrong. The thought of what came way too close to happening proved one thing: nothing would ever come between him and his wife again. And he'd always made sure she knew he loved her, so there shouldn't be a doubt, but he had a feeling he might be going a bit overboard in that regard from here on out.

Tilly and Keaton stood nearby, but he didn't see Kipling. He hoped his brother was okay. He thought back, trying to remember where he could have been in the room when he shot the guard, but he couldn't do it.

He looked up to Tilly and Keaton. "Bea?"

Keaton walked over to his side, worry lines etched on his face. "She's being examined. She refused for a long time, but the shock eventually got to her, and the doctors insisted she be checked out. She still put up a fuss; she wanted to be here when you woke up."

He felt the tension leave his body. But then a new worry occurred to him. "Is she okay?"

Keaton's smile assured him as did the pat on his good shoulder. "She's going be just fine. A little shaken, but that's to be expected. Seeing you awake and talking will do a world of good, I'm sure."

"Kipling?" he asked, while silently praying that his brother was okay as well.

"He's fine," Keaton assured him. "He just went to the bathroom. He'll be back in a few minutes." His jovial expression turned serious and his voice was somber when he added, "The guard, however, was dead at the scene."

He certainly hoped so, but didn't voice that hope out loud. "I thought he would be. I had to shoot to kill him. He was going after Bea with a knife." He searched his mind, trying to find any remorse over what he had done. Whenever he started to feel guilty, he pictured the look in the man's eyes as he stood behind Bea with his knife poised and ready to strike. He shivered, knowing that image would haunt him for a long time.

No, he didn't feel guilty at all. In fact, if faced with the situation for a second time, he'd take the man down again in a heartbeat. The exact same way.

"Alyssa came by." Keaton poured him a glass of water. "She's going to want to talk to you, obviously. The nurses chased her out, but I have a feeling Kipling was getting ready to do the same thing." He added the last part with a chuckle.

Knox nodded. He knew he would have talk to the police eventually. He would tell them the same thing, that, yes, he shot the man and he'd do it again in a second.

"No, I'm not going home," he heard from the hallway and smiled. Bea. "I'm going to see my husband. No, you can't talk me into doing something else."

The door opened and closed, and none too softly. "I swear," Bea said. "If one more person tries to get me to go home, I'm going to punch them."

She walked farther into the room and saw him. Her face lit up and she gasped and ran to the side. "You're awake. When did that happen? Are you okay? How do you feel?"

She reached her hand out but pulled back quickly as if afraid to touch him. He took her hand instead.

"Let's see if I can remember all the questions," he teased. "About five minutes ago. I am now. And much better now that you're here."

She dropped her head but not before he saw tears fill her eyes. "You were so silent and still. I was afraid you weren't going to wake up. That he'd hurt you too badly." She sniffled.

"No." He squeezed her hand. "It would take a lot more than that man to keep me down."

From the corner of his eye, he saw Keaton and Tilly slip out of room. Bea held his hand in a death grip and tears were running freely down her cheeks now.

"I'm so sorry," she said and wiped her nose. "I never meant for you to get or see those divorce papers. I honestly forgot all about them. Forget that I'd even asked for them to be drawn up. I was so busy with all the other stuff going on. The threats and everything surrounding them nearly consumed me. I worked so hard to stay away from you, the fact I'd actually requested them left my mind. I'm sorry if it hurt you when you saw them. That was never my intent."

She was babbling. He didn't think he'd ever seen her in such a state before. He stroked her hand with his thumb. "Bea," he said softly.

She stopped talking and sniffled again, but didn't say anything.

"I'm not upset about the divorce papers," he said, as she looked at him in shock. "I understand why you had them drawn up. I don't like it, but understand it. I know that you are looking out for me, trying to keep me safe."

"Thank you," she said softly.

"But I don't want our first instinct to be to walk out when things get tough. We have to be honest with one another and work through the issues. Talk about them." He swallowed around the lump in his throat. "I love you too much for anything less."

"I love you, too." She sniffled. "And I need some tissue before I get snot all over you."

He laughed. "I'm sure there's some around here."

She found the tissues on a tray near his bed and wiped her nose. "I also really want to hug you, but I'm afraid I'm going to hurt your shoulder."

"I'll risk it," he said. He lifted his good arm and stretched it out toward her. "Come here."

She went willingly into his embrace and though it was awkward, they managed to hug without disturbing his injured arm.

"I can't wait to get you out of here," she said. "Get you back to Benedict House. Pamper you all day. And night."

The beachfront property he had bought and never told her about came to mind. "About that," he said, "I have a surprise for you when I get out of here."

"To be honest, I've had enough presents for one lifetime."

He laughed. "True. But you haven't seen this prize yet and I guarantee you're going to love it."

She looked at him skeptically. "I'll take your word for it, and when you get out of here, you can give me your surprise."

"Oh no," he said, taking note of the bewildered look she gave him. "This isn't a surprise I can just give you. We have to travel there."

"In that case, color me intrigued." She leaned over and gave him a quick kiss, right when the door opened and a nurse walked in.

"I heard someone was awake," she said.

"Yes, and ready to get out of here," Knox said.

"Let's see what we can do to make that happen."

Two weeks later, Bea sat in Knox's car while he drove her to the surprise he'd brought up in the hospital. She still didn't know what kind of surprise it was or why they had to get in the car and drive to it. Knox had practically been bouncing up and down all day in excitement. She had to admit, seeing him so excited made her that way, too.

Or at least she was excited until he pulled a blindfold out.

"No thanks." She crossed her arms, deciding to tease him. "I'm not into that kinky shit."

He held the blindfold out by the strap to show her. "This isn't kinky shit. I just don't want you to see where we're going before we get there."

She smiled beneath the fabric covering her eyes. Honestly. It was just a figure of speech. But deep inside, she loved the possessive way he was around her.

For a time after they'd got in the car and started driving, she tried to keep up with where they were. She totally sucked at directions though, so after the first few turns, she'd given up and just leaned back to enjoy the ride.

"Are we there yet?" she said, more to annoy him than anything.

"Not yet," he replied.

She counted to ten before asking, "How about now?"

"You're incorrigible," he said with a laugh.

"Coming from you, I take that as a compliment." She fingered the edge of the blindfold. "Just a quick peek?"

"No."

"A tiny little one?"

"No."

"How about a hint, is it bigger than a bread box?"

"Who uses a bread box anymore? But yes, it's much, much bigger than a bread box."

Much, much bigger. That was certainly a surprise in and of itself. She'd thought maybe he'd bought her some jewelry or something. But that theory ceased to make sense as soon as they got into his car.

They turned off the main road. She could tell by the bumping. Wherever they were didn't have paved roads. That made even less sense.

"Where are we?" she said, mostly to herself.

"Almost there," Knox said, and she could tell he had a smile on his face. He was thoroughly enjoying this. That made her happy. She told herself no matter what the surprise was, she was going to love it.

Knox stopped the car and she swore she could feel his excitement radiate off him. Knowing he enjoyed this so much, made her enjoy it as well.

"Stay there," he said when she attempted to open the door.

"Can I take it off now?"

"Not yet, Mrs. Impatient."

She gave a mock groan and a long drawn-out sigh. But Knox would have none of it.

"You only have to be patient a few minutes more." He helped her out of the car and the sound of waves crashing welcomed her.

"We're at the beach?" she asked, but Knox obviously wasn't answering any more questions.

"Come on," he said, walking slowly beside her. She shuffled her feet to make sure she didn't trip over anything. They weren't on sand yet, she still had gravel under her feet. But she could hear the ocean and, even better, she could smell it.

"Just a few more steps." He led her onto what she thought to be grass. She held the arm he didn't have hold of out to her side to help with balance.

True to his word, they came to a halt a few steps later. He didn't immediately remove the blindfold, but stood there. Bea took the time to listen to her surroundings. Wherever they were, it wasn't crowded with people. In fact, she would almost say they were the only two people around. She could still hear the faint crash of waves, but it seemed almost out of place with the smell of freshly cut grass.

Knox reached behind her to untie the blindfold and she wasn't one hundred percent, but she thought she felt his hands shake.

The blindfold fell away and the bright sunlight blinded her momentarily. She blinked a few times, trying to speed up the adjustment of her vision. Little by little it cleared to show a house in front of her.

It was a bit rundown. The wraparound porch looked

like it needed to be replaced, one of the front windows was broken, and the entire structure needed painting. But with a bit of work, it would look incredible. The acreage was impressive, she could barely see the neighbors.

"What do you think?" he asked.

"I think if you fixed it up, it could become quite the head turner."

Beside her, he nodded in agreement. "That's what I thought. When I bought it."

She wasn't sure she heard him correctly. *He bought it? Like bought it, bought it?* "You what?" she asked.

He reached between them and took her hand. "Before I proposed, I saw it and knew it was our house, though I didn't put an offer on it until after. With your sense of style, it'll be amazing when we finish with it."

But her mind couldn't get there yet. She was still stuck on the fact that he'd bought them a house. "You bought a house."

"Yes." His answer was a bit hesitant and she feared he'd gotten the wrong impression and thought she was mad. "I was going to tell you sooner, bring you out here, but then all that happened with the threats, and your father and I . . ." His voice trailed off.

"Knox," she said, turning to face him.

"Yes?"

"I love it." She threw her arms around him. "I mean, living at Benedict House isn't as stifling as I thought it would be. I like your brothers and Tilly's a lot of fun, but we're still living in a place that isn't completely ours. This place, it feels right."

He looked at her with such passion she felt it down to her toes. "I'm so glad you like it. I just knew when I saw it that it was the perfect place for us. We'll still have to stay at Benedict House while renovations are being completed."

Yes, but at the end, this house and land would be theirs. "I don't mind, it'll be worth it when it's all said and done."

"Do you want to go look inside?" he asked.

"Of course." She could hardly believe they were standing in front of their house. She couldn't wait to go inside. She somehow knew it would be perfect.

"Before we go inside," he said, "there's one more thing I want to ask you." He waited for her to nod before he continued. "Since we were kind of evil and got married without telling anybody, what do you think of having a vow renewal ceremony? We can invite everybody, all of our family and friends. Then maybe they'll finally get off our backs for not telling anyone about our wedding."

It was truly a wonderful idea, Bea felt a bit perturbed she hadn't thought of it first. She rested her hand against his chest. "I think it's perfect. I would like to have it here, but I don't think we'll have it ready in time. Frankly, I don't want to wait too long to marry you again."

He grabbed her hand and held it tight to him, not letting go, as he dropped his head and gave her a claiming kiss. She wrapped her free arm around him, digging her fingers into his hair and being so very thankful that the neighbors couldn't see them from where they were.

When they finally broke apart, he continued to hold her hand and led her to the front door. "Just wait until you see the master bedroom. It's covered with windows and has a huge balcony. You can see the ocean and at night we can leave the door open and hear the waves crash as we go to sleep."

They stepped inside and even though she knew she was looking at everything through rose-colored glasses, she didn't think the house could be more perfect. Or at least it would be perfect when they finish with it.

They went from room to room, talking in excited whispers about what they would change and how it would look when they finished. Just as he had mentioned, she loved the master bedroom. It was so easy to imagine them having breakfast and drinking coffee on the balcony overlooking the ocean.

And she loved the closet space and was surprised that he didn't bring it up, especially since she was always complaining about how small hers was. This one was huge. She joked they could have a party in the closet, or least make it into a guest bedroom. They went back downstairs to the kitchen, and she started planning how she would lay out the countertops.

The only appliance in the kitchen was a stove. It was electric, but she thought they could switch it over to gas during the renovations. It was a shame for the oven to go to waste though. She pulled open the door to look inside, thinking that if it was nice enough and still worked, she could give it to a homeless shelter. She frowned as she looked inside. What was an envelope doing in the oven?

"What in the world?" she asked and held it up for Knox to see.

"That was in the oven?" he asked. "I looked in there the last time I was here and I didn't see it."

Her heart began to pound and she felt clammy. That meant somebody had been inside the house. Someone

Knox had not invited that he did know about. He walked over to her and placed his hand on her shoulder.

"Let's not assume it's a bad thing." His words were meant to comfort her, but they did not. Not after everything they had been through.

"What else could it be? No one's going to send us a housewarming gift and leave it in the oven."

He took the envelope from her hands. "Let me open it."

There was no writing on the outside, no indication of who it was from, or where it came from, or how long it'd been there. He opened it and took out a single sheet of paper.

"It's another birth certificate," he said.

She waited for him to say something else, but he didn't. He just stood there, looking at the paper, but now his expression had gone pale. It freaked her out.

"Knox?" she asked, but he didn't respond. "What is it?"

He didn't say a word, but handed her the sheet of paper and mumbled something about needing to sit down. Concerned, she took the paper and looked down.

It was very similar to the last certificate Knox had been sent. Except this one had more than "Baby girl" listed as the name.

"This can't be right," she said, turning it over as if expecting to find an explanation on the other side.

"It looks pretty official to me."

It did to her as well, which was even more concerning. She ran her finger over the raised seal. "How is this even possible? Wouldn't you have found out before now?"

"I don't know," he said. "But unless she's lying and that's a fake, our sister is very much alive."

"And I think in a whole lot of danger as well."

"Damnit. Why didn't she tell us? Why all the secrecy? It doesn't make sense. None of this makes sense."

Bea didn't know how to answer any of his questions. He probably wasn't looking for her to respond anyway. Right now he was in shock. And with good reason. Besides, how could she answer any of his questions when she had ten thousand of her own? Not the least of which was what they were going to do with this information.

Without waiting for her to say anything, he took his phone out of his pocket and dialed someone.

"Kipling," he said. "We have a problem. I need you to pull every string you have, turn over every rock, call in every favor." He took a deep breath as his brother replied. "It's urgent. It's about our sister. She's alive. And it's Jade."

READ ON FOR AN EXTRA BONUS SCENE

Bea Jacobs had always considered herself to be the epitome of calm and sensible. She credited those as being the two main characteristics that helped her to become valedictorian of her high school class. Later, they aided her in graduating summa cum laude from Duke Law. Really, she decided with a snort, she was an utter and complete bore.

The only thing was, utter and complete bores rarely flew to Vegas to elope.

What the hell was she doing? She glanced to her side where Knox Benedict, her finance, sat looking at her with an amused expression. "What?" she asked.

He leaned closer to her so the flight attendant currently taking drink orders from the passengers in the row in front of them in their first class cabin couldn't hear. "I was sitting here thinking about how happy I was to be on the way to Vegas because I'm going to marry you there, and I look over at you and it looks as if you're getting ready for a root canal."

"It's only because this is so far out of my comfort zone."

He picked up her hand and kissed it. "I know and I'm so happy you're willing to do it."

"Of course I am. Because that means I get to marry you." She leaned in for a kiss. When Knox walked into her life, not so long ago, marriage was the last thing on her mind. Truth be told, she hadn't been looking for any type of relationship. Her life was full enough with work. She was working to become partner at her current law firm and she was very likely going to run for Congress in a few years.

Wow, she really was an utter and complete bore.

"What's that look for?" he asked.

She took his hand. "I just realized what a stick in the mud I am."

"I'm trying to figure out why that has put such a devious expression on your face."

She dropped his hand and ran her finger from his knee to midway up his thigh. "Because for the next seventy-two hours, I'm giving myself permission to be a bit wild."

"Excuse me," the flight attendant interrupted whatever Knox had been getting ready to say. "Can I get either of you something to drink?"

It was just after ten in the morning and Knox asked for a bottle of water. A perfectly rational choice. Very sensible.

Utterly boring.

However, she was on her way to Vegas to get married. And she had just declared that she was no longer going to be boring. She looked at the flight attendant and smiled. "I'll have a Mimosa please."

The flight attendant nodded and left to get their drinks. She looked over at Knox. He was looking at her with amused expression on his face.

"I know," she said. "It's not very wild. I mean, especially when compared to all the crazy things the Benedict brothers do. But it's a baby step in the right direction. Wouldn't you say?"

Knox looks at the woman at his side. His fiancée. This gorgeous, smart, capable woman he had somehow convinced to marry him. "You're drinking before noon," he said. "I'd say you're well on your way to becoming an official Benedict."

She didn't say anything, but continued to look at him with that slightly devious look. The one he wasn't quite sure what to make of. One that turned him on. A lot.

Before he could say anything, the flight attendant had delivered their drinks, and moved on to the people behind them. He sat back in his seat; they still had hours before they reached Vegas, and closed his eyes. He was a little tired. He had been awake a good deal the night before, preparing for the weekend in Vegas, ensuring things at home and at Benedict Industries was taken care of.

Now it was just him and him his almost wife. In less than forty-eight hours, she'd be his. Her hand continued its way up his thigh. He smiled. And he'd be hers.

As if she'd heard him, her finger moved slightly, still headed in the same direction, but now traveling along his inner thigh to get there. He was uncomfortably aware of how much he wanted her.

"Bea," he said, but even to his ears it sounded more

like *Please don't stop.* He was mildly surprised and unexpectedly disappointed when she did stop, but thankfully didn't remove her hand.

He took a deep breath and somehow managed to nearly choke on nothing but air when he felt her warm words tickle his ear, "Tell me, Knox Benedict, are you a member of the Mile High Club?"

By the time he'd collected himself, Bea sat all prim and proper in her own chair, with her hands clasped in her lap, and yet mischief still danced in her eyes.

"I'm not sure whether that was a yes or no," she whispered. "Regardless, nothing of the sort will be happening anytime soon seeing as how you managed to capture the attention of the entire plane just now."

He took a sip of water and matched her body language with his. Relaxed. Looking straight ahead. *As you were, folks, Nothing at all to see here.*

Damn it all.

"The answer to your question is *no*," he said, eyes closed, and trying to calm down the lower half of his body. "Although if I had to guess, I'm the only Benedict brother who can say that."

"You poor thing." He heard her turn a page in what sounded like a magazine. She was reading? He couldn't believe it and yet her voice sounded as if she were still laughing at him. "We'll have to see if we can remedy that. If you can somehow manage not to tip off the entire plane to our plans."

He peeked at her with one eye and couldn't help but grin. Yes, she was still laughing at him.

Bea admired Knox's ass as he closed the door to the suite behind the bellhop. He had a mighty fine ass and by this time tomorrow, it would be her ass. He turned around to find her still staring.

"What?" he asked.

"Just appreciating your ass." She craned her neck, teasing him. "Damn, I can't see it."

He didn't move his body, but crossed his arms instead. She walked to where he stood and put her arms around him, low enough to run her hands over his backside. "I know what your problem is. I didn't get to make good on my Mile High promise. Well, it's not my fault that guy sitting the next row over knew your dad and wanted to chat the entire flight." She thought back to the long flight and how her poor finance spent the majority of it talking to the elder gentleman because he was too polite to do otherwise.

Knox cupped her cheek, slid his hand to her chin and tipped her chin up. At that angle, she felt she could see through his eyes down into his soul. Sure he was a handsome man, but she knew he was so much more. She had the privilege of knowing the Knox only a few knew existed. She saw the man past his eyes and he was even more handsome.

"You're looking at me funny," he said.

He took her breath away. He always had. Starting from that first day in in his office when they met on opposing sides of a law suit.

She had to lick her lips to speak. When had her mouth grown so dry? "I love you so much."

He drew her close and she sighed at how perfectly they fit together. Did every almost-bride feel the same? She hoped so, but somehow doubted it. Then his lips

were on hers and she didn't want to think about anything other than his kiss.

He pulled back, running a hand along the curve of
her spine and awaking her skin to his touch. The way
only he could. She shot him a knowing grin and
brought her hands to the button on his kakis.

"Fortunately for us, there are only two of us here.
No talkative old men. We're not on a plane, but better
late than never." She planned to drop to her knees as
soon as she undid his pants, but he groaned and pulled
her hands away.

"We can't," he moaned.

"Why not?"

He chuckled. "Because I made reservations for you
to be pampered at the spa for the next three hours."

Any other time, she'd jump at the chance for such
an extravagant afternoon.

He brushed his lips against hers. "I could have in
no way anticipated that what I thought was a delightful surprise would come back to bite me the ass."

She laughed. "There you go teasing me with your
ass again. It's very cruel, you know?"

Just before noon the next day, Knox was afraid to blink
for fear he'd wake and find that Vegas was a dream
and the exquisite creature at his side getting ready
to be pronounced as his wife was a figment of his
imagination.

He wished there was a way to remember every detail of this day, forever. He never wanted to forget how
breathtakingly perfect Bea was in the long white gown
that hugged her curves to perfection. Or the look in her

eyes as she met his and recited in the lawyer voice she had that turned him on whenever he heard it, how she vowed to belong to him and only him for as long as they both lived.

For the first time in his life, forever wasn't nearly long enough.

WANT MORE *SONS OF BROAD*?

Read on for the second novella
in this swoon-worthy series

HIDDEN FATE

CHAPTER 1

Brent Taylor considered himself an easygoing man. However, he knew that if he could get his hands on whoever sent his girlfriend roses, he'd rip them from limb to limb. It wasn't that he was overly possessive. Though the thought of anybody other than himself sending Janie Roberts flowers would upset him, it was the note attached to the flowers currently sitting on her dining room table that had the potential to send him into a murderous rage. The note that indicated her life was in danger.

"I should call this in." Janie looked at him, her face was pale, but there was a firm resolve in her voice. Her gaze shifted to the note she'd put on the table.

Rose are red.
Violets are blue.
These roses will die.

Just like you.

"Is this in relation to the case you were working?" Brent's half sister, Bea Jacobs, asked.

Janie had asked Brent to bring Bea to dinner. This was the first time both women were meeting.

"I can't imagine it not being about the case I was working," Janie said. "But why now? I've been fired."

She'd been fired because she had been dating him. The unsolved mystery of kidnapped women had escalated into a murder a few weeks ago. Janie had been working as an undercover bartender at the club where several of the women had worked. That's where Brent had met her.

He'd been considered a suspect at the time and her boss had put her on administrative leave after finding out they were involved. Brent had actually been cleared by then, thanks to DNA evidence. Skin scrapings from underneath the fingernails of the victim were believed to be from the killer and had not matched to Brent. But Janie, being Janie, had not been able to leave the case alone and was fired when her boss caught her investigating in the club.

"It could be several reasons." Brent walked over and sat beside her, putting his arm around her as he answered her question. "He may think that you're more vulnerable now. Or he may think you know something."

"How could I know something?" She was trembling, which only made him more upset. "Alyssa and I don't even talk about the case anymore."

Alyssa Adams was her best friend and work colleague. According to Janie, she had recently been placed on the case.

"I don't know. And whoever is doing this isn't going

to know what you and Alyssa talk about." Brent said. "Either way, I was just thinking out loud."

Janie nodded. "I'm going to call Alyssa."

Janie walked to the far end of the room. If Brent had to guess, she was working hard to get her anger under control. Bea raised an eyebrow.

"Not quite what we had in mind for dinner." Brent scratched his head. "I suppose they'll have to finger-print us. We all touched the box."

"A small price to pay to find who's doing this." Bea was watching Janie with careful eyes. His sister was a lawyer, and she didn't miss much. "You're not going to let her stay here by yourself, are you?"

No, he didn't want to. He wanted her to come back to his house and stay with him. But he knew Janie was very hardheaded, and as a cop, she often felt herself above protection. Yep, she would argue with him.

He looked up as she walked over to them.

"They're on their way. She's off duty and was having dinner with Mac. He's coming, too."

Brent had met Alyssa before, but he'd never met her boyfriend. According to Janie, Mac was a good guy, and had proposed to Alyssa repeatedly. Janie had joked that Alyssa had an aversion to wedding gowns, and that's why she wasn't accepting his proposal. Alyssa just told her she wasn't ready yet, but Janie was starting to think more and more that there was something with Mac. But then as soon as she thought that, she'd change her mind. She had no proof and had never witnessed anything strange about him.

"Janie," Brent said. "Want to pack a bag and stay with me tonight?" She didn't say anything, but he could see the struggle on her face. The tough cop who wanted to prove she was fine and the scared woman who'd just had her life threatened and only wanted to be held.

He put his hands on her shoulders. "I'll admit I'm being a bit selfish. I don't like the thought of you being here alone. Call it testosterone. Call it being a bullish male, but I'd sleep so much better with you in my arms."

Tears filled her eyes, but didn't fall. He wasn't sure if she thought he was just giving her a way to agree to stay with him without her having to admit she wanted to do, but he'd spoken the truth. He didn't want her here alone. Hell, she didn't even have a security system. "Okay," she finally whispered.

He pulled her into his arms and kissed her forehead. "Thank you."

She relaxed against him and he swore he could feel her strength and resolve returning. He dipped his head and smelled her hair. Lavender.

She pulled back and looked to Bea. "Sorry."

Bea waved her apology away. "Don't even think about it."

"I wonder if Alyssa and Mac were able to eat." Janie stepped out of his embrace and headed to the kitchen. "I probably have enough for all five of us."

"All five," Bea said. "So tonight I'm not just the third wheel, I'm also the fifth."

Though Bea was rarely alone, she never appeared to find anyone she wanted to see beyond the second date. Her tone was light; Brent hoped she was joking.

"Don't worry, sis," he said. "Mr. Right is out there somewhere. You'll find him."

He meant for it to be a lighthearted remark, but she

didn't smile. Her cheeks actually flushed and suddenly she was looking anywhere except at him.

"Bea?" he asked, and then it hit him and he smiled. "You've found someone, haven't you?"

She opened her mouth to reply, but right at that moment there was a knock on the door. Janie sprinted into the living room.

"I'll get it," she said.

"Make sure . . ." he started, but then stopped when she gave him the *I'm a cop and I know what I'm doing* look. "Sorry."

She checked the peephole and opened the door. Alyssa came inside, followed by a tall and lanky man whom Brent assumed was Mac.

"Oh my God," Alyssa said, pulling her friend into a hug. "Are you okay? Where are the flowers? Let me see."

"Over here." Janie led her to the table.

"Hey, Brent," Alyssa said in passing. "That's Mac."

"Mac." Brent nodded at the guy who looked the slightest bit uncomfortable. Brent couldn't blame him. This wasn't how Mac had planned to spend his evening. But then again, that's what happened when you dated a cop.

"I'm Bea," his sister said, holding out her hand to Mac. "Brent's sister."

"Nice to meet you." But Mac's attention wasn't on Bea. He was watching Alyssa.

"We can look for prints on the letter," she was saying. "But I wouldn't hold out much hope. I'm off duty now—Mac and I were on our way to dinner—so I'll do the preliminaries and finish it up later. Her voice dropped to a whisper. "So sorry I brought him on official business. I knew it'd be quicker this way."

"That's what I was thinking." Janie nodded. "And the box is probably a waste of time. Most of us touched it. And please, don't apologize. I understand."

"You'll find my prints on the letter," Brent said. "I took it from her after she read it."

"Not a problem, we have DNA." Alyssa said, and then turned and sighed. "Seriously, Mac? Please don't mess with that."

"How did you get DNA?" Mac asked, putting the box back on the table.

Alyssa sighed. "I really can't say."

"But you haven't linked it to a person yet." Mac spoke it as a statement. Not a question.

"Obviously," Alyssa snapped. "We haven't made an arrest yet, have we?"

Mac held up his hands. "Just curious."

"It's not a good time."

An uncomfortable silence fell over the room. At least, Brent thought, Janie no longer looked scared. She stood with her arms crossed, watching Alyssa.

Alyssa sighed and ran her fingers through her hair. "Look, I'm sorry, guys. I'm just under a lot of stress. This case . . ." She shook her head, then took an evidence bag and put the letter in it. "I'm going to go on and take this by the lab. Come on, Mac. Since you touched the box, I need to get you printed for elimination purposes."

Mac's lips tightened into a thin line, but he looked back at Janie and he smiled. "See you later. Be safe."

"Thanks. Take care of my girl." Janie smiled and took the few steps over to him to give him a quick hug.

Brent lifted his head when he heard Janie ask, "What type of cologne do you wear, Mac?" Something about her voice sounded off.

"My cologne?" Mac smiled and lifted his shirt for a sniff. "I don't even know. It's new. Alyssa's partner wears it and gave me a sample. Do you like it?"

"It's unique," Janie replied in a tight voice.

Mac snorted. "I'll take that as a 'no.'"

Alyssa coughed from her position by the door.

"Got to go. See you guys later," Mac said. "Nice to meet you, Brent . . . Bea."

Janie locked the door behind them. "Wow, that was odd. I've never seen her like that."

"Probably just stress," Bea said. "It can do things to a person. That Mac guy was nice enough, though."

"Yeah," Janie said, but she didn't sound convinced. "I guess that's possible, but she's been in stressful situations before and I've never seen her like this. It makes me wonder if it might be Mac. Maybe there's something to the fact that she keeps turning down his proposal."

Brent tilted his head. He'd never heard Janie say anything but positive comments about Alyssa's long-term boyfriend and there was nothing he'd said or done tonight that seemed out of line to Brent. He frowned. Except for that weird argument about the DNA.

"Everything okay?" he asked, coming up behind her and putting his arms around her.

She leaned back into his embrace and he swore he could feel the tension leave her body. "Yes, it's probably nothing."

"Want to talk about it?"

She thought for a second and then replied, "No. No,

I don't think I do. What I want to do is pack up dinner and get a bag together and go to your house. What I do not want to do is spend another second here tonight that I don't have to."

He tightened his arms around her, wishing more than anything he could snap his fingers and make this whole thing go away. "Sounds like a great idea. Why don't you go pack, and I'll set out dinner here for us all? Then we can leave."

"I hope you won't let the events at my house keep you from coming back," Janie said, throwing a smile in Bea's direction. They had finished eating and Brent was cleaning the kitchen. "It's usually quite dull around here."

"Don't worry about it. I can only imagine how stressful this is."

"Yes." She waved to the couch for Bea to sit down. "What do you think about Brent going to Washington?"

Bea leaned back into the couch. "Part of me is shocked. He's such the quintessential Southern gentleman, you know?"

Janie couldn't help laughing. "True."

"But he said he's not going to sell his house." Bea shook her head. "Thank goodness. I'd have to kick his ass if he did that. You have no idea what I went through decorating that place."

Janie smiled. "He told me. It's beautiful, by the way." She wondered where Bea lived and if she had a home filled with antiques.

"It's a hobby of mine. I'm living in a much smaller apartment at the moment and don't have near the amount of furniture Brent does. He inherited most of it from his father."

Janie knew from past conversations with Brent that the two half siblings had different fathers. Brent's had passed away, but Bea's was a prominent minister in the Charleston area. From what she'd heard about him, he was all hellfire and brimstone. Which was odd since Bea seemed the exact opposite.

Brent had been offered a position on a federal committee working with several executives on measures that would lead to reducing preservatives and toxins from food, and Janie knew he was thrilled with the opportunity to make an impact. Plus, he'd be excellent at it. If only it wasn't in DC. But then again, she no longer had a job. She wasn't tied to Charleston.

Actually, if she thought about it, she rented her place and Brent owned his. He had more ties to the South than she did. Of course, she told herself, it helped that due to everyone's schedules, he'd only be in Washington for six months at a time.

"I guess you don't worry you'll never see him much?" Janie asked. After all, that was her fear. But she'd never been in a long-distance relationship, so maybe it wasn't outright fear. Perhaps it was fear of the unknown.

"A little, but I'm hoping it wouldn't be for long. I'm planning to run for Congress term after next."

Janie hadn't heard that. "Really? That's great."

"It's horribly ambitious and it's taking up so much of my time, even now."

"I say go for it."

"Thanks." Bea flushed a bit and her mouth opened,

like she was going to speak, but then she must have changed her mind because she closed it without saying anything.

"What does your dad think of your running for office?" Janie asked. She could only assume, based on things she'd heard about the man, that he would hate it.

"He's less than thrilled," she said with a grin and an eye roll. "But what else is new?"

"He doesn't want you to run?"

"He didn't want me to go to law school." Bea waved her hand. "He's completely stuck in the 1950s. He thinks I should be married with two kids and another on the way."

"Oh, wow."

"Right? I mean if that's what you want," she said with a shrug, "but I'm not at that point yet."

"I hear you. I'm not ready for kids yet, either."

Footsteps sounded as Brent made his way from the kitchen to the living room. "I made some coffee if anyone would like a cup. Decaf."

He flashed Janie a smile and raised his eyebrow. She nodded. She'd been a little apprehensive about meeting his sister, but she was great. Not that she should have been worried; after all, Bea shared half of Brent's DNA.

He stood in the doorway grinning and though Janie knew he was worried and it probably took a lot of effort to smile, she appreciated his doing so.

"It's rare that I get to have a free night with my two most favorite women," he teased as he came over to the couch where they were sitting.

Bea playfully batted his hand away when he tried to

take it. "It could have happened a lot sooner than now if you hadn't been hiding Janie from me."

"I was afraid you'd scare her off."

"No way. If you hadn't scared her off, nothing I would have done could."

Janie wouldn't have believed it five minutes ago, but she actually felt relaxed and lighthearted as they made their way to her kitchen for coffee.

Later that night Brent and Janie lay in his bed, not really sleepy and just talking. Brent still felt on the edge but Janie seemed so peaceful the last few hours.

"I'm so glad you decided to stay over tonight," he started out by saying. "I feel so much better with you here."

She twisted in his arms and propped up on her elbow beside him. "I might actually sleep tonight, and that wouldn't have happened if I stayed at home."

He sucked in a breath as she started running her fingers on his chest. "I have a proposition for you," he said.

She laughed. "Aren't you supposed to proposition me *before* I get into bed?"

"It's not that kind proposition," he said with a smile.

"Damn."

"Two things actually." He decided to bring up the one she was most likely to agree with first. "Come with me to DC this weekend." This coming weekend he would have to find a place to live if he wanted to start the position on time.

"Are you looking for apartments?" she asked.

"Yes, and I really need to put an offer on something this weekend. I would love your input." He wasn't sure what they would do when he started the new position. He wasn't overly thrilled by the thoughts of a long-distance relationship, but he'd do whatever it would take to still have Janie in his life.

He remembered the night they'd met. She'd been working undercover at a local club and he saw her. All he knew right away was that she was beautiful. But it was when she quoted Aristophanes that he felt he had to get to know her. She was refreshing. Strong, self-assured, and smart, she neither seemed impressed by his money nor did she seem to want him for his wealth.

"You would?" she asked.

"Yes. I know I won't get you out of the South permanently, but I do hope you agree to visit me in Washington. A lot."

"Yes, of course I will."

"Well, in that case, I definitely need your opinion on where I'll be living."

She leaned over and kissed him briefly. "Okay, I'll go. When do we leave?"

"Friday morning around ten?"

"Sure, I mean, it's not like I'm working or anything." Though she probably meant for her statement to be lighthearted, it didn't come across that way.

Bea was a lawyer. Brent had been hopeful that she would be able to look over Janie's case and find a way to get her reinstated at the police department. He didn't have a chance to talk to her tonight, not with everything that was going on, but he didn't think it looked that hopeful. He would need to call her in the morning, though, just to make sure.

"I'm sorry," he said. He couldn't help but feel partly responsible. After all, she had been placed on probation because she was seeing him. At the time, when they first met, he had been a suspect in multiple kidnappings, along with one murder.

Janie's boss hadn't taken too kindly to one of his top investigators having an affair with a potential suspect. Brent couldn't fault him on that, but he didn't like the outcome. He especially didn't like that Janie was without a job because he knew how much she enjoyed being a cop. It was her passion. And she was damn good at it.

His mind drifted away. He couldn't help but think that if he moved to DC, and he happened to convince Janie to move with him, she could find employment in Washington.

"What was item number two?" she asked, bringing him back to the moment.

He took a deep breath, "I'd like for you move in with me."

Her expression grew serious; even with the low light in the bedroom he could tell. He pushed a lock of hair back from her forehead. "Thinking?"

"If I hadn't received the roses tonight, would you still be asking me to move in?"

She had him there.

"Eventually." It was the most honest thing he could say. The truth was, he hadn't planned to ask her to move in tonight. Not before she got the roses. "But you did, and the way I look at it, the roses are like a catalyst. I was going to eventually ask you to move in, I just did it quicker than planned. I can't be in Washington knowing you're here alone. I need you and I couldn't stand myself if something happened and I wasn't able to protect you."

She sighed and rolled over to her back. "Thank you for being honest."

"Janie," he said, sitting up so he could look at her and she could see his eyes. "I will always be honest with you. Was it my plan to ask you to move in with me tonight? No. That doesn't mean it's a bad idea. And it doesn't mean that I don't want it."

"I see what you're saying. But part of me takes issue with being asked to move in only because someone is after me." She held up a finger when he started to protest. "Or that you didn't realize you wanted me to move in until someone came after me."

Of course she would take issue. What person wouldn't?

"I can't fault you for that," he said. "How about this? Don't make any decision tonight. Just sleep on it. Take a few days to think about it. Maybe take the weekend. You might find yourself unable to live without me after spending the weekend with me."

That actually got him a smile. "Okay, Mr. Big Head. I'll take the weekend to think about it."

"Mr. Big Head?" he repeated, glad to hear her joking.

"It was the best I could come up with on short notice."

Her hand stroked his chest and he realized he was wide awake. On the upside, it appeared Janie was as well.

"I'm not sleepy at all," he said.

She stretched against him, lazy, like a cat enjoying the sun. "Me neither, but I'm not about to get out of this bed."

"I wasn't about to suggest anything remotely related to getting out of bed," he assured her, settling back down on the bed, this time taking her with him and rolling them so she was on top.

"Oh, yes." She looked marvelous above him. Fierce and strong and sexy. "This is so much better than either sleeping or getting out of bed."

As it turned out, it was much, much later before they finally made it to sleep.

After Brent left the next morning, Janie called Alyssa. Taking a sip of coffee, she waited for her friend to pick up the phone. Hopefully, she'd be in a better mood this morning.

"Hey," Alyssa said after she answered the phone. "I was just getting ready to call you."

"You have any information?" Janie didn't think that it had been enough time for the fingerprints to be run, but with Alyssa so excited to hear from her, maybe she was wrong. She debated bringing up the cologne Mac said her partner wore. Just to see if she'd smelled it and to potentially ask if she thought her co-worker could be involved. In the end, she didn't because she didn't want to jump to conclusions without the proper facts.

"No," Alyssa said. "But we'll at least know if there's a match with the next hour or so." She paused before continuing. "I want to apologize for my behavior last night."

"It's okay."

"No, it's not. Mac and I had a fight, and I was completely out of place to take it out on you and Brent. I just don't know what got into him."

Janie was shocked. She never heard of Alyssa and Mac having issues before; they had always seemed like the perfect couple. Of course she knew all couples argued, but the two of them never seemed to have much to fight about. "Are you and Mac okay now?"

"We will be when he gets home," Alyssa said with a laugh.

"Going to make up, huh?"

"Something like that." She said the words, but still sounded frustrated.

"I'm sure after he's home for about five minutes, you two won't even remember what you were fighting about last night."

"I hope you're right. We've been fighting a lot lately."

This was news to her. "About what?"

"He's been spending a lot of time working. A lot more than normal, that is. Last night was the first night in a week that he hasn't gone to the office."

Janie recalled he was a CPA, but she didn't think it was anything that required that much time when it wasn't tax season. She wondered if he was having an affair; it would certainly explain all his overtime.

"Is it a project that he's working on?" Janie asked.

"No, he said that there have been several people who have left the company recently. Apparently, everybody's required to stay late." Alyssa sighed. "I don't know what my problem is. I mean, I know he's not cheating on me."

Janie was curious as to how she knew with certainty that Mac wasn't cheating, but she didn't think that was the kind of talk her friend needed right now. "Anything I can do?"

"No, just take my apology for last night. If I act like an ass again, call me on it."

"Deal."

Both women laughed. When they stopped, Alyssa asked, "Any plans for today?"

"Yes. I'm going to run by my apartment. There are a few items I left when I packed to come to Brent's."

"Okay. I'm going to get off here and run these prints downstairs. I'll call you when the results come in."

They said their good-byes. Janie knew the odds of getting any usable prints were slim to none, but she felt a little better. At least something was being done to figure out who was behind all this.

Brent decided to stop by Bea's office in the morning instead of calling. He yawned as he pulled into the old historic home that had been turned into a law office. Bea was a practicing attorney, but she had plans to run for Congress in the next election.

There were no other cars besides Bea's in the parking lot, so he was surprised when he heard voices coming from her office. Even more surprising was it didn't exactly sound like a business meeting. It was definitely Bea, though, and she was with a man. Not only that, but she was giggling. He didn't think he'd heard her giggle like that since she was in middle school.

He loved her, but she had always been very studious, even as a young child. He had grown concerned in recent years that she was all work and no play. While she would date on occasion, she never seemed serious about anyone.

It had actually been one of the reasons he'd hesitated on taking the DC job. If he left town, who would make sure she got out of the office every once in a while?

Their mother had passed away years ago, and while her father was still nearby, he was a very conservative minister. Brent couldn't see him telling his daughter to get out on the town more often.

But if Bea was in a relationship, he could move to DC without that worry hanging over his head.

At the moment, though, she didn't expect him to drop by and she'd be embarrassed if he heard too much. He walked to the closed door and knocked. "Bea? Are you in there? I saw your car."

From the other side of the door, the giggles stopped, followed by hurried whispers. Damn, what had he interrupted? He changed his mind; he was definitely going to tease her about this.

"Just a second!" Bea called out.

"I'll go get us coffee. Be back in ten."

When he returned, closer to fifteen minutes later, she was alone. Waiting.

He followed his sister into her office, and took a seat across from her large wooden desk. She sat on the other side, straightening papers, and still refusing to meet his eyes.

"Did you need something?" she asked.

"I want to talk about Janie."

She nodded, switching to all-business mode. "I looked over everything that you gave me, and unfortunately, there's nothing that can be done to get her job back."

He was afraid of that, actually, but felt he owed it to Janie to at least try. "Thank you for checking it out." He drummed his finger on the desk and across from him Bea lifted an eyebrow. "I'm also interested in your take on what happened last night."

Bea shifted in her seat, leaning back and eyeing him carefully. "About what?"

"What do you think about that Mac guy?"

She shrugged. "He seemed friendly enough. His girlfriend had a major attitude, though."

"I've met Alyssa before and last night was definitely not indicative of her normal personality," he said, and then added, "I can't help wonder if it has anything to do with Mac being around?"

Not only that, but he couldn't get out of his mind the way Janie looked when she asked Mac about his cologne. It was more than idle curiosity. She looked fearful. The biggest issue being that Alyssa's partner also wore it. Did that mean both men were involved? Was that even possible with both men being so close to Alyssa? He needed to think about it more. He did not share any of that with his sister.

"Maybe," she said. "But usually you'd think she would have been more professional around people she didn't know very well."

"I think I'll mention checking him out to Janie."

"Wow," Bea said. "Big jump much?"

"What are you talking about?" he asked.

"Just playing devil's advocate here." She said it with a hint of mischief in her expression. It had been a favorite game of hers growing up. It used to drive him mad that she would argue so vehemently for a position she didn't even believe in. Looking back now, he could see it was an excellent game to play in preparation for her career in law.

He crossed his arms. "Go ahead."

"I was just thinking, you say Mac's a nice enough

guy and it's not like Alyssa has only been dating him for a short period of time. Surely if there was something peculiar or questionable about him, Janie would have seen it, assuming Alyssa didn't."

"I see your point, but the truth is, maybe I'm not expecting to find anything. Maybe I'm ninety-eight percent certain he has nothing to hide, but there's that two-percent chance he is hiding something. I have to know."

"There are plenty of people with more than a two-percent chance that they're hiding something. Are you going to look into them, too?"

He gave her a grin. "I just might."

She put her hands up in mock defeat. "Okay, okay. Just be careful. I'm gone for a couple days and won't be around to bail you out."

Brent exaggerated his shocked face. "You? Taking a vacation? A real one? I think I should play the lottery."

"Stop."

It hit him then, where she was going. Or maybe not where, but at least with whom.

"Is that guy who was here going with you?"

"I told you I'm not discussing him with you right now. All you need to know is that I'm going away for a few days. I'll call you when I'm back."

"Just as well," he said. "Janie and I are heading to DC for the weekend. I have to find something if I'm going to take the position."

"When are you making the final decision?"

"This weekend." After he discussed it with Janie.

As if reading his thoughts, Bea added, "I like her. She's a keeper."

"I think so, too." But it made his day that his sister felt the same.

He couldn't help it. He had to stay and watch. They thought they were being so smart, keeping Janie at her lover's house. He laughed. Right. Like he couldn't figure that one out. Like she was safe there.

He might let her think that for a bit. Then when her lover took her to DC, he could show them just how unsafe she was.

He was enjoying this more than he thought he would when The Gentleman gave him the assignment. He'd especially liked what he'd done today.

He was actually surprised when he saw her pull up to her apartment moments after he left. Good thing he'd worked quickly. The downside was the kill was still fresh and it would have been so much more dramatic if it could have decomposed a few days. But still, this way he was able to watch for her reaction.

She was unlocking her door now. He pictured the layout of her apartment in his mind. The living area with the kitchen in the back of the open-concept style. She'd pass through that area none the wiser. But when she turned and entered her bedroom—

His thoughts were interrupted by a shrill scream.

Yup, just like that.

He despaired that he couldn't wait around for Brent and the police to show up, but it was better for him not to take that risk. But that was okay. No matter what, he'e accomplished what he wanted. Janie could pretend she was tough and strong. She might even have fooled a few people in her past. Now everyone knew the truth. She could be broken by the sight of dead cat. He almost laughed, but didn't. After all, there was no way to tell who was watching.

He slipped around to the back of the apartments and across the nearby neighborhood park where he'd parked his car, whistling as he went.

CHAPTER 2

"It's fortunate you didn't arrive any sooner than you did," the officer was telling a still shaken Janie. "From the looks of it, that cat hadn't been dead for very long."

"Was that necessary?" Brent asked as Janie dry heaved again. They were outside her front door. He took a wet cloth one of Janie's neighbors had brought out and pressed it to her forehead. "Deep breaths, baby. It's okay. No one's going to hurt you. Not as long as there's a breath in my body."

He had just left Bea's office and was heading out to Janie's favorite seafood restaurant to pick up some soup for her to have for lunch when she'd called him.

Why she'd decided to stop by her apartment without telling him, he wasn't sure, but when she'd arrived, she'd found a dead cat on her bed. Worse, its throat had been cut and blood was damn near everywhere.

He'd kept her on the line as he broke every speed limit in Charleston to get to her. By the time he'd arrived, the police were already on site.

He was surprised Alyssa hadn't shown up. Surely,

her best friend would have heard about the call and would check on her?

Brent rubbed Janie's back. "Do you need anything out of your apartment?" He looked at the officer. "Is it okay to go inside?"

"I don't need anything," Janie whispered. "I don't want anything in there. You can burn it all. I've never stepping foot in there again."

It was probably the shock talking. Brent had already made up his mind he was going to have the apartment cleaned while they were in DC. Maybe after some distance and a thorough cleaning, she'd be able to face it better.

But she didn't need to know that now. "It's okay. You don't have to go back inside. We'll go back to my place and you can rest."

"I don't want to rest. I want to find this sadistic son of a bitch and rip his balls off."

"Ah, there's my girl." Brent brought his hand up to her cheek. "Still on for DC, though, right?" he said with a smile.

His heart cracked when she gave him a small smile. "Yes."

He pulled her close and kissed her forehead. She nearly hummed as she snuggled in close.

"Do you need us for anything else?" he asked the officer. "I'd like to get her home."

The officer assured him that they could leave and they'd be notified if anything was found. Brent couldn't help but think they had to find something. Whoever left the cat had done it in broad daylight. Didn't it stand to reason someone would have seen the culprit?

He kept his arm around her as he led her to his car.

He got her settled into the passenger seat before getting in the car himself. Once he closed the door, he snuck a quick glance to make sure she was okay.

From all appearances, she was. She had some of her color back and there was a curious expression on her face.

"What?" he asked.

"I liked what you said back there," she said. "That you'd like to get me home."

"My home is your home." He reached out to put his hand on her knee. "I meant what I said, I'd like for you to at least consider moving in with me."

She took his hand and entwined their fingers, but she didn't look at him, choosing instead to focus on their hands. "I know you said it, but hearing you back it up just now means so much more to me."

"Does that mean you're thinking about it?"

"Yes," she said, finally smiling. "It does."

That night, they went on a walk around Brent's neighborhood. He suggested it because Janie loved looking at all the historical homes and he thought the fresh air would do her some good.

She certainly seemed to be in better spirits. There was a sparkle in her eyes again and her steps were light as they walked. She even teased him a time or two about moving to the north and "becoming a Yankee." He laughed and told her he didn't think it was possible to be a Yankee and also to own a historic home in Charleston.

"I don't know," she said. "That's a pretty shaky argument to me."

"Give me some time and I'll think up a better one."

They passed a few minutes in silence before he spoke again. "What do you think about leaving for DC a few days early?"

"How early?" she asked.

"Like tomorrow early." There was no reason not to go that he could think of and part of him couldn't help but think she'd be safer out of town.

"I think that's a great idea," she said.

"Good. We'll pack when we get back home."

They turned to head back and out of the corner of his eye, he'd have sworn he saw someone duck into the shadows. He glanced at Janie, but she was looking in the opposite direction at a house.

It wasn't dark yet, but it would be soon. He walked a bit faster, inwardly cursing himself for being so flippant about Janie's safety. What was he thinking to bring her out? They were too exposed walking as they were. He knew she normally carried a gun with her, but he'd be lying to say it didn't make him nervous.

"Brent?" she asked and he realized she'd asked him a question. Repeatedly, from the way she said his name.

"Hmm," he mumbled, trying to act as normal as possible while keeping an eye on their surroundings.

"I asked what time we were leaving tomorrow." She narrowed her eyes. "Are you okay? Did you see something?"

He couldn't lie to her. He respected her too much to do that. Besides, he knew her strength and knew she could handle the truth. "I'm sure it was nothing."

"But you did see something?" Her eyes darted around the street.

"I'm not sure what I saw, which is why I didn't say

anything. Regardless, I'll feel better once you're safely inside the house."

The change to Janie was immediate. Gone was any sign of lightheartedness. She moved with one goal in mind—getting to the house. Every step was accompanied by a sweep of her gaze all around the street. Brent knew her sharp eyes would miss nothing. God, he hated this. It broke his heart that she was going through this.

He also knew getting to DC in the morning was the best move he could make at this point. Even the top-of-the-line security system his home boasted suddenly didn't seem adequate to protect her.

A movement in the bushes at his next-door neighbor's yard made them both freeze.

"I didn't imagine that," she said.

No, unfortunately, there was no way he could pass that off as a figment of his imagination. "Do you have your gun with you?" he whispered.

"Yes." Her hand shifted to her hip. Obviously, the tunic top she wore covered up her holster.

He could tell Janie didn't want to bring her gun out in public, but she kept her hand on it as they drew closer to the bush. He could see her breathing heavier with each step forward.

Three steps away from the bush. Her hands started to shake.

Two steps. He held his breath.

One step.

A massive ball of black fur jumped out from behind the bush and landed on the street in front of them. Janie pulled her gun, but somehow managed not to shoot the cat now standing in their way.

"Oh my God," she said. "That cat scared the life out of me."

Brent put his hand on her back and quickly guided her to the front door. The cat the day before had been white. He watched her carefully to make sure she was okay. "Me too. I've have never been more happy to see a black cat."

Once they were both inside, he closed and locked the doors, and armed the security system. He took a quick peek out the window, just to see if there was anything in the shadows that shouldn't be. He didn't see anything. Unfortunately, he knew enough to know that whoever was chasing Janie wouldn't be seen unless he wanted to.

"Let's pack," he said. The morning in DC wouldn't come soon enough for him.

They arrived in DC early the next morning, thanks to Brent's insistence of a private jet. Janie had balked at first, but he played it off like he always traveled on one and she finally relented. He told himself he had just stretched the truth a little. Yes, he sometimes flew in a private jet, but more often than not, he went commercial.

Yes, he was paranoid.

Yes, he was overprotective.

Did he care? Not at all. He'd do what he had to do in order to keep Janie safe.

The hotel they were staying at allowed them to check in early. He loved the way Janie's eyes grew big when he opened the door to their suite.

"Brent," she said in amazement. "This room is ridiculous. Seriously. It's bigger than my apartment."

"Humor me." He walked up behind her and put his

arms around her, dropping a kiss on her neck. "I like pampering you."

She was so different from the type of women he normally dated. Most of them expected such things. And while he didn't used to mind it, experiencing what a joy it was to do things for Janie made him realize how shallow those women were. Which proved how shallow the relationships had been.

Janie was a strong-willed woman who could kick some serious ass. That was probably why it pained him so much to see her scared. He knew how much it took to break her confidence.

But it was more than her strength. She was also smart and funny. She knew more about the antiques in his house than he did and she appreciated his iced-tea-making abilities. He loved her often sarcastic sense of humor, not to mention her knowledge of Greek theater.

He watched her as she walked over to the large picture windows overlooking the Potomac. She'd had a hard time lately. Not too long ago, a homeless man she'd grown close to had been murdered. Probably by the same person who was after her now. And she'd been suspended from her job. How could he not want to protect and spoil her?

Someone knocked on the door and he smiled. Speaking of spoiling, his first surprise was right on time. She raised her eyebrow as he went to open the door, but didn't say anything. They were both hopeful that whoever was threatening her wouldn't know that she'd left town. Another reason he'd wanted to take a private jet.

He checked to make sure it was the deliveryman he was expecting, though, just to be safe.

"Your package, Mr. Taylor," the man said, handing

him the box with the well-known Charleston designer-shop logo on the side. Brent tipped him and turned around, not wanting to miss Janie's expression when she saw the box for the first time.

He wasn't disappointed. Her gasp of shock made him want to surprise her again and again. He held the box out. "A little something for you."

"Little?" She took the box and put it on the couch, her finger traced the logo. "You shouldn't have."

"I most definitely should. We're going out tonight and you need something to wear."

"Where are we going?"

"It's a surprise." He nodded toward the box. "Open it."

She gave him a big grin and lifted the lid. He knew he'd done well when her hand flew up to cover her mouth. Tears danced in her eyes when she looked up at him. "You remembered."

His chest ached just looking at her and all he could do was nod. She lifted the outfit from the tissue paper almost reverently. "I can't believe it."

The night of their first date, they'd met in downtown Charleston. She'd arrived first and he'd found her eyeing that cocktail dress through a store window. When he mentioned it to her, she'd brushed it off by saying she had nowhere to wear it. Be that as it may, he couldn't stop imagining how she'd look in the silver silk gown with the flowing skirt. While setting up the DC trip, he'd gone back to the store and arranged to have it delivered.

"You really shouldn't have," she repeated. "But thank you."

"You're very welcome. Want to go try it on? I can't wait to see it on you."

He knew he was in trouble when she turned her teasing eyes on him. "I think if you're not telling me where we're going, you don't get to see me in this gown."

She had him there. "You drive a hard bargain."

She shrugged. "Fair is fair."

He wasn't sure how fair that was, but he was willing to go along with it if it meant she'd keep that smile on her face. He crossed his arms. "I can live with that."

"Let me hang this up." When she came back, she wrapped her arms around him. "Do we have anything we have to do today?"

He murmured against her lips, "Not that I can think of."

"Good," she said, before kissing him.

It wasn't a kiss born of urgency, but rather a slow and gentle prelude. She tilted her head when he deepened the kiss, as if needing for him to take more of her. He was more than happy to oblige and when her fingers fumbled with his shirt, he moaned at the feel of her hands on him.

"Janie," he whispered. "You feel so good. I love it when you put your hands on me."

"How fortunate," she said. "I love to put my hands on you."

She kissed him again and he smiled as he replied, "Prove it."

She took it as a challenge and he nearly came on the spot when she unbuttoned his shirt and pushed it off his shoulders. He also loved it when she got aggressive with him.

"Mmm," he hummed in pleasure when she slipped a hand between their bodies and palmed his erection. "So good."

Most of the women he'd been with were content to let him lead in the bedroom, and many times, they'd just lie there and let him do all the work. Janie was a breath of fresh air. She wasn't afraid to tell him exactly what she liked and what she wanted.

"I want to feel your skin on mine," he said. "Take me out."

He also liked that she truly wanted to please him as much as he pleased her. She would often tease him when he asked for something directly, but only to heighten his anticipation by making him wait.

Within seconds, his pants were undone and she had taken hold of his shaft. He nearly lost it at the feel of her thumb stroking the slit on his head.

"Oh, yes." His eyes almost rolled to the back of his head. "Just like that."

"I want you to come in my mouth," she said, and his eyes flew open at the very thought of it.

"Are you sure?" He'd never been with anyone who particularly liked for him to do that. For damn sure, he'd never had anyone ask him to do it.

She looked at him with dark, lust-filled eyes that held only the truth. "I wouldn't say it otherwise."

"I don't want you to do anything you aren't comfortable with," he said. She kept stroking him the entire time they were talking and it was getting harder and harder for him to carry on a conversation.

This time she didn't say anything, but dropped to her knees, keeping her eyes on him as she did. Only when she reached the floor did she look away. He watched and felt himself grow longer and harder until she took his entire length into her mouth and his eyes closed involuntarily.

Fuck. Her mouth felt so damn good.

He dropped his hand to rest lightly on the top of her head. Not to hold her in place or to guide her, but because he wanted the connection of somehow touching her as she pleased him. The thought shocked him a bit. Before, he'd never cared about anything other than the actual blow job. Never had he ever cared about any connection other than the feel of his partner's mouth on his dick.

All that was different with Janie. He forced his eyes to open and look while he dug his fingers into her hair and massaged her scalp. She hummed in pleasure, her hand dropping between her legs. The thought that she was getting turned on by what she was doing made his balls tighten and he knew he wasn't going to last very much longer.

He held still, forcing himself not to thrust, but allowing her to work him over. She took him all the way in her mouth until he felt the back of her throat. He sucked a breath in through his teeth and he fisted her hair.

"I'm getting ready to come," he warned her, still wanting to give her a chance to change her mind if she wanted.

But she would not be swayed. She grabbed his upper thigh with her free hand, not allowing him to get away. He wasn't sure he'd ever experienced anything hotter and he groaned, releasing down her throat.

She didn't pull off, instead, she swallowed rapidly, taking everything he gave her. Even when he'd finished, she was still attentive. She gave him several licks, finally placing a kiss on his tip as he slid out of her mouth.

Normally after such an intense orgasm, he'd feel completely spent, but seeing the look of satisfaction she had, and the way she rocked triumphantly to rest her butt on her heels, revived him. He held his hand out to her and pulled her to her feet.

"That was incredible," he managed to say. "I'm going to need some time to recover, but do you know what I'm going to do in the meantime?"

Her only reply was to lick her lips.

"Damn it, Janie." He led her to the bed. "Keep that up and I won't need any time to recover and I do want to give you at least two orgasms before I fuck you." He nodded to the bed. "On your back."

She gave him a saucy smile. "I definitely won't argue with that."

"Good." He pushed her thighs apart. "Now hold on."

He turned his attention to bringing her as much pleasure as she'd brought him moments before. Taking his time, he used his fingers and his mouth to work her over. He loved how she responded to him, her body softly opening to his touch and the way she writhed under him.

Several times, her legs tried to close, but he held them open, determined to make good on his statement to make her come twice before moving on. When she came the first time, it was with a soft cry of surprise. He took that as a challenge and doubled his efforts.

Her second time was neither soft nor quiet. It couldn't have come as a surprise, either. Surely by then she had to know he'd been telling the truth when he'd told her of his intent.

Likewise, he'd been correct in other ways as well. By the time he'd made her come the second time, he was hard again. So, while she shook in the aftermath of her fading orgasm, he rolled her to her belly, slipped on a condom, and positioned himself behind her.

"Think you can come again?" he asked, stroking her backside as she got up on her hands and knees.

"I don't know," she admitted. "That'd be three in a short period of time. I think it'd be a record."

"In that case, it's a given. You're doing it." He passed a hand between her legs and smiled to discover she was wet again. She rubbed against him when he found her clit. "Oh, yes. You're definitely coming again."

"Oh, shit," she panted when he pushed inside her. "I think you're right."

He started working his hips, thrusting into her. "I know I am."

After coming in her mouth, he was able to take his time the second time around. He stroked his hips with long and precise motions, making sure he brought her as much pleasure as possible. She didn't even try to hold back this time, but moved her hips along with his and when she came, he followed close behind.

As he gathered her in his arms, he wondered how he'd be able to convince her to move with him, because he didn't think he could do the long-distance thing with her. He wanted her forever.

He watched them through his binoculars from the hotel across the street. They had put their guard down. He could tell because they were smiling so much. At first that made him mad. How dare they be laughing and smiling after he'd sent her a death threat? Did they think he was joking?

But the more he thought about it, he liked the fact

that they were relaxed. It wasn't that they thought he wasn't serious. They thought they were safe in Washington. Which really meant they were much more stupid than he originally thought.

He wasn't sure yet how he was going to take advantage of the fact that he knew where they were and they didn't know it. Should he surprise them with something left in their hotel room? Wait until they got back from dinner? Or would it have more of an impact if he waited until the next day? If he let them enjoy their false sense of security before jerking it out from underneath them?

Hmmm, so many tempting ways to go about bringing Janie down. Which one would be the most fun?

The buzz of his telephone made him sigh and put his binoculars down.

UNKNOWN CALLER

Hell, he knew exactly who that unknown caller was. Though sometimes he wished to God he didn't.

"Hello," he answered.

"I heard you left town rather quickly," The Gentleman said. "I thought you might be doing something stupid."

Interesting. Did he really think he'd try to run?

"No, sir. Just playing with my prey."

There were a few seconds of uncomfortable silence before the caller spoke again. "You know your time is limited?"

"Yes, sir," he replied, deciding he had liked it better when The Gentleman wasn't so obsessive. Still, as long as he didn't know about the DNA evidence he'd unknowingly left behind, he wasn't going to complain. Because that was the only DNA that had ever been collected on him, the police department wouldn't be

able to identify with it. All he had to do now was to ensure there was never any collected that could be tied to
him. Risky, but possible.

Hell, whom was he fooling? He'd never even think
about complaining to The Gentleman.

"You see, sir." He should explain his thinking; that
way he wouldn't appear incompetent. "I could extermi-
nate her anytime I wanted to. But I want to do more
than that. I want to scare her, to become her worst
nightmare. To become the shadows she sees in the
middle of the night. And only then, when she's out of
her mind in fear, will I take care of her."

The Gentleman chuckled. "You sound almost dia-
bolical."

"I take that as a compliment coming from you, sir."

"Yes. Quite. The only thing I'd be careful of if I were
you is being too sure of yourself. Brent Taylor is a
powerful man and he will be a challenging adversary,
especially when paired with her."

He snorted. "He can't be any worse than the Charleston PD."

"Ah, there it is. The cockiness. The Charleston PD
is a disgrace. They have botched up more cases than
they've solved. Why do you think I've stayed in this
god awful climate?"

"I always assumed it was a fondness for the food, sir."

But The Gentleman wasn't laughing. "You would be
wise to treat this assignment with a bit more respect.
Don't think that just because you're out of town means
I don't know exactly what you're doing."

His mouth grew dry. Clearly, he'd lost his head to
even think about joking with The Gentleman, much
less to actually do it. "I would never think that, sir."

"Excellent. And just so you know, I'm keeping an eye out on our mutual friend as well."

There was a mocking tone to his voice when The Gentleman added, "I've been thinking. I've changed my mind about killing her if you screw this up. I think she would fit well in my collection."

He closed his eyes against the thought. She'd fare even worse then. Most women The Gentlemen selected for his personal collection didn't last two months.

"I won't fail, sir," he ground out.

"See to it that you don't," The Gentleman said, and then hung up.

Brent whistled when Janie stepped out of the bedroom later that night wearing the gown he'd surprised her with. "You look divine."

She flushed slightly, which he thought only added to her charms. "Thank you."

He held out his arm. "Shall we?"

A private car waited for them and though she didn't say anything, he enjoyed watching her eyes dart back and forth as she took in the sights. After a while, she leaned back and took his hand.

"It's been forever since I've been in Washington," she said.

"How long?"

"I think I was a senior in high school."

"Class trip?" he asked, curious as always to learn more about her.

"Yes. I think that trip in part helped me decide I wanted to be in law enforcement."

He tried to picture a young Janie Roberts and found

he couldn't. He'd have to ask her to show him her old school pictures.

"We went and toured the FBI building." She looked at him. "They used to do that, you know, let you tour. It was fascinating. Or at least it was to me. I remember seeing everything the agents did and thinking, 'I want to do that. I want to be someone who puts the bad guys away.'"

"And now you are."

Her expression changed immediately from wistful to sad. "I used to." She turned to look out the window. "I don't anymore."

"You know that's only temporary, don't you? You'll get your job back. Or maybe you'll find a new one. In DC."

Her surprised reaction smacked him upside the head. What was he thinking, dropping that like that? The plan had been to suggest she move to DC with him after the weekend together. Not before.

He took her hand. "It's only something to think about. Nothing you have to decide right now."

She nodded, but she bit her bottom lip. He'd learned that she only did that when she was nervous or in deep thought. He hoped it was the later in this case and not the former.

"Look." He stroked her hand. "Forget I said anything and let's enjoy the night."

She gave him a weak smile. "You still haven't told me where we're going."

He couldn't help but laugh. It was so like her. She wanted to know every detail, every fact. It was probably one of the things that made her a great cop, but it totally sucked the life out of trying to surprise her.

"You've waited this long," he said. "Don't you think you could wait another five minutes?"

"I'm sure it'll be more like ten in this traffic."

Out the window, traffic was horribly gridlocked. It would probably be more like twenty. "You really don't want me to tell you, do you?"

"No," she finally admitted. "But it's so much fun to tease you about it."

"Tease is you in that dress."

"Well, you only have yourself to blame for that one."

"I did bring that on myself, didn't I?"

Her only response was a raised eyebrow and he couldn't help not to laugh.

Minutes later, ten to be exact, they pulled in front of the restaurant he'd made reservations at. Much like the gown, he cherished her reaction.

"Plume?" she asked in amazement. "You made reservations at Plume?" She didn't wait for him to answer, but continued. "Alyssa said Mac tried to get them reservations for here once and they were booked for months. It was a spur-of-the-moment long-weekend trip, so he hadn't been able to plan that far out."

"It helps when you know the right people. If you like, you can tell Alyssa and Mac to let me know the next time they're in DC and I'll see what I can do."

She simply squeezed his hand and for the next few hours, they got lost in each other. For those few precious, almost stolen hours, there was no talk or worry about threatening notes or lost jobs. There was only Brent and Janie.

After dinner, he surprised her further by taking her to an upscale nightclub, where they danced until the early hours of the morning. Brent has happy to see

Janie's good mood continue. He truly believed after their night out that not only was her moving to DC a good idea, but that she would also agree.

When they made it back to their suite after finally deciding to leave the club, she turned to face him as he closed and locked the door. He barely had time to realize what she was doing before she put her arms around him and whispered what a great time she'd had.

Janie stretched against Brent with absolute contentment. Beside her, with his arms wrapped around her, Brent also appeared to be the very definition of bliss.

She shifted slightly and he stroked her arm. They didn't speak, but rather, let the silence communicate for them. There was an intimacy, Janie had discovered since dating him, that could only be found in silence. The communication of their bodies, even when they were doing nothing but enjoying the peace that came after making love, often spoke stronger than words.

It was there in his arms that she realized she was being an idiot when it came to moving in with him. In that moment, she couldn't think of one reason not to move to DC with him. What did she have keeping her in Charleston? There was no job, no family, and she couldn't see staying for friends. Not when she could have a future with Brent.

Once she gave serious thought to moving, she felt even better. It was almost as if everything clicked into place. She belonged here, in this city, with this man. Not only that, but she probably had better job prospects in DC than she did if she remained in Charleston.

The only downside would be the winters, but even that didn't seem so bad wrapped up in the warmth of

Brent's arms. Actually, the more she thought about it, the more snow sounded fun. If nothing else, it would be a nice change. Besides, Brent was keeping his Charleston home.

She rolled to her side, rose up on her elbow, and smiled at him.

He cracked one eye open. "You'll have to let me rest. I'm not as young as I used to be."

She laughed and gave him a playful swat. "That's not what I was thinking."

"Well, damn." He had both eyes open now. "I certainly was. Way to crush my ego."

"I'm sure your ego is fine. I was actually thinking about what you'd said."

He yawned. "I'm too tired. Remind me?"

"About me moving here with you."

With those words, he no longer appeared tired. His eyes flew open and he pulled them both up so they were sitting in bed. "What? What are you thinking?"

His excitement at the fact she'd been thinking about the possibility proved she was making the right decision. "I'm going to move with you."

No sooner had the words left her mouth, then he pulled her to him and covered her lips in a big kiss. "This makes me so happy," he said, pulling back just a bit. "What made you change your mind?"

A sense of peace settled over her, leaving her more content that she'd remembered feeling in a long time. "I don't know if I actually changed my mind. I never said I wasn't going to move in with you, just that I needed time to think."

"Ah, well, that was me then. Just thinking the worst." He kissed her again, but briefly this time. "I'll rephrase.

What was the determining factor that made the decision for you?"

"Several things. There's not much for me in Charleston anymore. I mean, I'll always love the city, but I don't have a job . . . you're moving . . ." She shrugged. "And I want to spend every night like this and wake up in your arms every morning."

"I feel the same." He brushed her cheek softly. "We have a lot to do to get both of us moved. And not only do we have to find a place to live, but you'll be wanting to look for a job."

"Mmmm." It was much too difficult to think about practical things like packing and jobs when his lips were *right there* and looked so kissable. "Later."

"Later?" His forehead wrinkled.

"Later." She pushed him on his shoulder back down onto the bed and then straddled him. "I hope you had a chance to rest, because sleep is the furthest thing on my mind at the moment."

There was no need for him to answer; his hands were already moving across her body, speaking with his touch. For the next little while, they allowed their bodies to communicate for them. And when they finally fell back to the bed, exhausted, Janie could easily picture her future in this city and with this man.

CHAPTER 3

Brent took her to his favorite brunch place the next day before they went house hunting. Though they slept in, neither of them had gotten very much sleep the night before and he wondered how long they'd be able to look at places before they decided to call it a day and schedule the remaining properties for another time.

As he suspected, Janie had a sharp eye and was able to look beyond the current state of the places they viewed to see the space they could become. His agent had booked four penthouse apartments for them to visit. They toured the first two and Janie quickly pointed out things he would have to change. They were on the way to third when his phone rang. He frowned at the unknown number, but answered it anyway.

"Hello," he said.

"Mr. Taylor?" someone asked.

"Yes."

"This is Herb from the St. Regis."

Ahhh, the hotel. He probably had a package waiting for him or something.

"Yes, Herb. How are you?"

"Mr. Taylor," the man from the hotel said, and Brent wondered if he was making it up that the man seemed slightly irritated. "We need you and your guest to stop by the front desk when you return."

"Is there a problem?" Brent asked. Odds were it wasn't a package if it was requested they both stop by the desk.

"I don't want to get into specifics over the phone." This time Brent was certain there was something off in the man's tone. After hanging up the phone, he told Janie they were going to have to cut the house hunting short. She seemed disappointed until he told her he'd ask the real estate agent to reschedule the showings for the next day.

"What do you think it is?" she asked, taking his hand as they walked into the hotel lobby.

"I'm not sure. Honestly, I've never been asked to stop by when it wasn't to pick up a package or something."

"I hope it's not . . ."

He squeezed her hand in understanding.

He thought about going up to their room and stopping by the front desk later, but the hotel employed several off-duty cops as security guards. Looking toward the elevator, there was one in his usual spot. He and Janie might slip by, but why take the chance?

Besides, if the reason they were asked to stop by the front desk had anything to do with the threats on Janie in Charleston, he wanted her to hear as well.

"I have a gut feeling it's not a package," she said.

"I know," he said softly and squeezed her hand. "Me, too."

As they approached the front desk, one of the employees working picked up the phone and called someone. All the while watching them. Beside him, Janie held on to Brent's hand tighter. Before they could approach anyone, a woman Brent recognized as a manager rushed over to them. By the time she made it to the front desk, Brent had had more than enough.

"I've been a loyal customer for years, Mrs. Hall," he said to the manager. "I'm not sure what's going on now, but I'd appreciate it if someone would tell me what's going on."

The manager appeared unruffled. "Yes, sir, Mr. Taylor. I do appreciate your patience."

He nodded and glanced around the lobby. He was starting to think the delay at the front desk had nothing to do with him and everything to do with Janie. And if that was the case, he didn't want her out in the open of the public lobby.

"If you and Ms. Roberts would step in here, please." The manager waved to a small office to the right of the front desk.

Brent took a deep breath and kept his hand at the small of her back as he walked with Janie toward the open door the manager indicated.

Though the manager motioned to two chairs in the office, Brent remained standing. He crossed his arms as he waited for an explanation of why the perfect day he'd planned had taken a turn for the worst.

"I apologize for any inconvenience," the manager said. "But we wanted to keep this as quiet as possible."

He'd reached the end of his patience. "Pardon me, but exactly what are you wanting to keep quiet?"

She reached into the desk and pull out a sheet of paper. "Our staff went into your room to prepare it for the evening and they found this had been slipped under the door."

Brent took the paper, his eyes recognizing the image in front of him at the exact moment he heard a cry of despair come from Janie. He flipped the picture over, but it was too late. The image of Janie, naked and above him in bed, with the words "Time is up, police bitch," written in red would stay with him forever.

How he managed to keep his temper under control, he wasn't sure, but his voice sounded eerily calm to his own ears when he replied, "Yes, I can see why you wouldn't want other guests to know that the possibility of someone taking pictures of them exists."

The manger flushed. "We haven't contacted the authorities. We thought it best to talk to you first."

Brent stood, picture in one hand and reaching for a pale and shell-shocked Janie. "Thank you. I have a feeling we know who this is, or at least what it pertains to. Be sure to keep us informed going forward."

Janie stood and took his hand, but her movements were robotic. He led them quickly to the elevators and he was surprised that she made it into their room before breaking down.

"Oh, God." She crumpled to the couch, covering her face and sobbing. "He knows I'm here. I'm not safe anywhere."

He held her close, not saying anything, but rubbing her back and plotting in his mind different ways he could kill the bastard behind this.

"He knows we're here," she continued after a few

minutes. "Which means he's somehow followed us, scoped out a place where he could watch us, and then took those pictures."

Listening to her talk had brought up a new question. "How the hell did he know what room we're in? We haven't told anyone."

"It's not like we were exactly careful, you know," she said in a deadpan voice. "The room has those huge windows near the bed. Chances are he just got lucky."

"I'd like to get my hands on him."

"Stand in line." She looked up at him with a grim expression. "He's probably still here."

He looked up and cursed under his breath. The curtains weren't drawn. Whoever it was, might be watching them now.

"I'll be right back," he promised Janie, shifting her so she sat on the couch.

He walked to the large widow, his eyes searching for anything out of place. Not seeing anything, he moved so he could observe the tall office building across the street. Most of the rooms were dark, so it didn't take long for him to spot what he was looking for, high in the building. A man stood, staring out his own window and though they were too far to tell with any certainty, Brent was almost positive he was looking his way.

Brent cursed under his breath.

"Do you see something?" Janie asked, coming up beside him and slipping her hand him his.

"Three o'clock. Almost eye level."

He knew as soon she saw him. Her body tensed and she squeezed his hand. "It's him, isn't it?"

"More than likely."

They stood for several long minutes, watching the man partially obscured by shadows. As they did, Brent started to feel uneasy. He couldn't put his finger on exactly why, until Janie nailed it on the head.

She reached out as if touching the window would somehow sweep the shadows away. "Something about the way he stands looks familiar."

"Yes," he said, realizing she was right.

"It's somebody we know." She shivered and he wrapped his arm around her.

He wanted to protest and tell her she was wrong, but deep inside, he knew she wasn't.

CHAPTER 4

"I'm not sure I want to look at any other places," he told her the next morning over coffee.

"You don't?"

"To be honest, I'm not comfortable with you being in public." Before she could say anything, he added, "Did you like any of the places we saw yesterday?"

She crossed her arms across her chest. She knew both his tone and body language and, at the moment, both of them were telling her that she'd get nowhere by arguing. But she didn't want to give up yet. "Don't change the subject. I can't live locked away forever."

"I wasn't planning on keeping you locked away forever, only until we find out and catch who's behind these threats."

Janie thought she knew what the underlying problem was. Brent thought she'd be safe in DC and he was shaken to learn she was just as vulnerable. In his mind, he probably wanted to get her back to the city he felt most comfortable in and believed he had the most control over.

"I think by running back to Charleston, we're letting this guy have too much control over our lives," she said. "I think it's clear we can't run from him. He'll only follow us."

He sighed and walked over to her, and placed a hand on either of her shoulders. "Janie, I love you. I've waited for you my entire life and I'd almost lost hope I'd ever find you. Can you blame me for wanting to keep you safe?"

Her resolved melted at his words. "Not when you put it like that."

"I know you're a cop and that you're a strong, kick-ass woman. I love that part of you. And I'll admit I'm a bit caveman over keeping you safe. It's just that I can't imagine life without you anymore."

His eyes pleaded with her and she didn't doubt his sincerity. To be honest, it felt rather good to have someone look after her for a change. So much of her life had been spent being in charge and having to look after everything and everyone. For once, couldn't she just step aside and place things in Brent's extremely capable hands?

"Okay."

He gently rubbed her shoulders. "Did you like any of the places we saw yesterday?"

"I liked the second one," she said.

"The penthouse with the private rooftop space?"

"Yes, I think I can deal with the busyness of DC if we have a private little getaway."

"I agree." He leaned down and kissed her neck. "I'll call the agent now."

The trip home was much less intense and they spoke at length about the move to DC. Brent thought he could be ready to move in a matter of weeks, and while it would be a stretch for Janie, she thought she could get everything together and be ready the same time he was.

Everything felt so completely normal, so everyday, that it was easy to forget she had a lunatic stalker who'd threatened her life. In fact, they didn't bring up the photo he'd left, what they saw out the window the night before, or anything related to the man in question.

That peace vanished as soon as they pulled up to Brent's house and saw the white paper box on his front porch.

She felt sick to her stomach. Brent cursed under his breath.

But as they parked the car and walked up to the door, Janie's unease was joined by a sense of *Well, of course there's a package waiting, what else did you expect?*

"I don't suppose we'll be fortunate enough for there to be a return address so we can just mark the thing 'return to sender' without opening it, right?"

"I'd feel better about your safety if we could go inside," he said.

"No," she said. "If he's here, I want the asshole to hear. I trust Alyssa, but I get the feeling her hands are tied. It's not her fault the Charleston PD is incompetent and unable to take care of this efficiently. So we're going to do it." She kicked the box and it opened, revealing a floral arrangement meant for a funeral. The ribbon on it said *Fourteen Days and Counting.* "This shit stops now."

With that she stomped on the flowers, kicked them out of her way, and reached for Brent's hand. He took it, and even though she tried not to, she couldn't help but look over her shoulder at the crushed roses that were now scattered across his porch. Nor could she keep her eyes off the ribbon that proudly announced how long she had to live.

Fuck. He'd messed up. Just like Janie had thought, he'd been hiding nearby, waiting for their arrival and to hear what they thought about his gift. Needless to say, it hadn't gone as well as he'd hoped.

Was she really going to go rogue and cut out the police? That would be a nightmare. Working within the confines of the police department did more than ensure he knew what was going on, it also provided lines he knew she wouldn't cross. But if she turned away from that, he'd be operating totally in the dark.

Damn it all to hell, he'd grown too cocky, too sure of himself. He'd done exactly what The Gentleman had warned him not to do. He'd grown complacent, sure of his ability to outwit Janie, Brent Taylor, and the entire Charleston PD. But he'd also counted on his ability to be one step ahead of everyone.

His phone buzzed. Of course it did. Because The Gentleman had some sort of sixth-sense ability to sniff out when he found himself in a shit storm. He gave serious thoughts about not answering it, but he knew that would only result in a bigger one.

"Hello." The caller kept it simple and to the point. "I see our friends arrived home."

The back of his neck grew prickly as if someone was watching, but he squeezed his eyes so he wouldn't be tempted to look. Likewise, he shoved his free hand in his pocket so he wouldn't reach for his neck.

"Yes, sir," he answered. "I was just watching them arrive and stayed to see their reaction to my latest gift."

"Would that gift happen to be the funeral arrangement littering Mr. Taylor's front porch?"

"Yes, sir." His stomach twisted. He was nearby. "Apparently, he and Janie didn't think much of it."

"I fear you're taking this assignment far too lightly. Like you think you're playing a game."

"No, sir. I don't." *At least, not anymore.*

"Make no mistake about it. There will be funeral flowers needed fourteen days from now. The question is, who will they be needed for?"

Janie stepped back and looked at her work. She'd completely taken over one of Brent's guest bedrooms. Along one wall was a time line that ran from the disappearance of the first girl, all the way to the flowers she'd received today. On another wall, she'd hanged a poster board with everything they knew about the suspect. Yet another wall was decorated with every known victim.

Brent came up beside her and gave a low whistle. "Wow. This is amazing."

Janie looked from the time line to the list of details about the suspect. "It's here. I know it is. The answers we're looking for. Everything. We just have to find it."

"Why does it feel like a needle in a haystack?"

"Because it is." She walked to the suspect details with a pen in her hand. "I keep coming back to that moment in DC when we saw him and we both thought he looked familiar."

"Me, too," Brent said. "I thought if we could come up with a list of people we both knew, it'd be a good place to start."

"I thought the same thing." She pointed to a garbage

can, so stuffed with wadded-up papers it could no longer contain them. "We know too many damn people."

"Why don't you take a break and we'll relook at this over dinner?"

She stretched her arms above her head groaned. "I'm going to run by my place and start getting ready for the move. I sent Alyssa a text about fifteen minutes ago and she's going to be here soon with Mac to take me."

Even with her friend, who was an active law enforcement officer, and her boyfriend, Janie still felt anxious on the ride over to her place. Was her stalker following her in Alyssa's car? She wanted to turn around and look out the back window, but on the off chance the bastard was, she didn't want to give him the satisfaction.

"Any leads?" Janie asked Alyssa. "Off the record?"

Alyssa sighed and shook her head. "I wish I had some good news to share, but there's nothing concrete at the moment. Every time we have a new bit of information, I think it's the one that's going to bust this case wide open. And every time, it goes nowhere. The DNA we have doesn't match anyone in the system. We did find a partial print on the last batch of evidence collected, I'm sure it won't lead anywhere. but I still hope it does."

"I feel like we're so close." Janie gazed out the window.

"We are," Alyssa said, but her hope sounded forced. "Sooner or later something has to turn up."

Yeah, Janie thought. She was sure it would. She only hoped she was still alive to see it.

Mac pulled into the parking lot of her apartment and

dread filled her belly. She knew without stepping foot into her place that there would be something waiting for her inside. What would it be? Another dead animal? More flowers? Part of her didn't even want to go inside. But she had to, at least one more time.

If it was at all possible, this would the last time she went into the apartment. She would do everything in her power to get everything wrapped up today. God, she hoped she could do it. She closed her eyes. She could do this. She was strong.

"Are you sure you're up to doing this?"

She looked up to see Alyssa staring at her through the rearview mirror. Her friend's face was filled with concern.

"We can do this later, you know," Alyssa continued.

"No." Janie undid her seatbelt and opened the door. "We do this today."

Alyssa looked at Mac, and Janie didn't miss the unspoken message sent between the two of them. She wondered what that was about.

"Okay," Alyssa said. "But I go in first."

"Why you?" Mac asked. "Why not me?"

"You think you should go first because you're a man?"

"I never said that," Mac said.

"You meant it that way. I'm going first because I'm a law enforcement officer."

"Damn it all to hell, Alyssa," he said, and he sounded more angry than Janie had ever heard. "Does everything have to come down to showing me how badass you are? You're a cop. I get it."

"I don't know what you're talking about."

Mac shrugged, and Janie realized she'd been distracted from her own thoughts by the tension between Alyssa and Mac. Something was definitely going on between the two of them. She wondered if Mac was still working all the time. Didn't it say something that he wasn't working now?

She got out of the car and followed behind Alyssa, who was walking so fast toward her door that she was almost jogging. Mac hung back and waited for Janie. He gave her an apologetic smile. He didn't say anything. Probably because he didn't want to say anything about Alyssa to her best friend. However, nothing could stop the sense of unease she felt growing with each second.

She tried to put her finger on what it was that made her uneasy. Was it because she had once more witnessed an argument between Alyssa and Mac? Maybe Mac himself? Or, most likely, something not having to do with either, but something else entirely? Like she still hadn't relayed to Alyssa her concerns about her partner? Or she just didn't want to go into her apartment?

They walked slowly to her apartment and Janie wasn't sure if she was relieved or disappointed that Alyssa hadn't opened her door yet. Alyssa had a key to her place; they'd exchanged them years ago.

"I didn't want to open it without you being here," Alyssa explained.

"I know and I appreciate that."

Alyssa put an arm around her. "There's going to be something inside, isn't there?"

"I don't know for sure, but my gut thinks so." She took a deep breath. "I'll open it."

"Okay, but I'm going in first."

As much as she'd like to pass that off to Alyssa, she

knew she had to be the one who opened the door. It was her apartment and she'd be damned if she'd let some sicko keep her from it.

Alyssa smiled. "I'll be right beside you."

"I'll stay out here," Mac said. "Make sure no one's watching or followed us."

Just as well, Janie thought. If she totally freaked out, only Alyssa would see.

The door was unlocked and she never forgot to lock her door. Had she not already convinced herself that something would be waiting inside, that would have done it for her. She glanced at Alyssa, who had her gun in her hand.

"Ready?"

Alyssa nodded.

Janie opened the door and stepped inside, Alyssa followed close behind.

"Holy shit," Alyssa said, speaking what Janie was thinking.

Plain white delivery boxes littered the floor, every one of them opened to reveal dead roses inside. They stepped gingerly around the boxes, not wanting to disturb anything more than necessary.

Janie signaled to the bedroom and Alyssa nodded. They needed to make sure they were the only two people inside before they did anything else. A careful search showed whoever had ransacked the apartment was long gone.

Making their way to the living room, they compared observations.

"I didn't see a note," Janie said, trying to remain calm. The sight of the roses made her stomach flip.

Damn it, they were just roses. At least he hadn't left another dead cat.

"He probably doesn't think he needs one," Alyssa said. "The way he sees it, there's little doubt you'd believe it was anyone else."

"Possibly, but do you think it's more? Like maybe he thought he was revealing too much in them?"

Alyssa was quite as she thought. "I don't want to rule anything out at this point. I don't remember anything sticking out, but it won't hurt to look again."

"Thank you."

"I'll call the station and get a team out here." Alyssa put her gun away. "You probably shouldn't touch anything until they do."

"Really?" Janie raised an eyebrow and took out her phone. She needed to let Brent know what was happening.

"Sorry. Old habit."

As she waited for Brent to pick up, she heard Alyssa step outside and say something to Mac.

"Hey," Brent said. "What's going on?"

"He's been busy," she said.

Brent cursed. "How so?"

"It appears as if he's bought damn near every white box in the city and filled them with every dead rose he could find." Her words were light, but she knew he picked up on the slight edge in her voice.

"I'll be right there," he said and she almost told him it wasn't necessary, but she desperately wanted to feel his arms around her. "After the police leave, take what you can, and make a list of everything else you want to keep. I'll call a cleaning service and a moving company.

They'll take care of everything so when you leave today, you won't have to go back if you don't want to."

"How do we know they'll be safe? I can't stand the thought of someone getting hurt because they were in my house if he happens to go by again."

"Don't worry about that. I know the owner personally. I'll explain the situation and ensure everyone is safe."

She closed her eyes. He was so good to her. "Thank you," she whispered, wondering how it was possible she'd ever thought about not going to DC with this man.

CHAPTER 5

Later that night, Brent sat in the guest room with Janie. She never stopped amazing him. Just when he thought he had her figured out, she'd do something to remind him all over again how it was he'd fallen in love so fast and complete with her.

He knew the discovery at her apartment had scared her. But she refused to give into that fear and instead she'd returned back to his place with renewed vigor and determination to find the person responsible and to put a stop to them.

She was, hands down, the strongest woman he knew. And since he was raised by a strong woman, spent his summers in Greece with his strong grandmother, and had a sister with similar characteristics, that was saying a lot.

"I don't know why he's doing this," she said, looking over all the evidence she had pulled together.

"Tell me what you're thinking," Brent said.

"I'll give you a quick list. First of all, I'd be surprised if he's working alone. I believe he's either working with somebody, or for somebody. I'm not sure which. Secondly, he's either with the police or he's very close to somebody in the police department. There have just been too many instances where he seems to know information that is either confidential or hasn't been released to the public. Like how he always knows where I'll be and for how long, how he always seemed to get away with seconds to spare and, I'm sorry, I just think it's strange that we only ever got that one DNA profile of him."

Everything made sense to Brent. He had to admit, the part about the police department both made sense and scared him. Assuming the person was on the police department, where did that leave them? The perpetrator would always be at least one step ahead of them.

"Also," she continued, "he's made a few mistakes. He's acting a bit irrationally. Seriously, all those boxes were overkill, and I believe he's showing signs of extreme confidence. While it's sometimes dangerous when they get like that, it's also when they make mistakes. Big ones. Mistakes will allow us to catch them."

It all seemed too much to hope for. She looked at Brent and took his hand, entwining their fingers.

"I would love to go to DC with all of this behind us," she said. "And not have to worry about it another day."

"Me, too."

Janie was studying the boards. "Another thing. I think our man will turn out to be well liked in the community, the sort to fly under the radar, and generally, one of the last people you think would be possible to do this. And yet, I believe he is highly volatile, has a short temper, and has shown violent tendencies in the past. Perhaps as early as childhood."

"Don't tell me he's going to blame all this on his childhood," Brent said.

"I'm sure a defense attorney would love that line," Janie said. "My hope is to shut him down before he gets to that point. I mean, I always prefer to have the suspects taken into custody as opposed to shooting them. But if it comes down to it, and I have no choice, I'll shoot to kill every day as opposed to letting someone like this get away."

"What are our next steps?" Brent asked.

"According to those flowers that were waiting when we got back from DC, he won't make a major move for at least a week."

She'd stopped in front of the end of the time line, but Brent walked to the beginning.

"I keep asking myself, why you? What did you see or what does he think you saw for him to be chasing you so relentlessly?" He turned to look at her. "Did you see anything? Any little thing that he might think is something?"

She ran her fingers through her hair. "I honestly can't think of a thing."

She started to stay something else, but her phone rang. She looked the display and smiled. "Hey, Alyssa. What do you have for me?" As Brent watched, her smile fell. "Of course. I don't know why I expected anything else." There was another pause and then she said, "I'm not holding out much hope, but let me know if it turns up anything."

"What was that?" he asked when she got off the phone.

"No prints on any of the boxes."

He nodded. That wasn't surprising.

"But," she added, "they're going to run DNA to see if anything turns up."

"Do you think it will?" He hated the hope he had at any new clue or direction that always got shattered later.

"Probably not, but at least they're doing something."

She looked tired and worn out. He reached out and she went silently into his arms. "Let's think about something else for at least an hour. How does a bubble bath sound?"

"Divine," she said with a half happy sigh.

"Come with me," he said, taking her hand and leading her down the hall. She sighed when they entered his bathroom. It was huge and always reminded her of a spa.

"You rest here while I get everything ready." He nodded to the plush stool sitting beside the tub.

"I can help, you know," she said.

He kissed her cheek softly. "I know. But I don't want you to right now. All I want you to do is sit right there and relax."

She smiled. He always took such good care or her. She sat back and watched him moving around the bathroom, humming to himself as he pulled out the bath wash and set a few towels nearby. He turned the water on and it wasn't long until the room was filled with the smell of summer wildflowers.

He looked over at her. "Are you ready?"

She smiled and held out her hand. "Yes."

"Be careful." He took her hand and helped her step into the bathtub. "I'd hate for you to slip."

His tub was a huge, massive number. An old antique find, with clawed feet that had been restored. The high back on one side was perfect for soaking. She dropped into it, up to her neck in warm sudsy bubbles. Her eyes drifted closed and she groaned.

"It's so good." She cracked one eye open. "But it'd be so much better if you joined me."

"Oh no," he said. "I'm enjoying sitting here, watching you way too much."

"You can still watch me if you join me."

He chuckled. "Perhaps. But then you wouldn't relax very much, now would you?"

"Relaxing is highly overrated."

"Be that as it may," he said with a grin. "Right now it is about you."

He didn't say anything else, but started bathing her with warm caresses and soft strokes. He was so gentle, he treated her as if she were made of fragile glass.

She couldn't remember the last time that she felt so cherished and cared for. By the time he finished, and he'd dried her off, and curled up in bed with her, she was completely relaxed and couldn't keep her eyes open.

CHAPTER 6

Janie had been a nervous wreck all week. She kept waiting for the other shoe to drop. Even though she had said she didn't expect anything, the truth was she kept waiting for something to happen. Each day that passed with nothing happening only served to drive her to look more closely the next day.

She told herself to stop and that she was only making matters worse. Each day, too, she waited for Alyssa to call with test results, but she should have known better than to expect them that fast.

Through it all, Brent was her rock. She truly didn't know how she'd do it without him. Even now as they got ready to go to the cookout Alyssa had invited her to just hours ago.

She thought she'd been doing a good job at hiding her nerves, but when he came up behind her and put his hands on her shoulders and asked, "Are you sure going to this cookout is the best thing to do?" she knew she hadn't fooled anyone.

"I'm fine," she managed to say with a smile. The psychopath who had been strangely quiet for the last week. She wasn't sure which made her more nervous: the plethora of notes he'd left in the beginning or not having anything sent to her in a week.

"This isn't funny, Janie," Brent said, catching her eyes in the mirror.

She turned around and captured his face in her hands and ran her fingers across the worry lines she found there. "I know it's not. But I have to laugh or else I'll be so scared I won't be able to function."

"That's why I wonder if it wouldn't be best for us to stay home."

She shook her head. "He wins that way."

"But you're alive."

"I don't think there's any place safer than a police department picnic."

"It's at a public park."

"She invited us three hours ago. There's no way anyone would have time to plan anything with that short a time frame." At first, Janie wasn't sure it was such a good idea, what with her being recently fired and all. But Alyssa had told her it wasn't an official departmental event and to be honest, there were several people she wanted to see before heading to DC who would be there.

Brent told her from the beginning that he didn't want her to go. But Janie had been persistent. Soon she'd be moving to DC with Brent and a part of her needed this cookout for closure, as a way to say good-bye to what had been a major part of life for a long time.

Brent knew this, though, and she wasn't in the mood to rehash the same conversation for the tenth time.

"You don't have to go," she said, inwardly hoping like hell that he didn't decide to let her go alone.

He looked almost angry when he replied. "Do you actually think I'm going to let you go by yourself?"

"I need to do this," she said. "I need to be able to go to DC having closed this chapter in my life."

He searched her eyes. "Okay," he finally said. "But we don't stay long and you never leave my sight."

She rose to her toes and gave him a quick kiss. "Thank you."

"I still don't have a good feeling about this."

"What could possibly happen at a public police department?"

"You're almost out of time," The Gentleman said when he answered the phone. "I'm looking forward to sharing your girlfriend's company in a week."

He took several deep breaths. He was close, so damn close. He couldn't afford to let The Gentleman goad him into making a mistake.

"It's all going to plan," he said. "Make no mistake about it: this time next week, Janie will be on a slab in the morgue."

Sooner than that if he'd played his cards right. Janie still thought she had a week left. He was going to make her wish he wouldn't wait that long.

Three hours later, dusk was falling. The picnic had been fun and not awkward at all like Janie had feared. She'd announced her plan to move to DC and everyone seemed genuinely happy of her. Brent had been the recipient of many back slaps at that, and ended up wearing a big grin most of the night.

They were standing around, talking. Janie looked over the group of colleagues she'd worked with for years and though she felt a little bittersweet about leaving, all she had to do was look at Brent and she knew she was looking at her future.

He caught her staring and smiled before glancing down at his watch. He gave it a tap and she nodded. They'd stayed longer than they'd planned and she knew it was time to head home.

She looked around for Alyssa. She wanted to thank her for inviting her.

"I'm going to go tell Alyssa good-bye," she told Brent, after finding her friend off to the side, talking with her partner.

Brent nodded. "I'll go with you."

She resisted the urge to roll her eyes, knowing he was only worried about her safety. Instead she held out her hand and waited for him to take it. "I'll just be a minute."

"Brent!" Mac walked up to them. "I need to ask you a question really quick. Hey, you guys aren't leaving yet, are you?"

Brent looked caught between Mac and Janie. Janie decided to make the decision for him.

"You two chat," she said. "I'm going to go say bye to Alyssa, I'll be back before you finish."

Brent hesitantly let her hand go and she turned toward Alyssa, not wanting to be away from Brent any longer than possible.

She froze. She smelled it. The cologne. Hadn't Mac said Alyssa's partner gave it to him or gave him the name or something? Trying not to be obvious about what she was doing, she looked around. She knew her partner was here. She saw him not too long ago.

She spotted him alone, not part of the crowd, but not entirely separate either. Brent was watching her, he might not like that she didn't go straight to Alyssa, but he wouldn't stop her.

The off duty office flashed a friendly smile at her approach. "Hey, Janie. So sorry to see you leave Charleston."

"I bet you are. Traveling to Washington's going to be a bitch for you, isn't it?"

She watched him carefully, but he revealed nothing when he spoke, "I don't know what you're talking about."

She took a step closer. "It's over. I know where you were last weekend."

"In Atlanta, watching the Braves. My nephew turned sixteen." He shrugged. "I don't know why that's any of your business though."

Her mouth dropped. "The Braves? Atlanta?"

He looked at her as his she'd grown two horns and a beard. "Yeah. Look, I hate to cut this this short, but I need to go talk to Watson over there. He got in some evidence I want to expedite. See you around."

She didn't say goodbye or watch him walk away. Instead she was running though everything she knew about the case, trying to pinpoint how she'd got it all wrong.

Laughter boomed loudly. Turning to see who it was, she discovered it was Mac.

Mac.

Suddenly, it all made sense. She thought the man might be a police officer. However, with Alyssa as his girlfriend, he'd have access to everything. He'd know what was found as well as the next steps. No wonder he was always a one step ahead of everybody. He had the perfect setup for snooping.

She motioned for Alyssa to join her. Her friend frowned, but told Mac something, and started walking.

Alyssa made it to her. "Are you okay?"

Janie kept her eye on Mac, not really sure how to bring it up. "I know this sounds weird, do you think—"

She couldn't get out what she was going to say because at that moment, an explosion ripped through the night.

Everything was chaos. The world was filled with darkness and noise. She fell.

Her ears buzzed. She wasn't sure what had blown up. It had been close by. There was smoke everywhere. It burned her eyes and made her cough. It took her a few seconds, but she realized she'd been momentarily blinded by the explosion. She wondered if she'd passed out.

Nothing seemed right. Where was everybody? Why couldn't she hear anything?

She tried to remember. God, it hurt to think. She rolled over and gravel dug into her knees. A groan escaped her throat. She didn't know she'd been on the ground.

"Brent," she coughed out. But she couldn't find anybody.

Was Alyssa nearby?

She struggled to sit up, but everything hurt and the odd buzz in her ears made her head ache even more. She slumped down, gathering her strength, when she became aware of a presence by her side.

She held still, hoping they wouldn't notice her and jerked when the presence touched her. That smell! Her throat seized in a moment of panic.

"Janie!" Brent looked around the increasingly frantic crowd. Where was she? He'd been watching her and then the explosion happened and now he had no idea where she was.

He desperately wanted to ignore the thought that this was somehow related to the threats she'd been receiving, but it was too coincidental. It had to be related.

Dread began to seep into his body. He'd known they shouldn't have come to this party. Why had he agreed to come? He should have told her no. Tied her to the bed and kept her there for days.

But no, she'd wanted to come and it was impossible for him to turn her down. Damn it. If anything happened to her . . . he shook his head, not even able to let his mind go there.

Alyssa walked by, talking on her phone. He jogged over to her.

"Alyssa!"

She stopped and turned around. "Brent." She frowned. "Where's Janie?"

The panic grew. He forced himself to speak as calmly as possible, "I was hoping she was with you or you knew where she was. Wasn't she with you when the explosion occurred?"

"Yes, she was with me and my partner. Who I can't find, either. Wasn't Mac with you?"

Mac. Right. He'd forgotten about him. "Yes, but he had to grab something really quick. What happened, anyway?"

"From what I've been told, it was a car bomb. Too soon to know whose car, though."

He didn't care who the car belonged to. Who could possibly be concerned about a car when all signs pointed to the conclusion that whoever was behind the car was also the man they'd been hunting?

"Oh, look." Alyssa pointed to two people quite a distance away in a small clearing. "Mac and Janie are over there."

Brent breathed a sigh of relief. "Thank goodness. I wonder how she got over there?"

"I don't know. I'm going to text Mac and tell them to stay there. It's too smoky over here."

Brent nodded. Damn, that was close. Janie would be safe with Mac. He would stay with her and he knew about the threats.

Still though, Brent wouldn't feel completely at ease until he could touch her. "I'm going to head that way."

Alyssa nodded, talking once again on the phone. Brent took two steps toward the tree Janie was sitting in front of when Alyssa's cry of distress made him stop. He turned to look at her. She was pale and her eyes were searching the area frantically.

"Alyssa?" Brent asked.

"Thanks," she said to whomever she was talking to and hung up. She didn't look pale now, she looked green. "Where's Janie? We have to get her."

Brent looked toward where Janie had been moments ago, but now he didn't see anything. Where could she be?

"Where is she?" Alyssa asked again.

He squinted, cursing because he still couldn't get a

visual on Janie. "She was with Mac, by that tree. I don't see either one of them now."

"Oh no. Oh my God."

Brent took off toward the tree. "What's wrong? What's the problem?"

"DNA is back on those boxes."

"Shh. It's okay," the presence said, and she realized it was Mac.

She tried to say his name, but her mouth was too dry and all she did was cough.

"Don't try to talk," Mac said. "Come over here, it's quieter and there's not as much smoke."

She stood on legs that were too wobbly in her opinion. He led her to a tree stump and she clumsily sat down. She had to get away. Damn it. Why was she so weak?

Looking around, she tried to find Brent, but all she saw in the direction they came from was a fireball. Mac handed her an open bottle of water and she gulped down half of it before she was able to talk.

She wiped her mouth with her forearm. "What happened?"

"A car bomb, from the looks of it."

"Was anyone hurt?" she asked.

"No," Mac said, but something flickered in his eyes.

All at once, she felt very exposed. When she tried to stand, she fell to the ground.

"Whoa!" Mac said, picking her up. "Easy. Where are you going?"

Her mind felt muddled. What was happening to her?

"Brent," she managed to get out.

"Let's get you back on the tree stump," he said, helping her to sit back down.

She shook her head. It felt as if the fog that had been surrounding her had somehow seeped into her brain. Her thoughts were so fuzzy. "Brent," she repeated.

"I don't think you're in any condition to walk all the way back," Mac said. "Come with me. I'll help you."

How had she gotten so far away from the main crowd? Did Mac carry her that far? She squinted, as if that would clear her mind. Were those fire trucks she saw? Why was she so dizzy?

The smell hit her as soon as Mac opened the door to the truck and just as quickly, her mind cleared. The cologne. She instinctively tried to back away, but her limbs wouldn't cooperate. They were still jelly.

"Inside, Janie." He pushed her roughly on her back, tying her hands. That still wouldn't work right. Then he shoved her onto her stomach into the backseat of the cab and slammed the door behind her.

Why couldn't she move her arms and legs? She rolled as best as she could and made it to her side and ice-cold fear kept her frozen in place. There on the floorboard was a generic white box. Exactly like the ones that kept being delivered to her.

The front door of the truck opened and Mac got in. He looked over his shoulder at her, but she no longer saw Alyssa's long-term boyfriend. In his place was her tormentor, her worst nightmare, and quite possibly her murderer.

"I'm a little disappointed," he said. "I didn't think it'd be so easy. Maybe when we get to where we're going you'll have a bit more spunk."

He turned back around and started the truck, whistling.

Janie forced herself to remain calm and not to give into the fear that threatened to consume her. She was a trained cop. She could handle this. The only other option was death.

Read on for an excerpt from the next Sons of
Broad novel

BROKEN

PROMISE

Coming soon from St. Martin's Paperbacks

"Dance with me."

She jumped. She'd been so intent on watching the couple on the dance floor; she completely missed hearing Kipling walk up behind her.

Without turning around, she replied, "No, that's okay. I'm fine." Because suddenly the thought of being that close to Kipling and having his arms around her, made her skin flush more.

"It wasn't a question."

She turned around to find him smiling and all but laughing at her. She decided to play along and raised an eyebrow. "Really? Don't you know it's not polite to go up and command a woman dance with you?"

The hint of a smile teased his lips. "I thought you knew me well enough to know I've never been one to be called polite."

She couldn't think of anything to say back so she stood there, feeling flustered. Damn Kipling Benedict. She should have left after the ceremony and not cared about being offensive.

He took a step closer toward her. "I see you standing here, watching the couples dance and yet you're not dancing. And I realize you didn't come with a date and I don't have a date." He shrugged. "We might as well have a go."

"No thank you," she said. "I don't want to be anyone's pity dance."

"Let's get one thing straight, why don't we." He leaned down and spoke in a low voice she knew no one else heard. "I do very many things and I do them for all kinds of reasons, but I never do anything out of pity, especially when it comes to a beautiful woman."

Her brain threatened to short circuit, she blinked. "Why would you . . ." She trailed off as his hand moved to stroke her shoulder.

"We've both tried to ignore it, but we know there's something between us." His voice grew rougher. "Let's give into it just for today. For one dance."

She looked toward the dancing couples, imagining his arms around her, and licked her lips, on the verge of saying *yes*. She shook her head. "It's not appropriate. I'm involved in several cases that have ties to your family."

"It's one dance, Alyssa." While he spoke, he still stroked her shoulder. The touch of his fingers made her want to feel his hands everywhere. "At my brother's wedding. There's nothing wrong with two single people enjoying themselves."

Why did she get the impression he was talking about more than a dance?

She closed her eyes, but doing so did nothing to diminish the way his touch felt. She could get lost in his touch without even thinking twice. To agree to a dance would be one step down a path that offered nothing but heartache and trouble.

"Yes," she said anyway.

His hand slipped off her shoulder and he held it out to her. God, she was actually doing this. She took the offered hand, noting how warm it was and she didn't think she was imagining the strength it contained.

He didn't say anything as he led them to the dance floor. She stared at him, not looking to either side for fear of seeing the other wedding guests' reaction. She didn't realize how stiff and uncomfortable she must look until he whispered, "It's not an execution, you know. A smile wouldn't be remiss."

She smiled, but it felt fake. What didn't feel fake was the way her body reacted when he slipped his arms around her. She lowered her head, hoping to keep to herself the fact that her skin flushed at such close contact with Kipling.

"If I'd known you would feel so good in my arms, I'd have asked you to dance long before now," he said.

She tried to imagine them dancing at any of the previous times they'd been together. The image of them dancing while she arrested him made her chuckle with its ridiculousness.

"There we go," Kipling said. "Now people will think we're having a good time instead of assuming I'm torturing you."

She pulled back to look at him and make a snappy comeback, but instead she found herself caught up in his eyes. They were the most mesmerizing color. A light brown that somehow appeared golden. How had she never noticed his eyes before and why did they seem so familiar?

The corner of his mouth uplifted in half smile. "Cat got your tongue?"

"What?"

"You looked like you were going to say something, but then you stopped."

Had she? "I don't remember."

"That's not good," he said. "I don't mind rendering you speechless, but affecting your mental capacity isn't on my agenda."

She'd like to know exactly what was on his agenda concerning her. She bet it was mind-blowing. But what was truly mind-blowing was the way he looked at her with such intensity. It was a bit unnerving and she was starting to understand why Kipling was so good in business. Not a lot of people could stand up to the scrutiny of his gaze. Fortunately, she'd had plenty of experience dealing with intense stares.

"Why are you looking at me like that?" she asked.

"Like what?"

"Like you're looking for something or waiting for me to do something."

"Am I?" he asked in such a way that proved he was, in fact, the most tedious man ever.

She decided not to even bother with a reply. She focused on a blank wall and willed the song to be over soon so she could start to pretend his arms really didn't feel as good as they did and that his body didn't seem oh so right pressed up against hers.

"Actually," he said. "I was wondering if you'd like to have dinner with me."

She stopped dancing completely. "Are you asking me out? Seriously?"

"For someone who didn't want to cause a scene, you aren't being the most discreet right this second."

She glanced around and saw that they had quiet a few eyes watching them. She smiled at them and nodded to Kipling to start moving again.

"Why would you ask me out?" she said.

"You know, I didn't peg you as the type to need an ego boost, but you're smart and attractive." The sincerity of his expression took her breath and she had to look away. "And I'm willing to bet underneath the layers of sarcasm, you have a delightful personality. I'd like to find out."

Now there was no doubt he was drunk or at least on his way there. "I arrested you."

"And you later released me."

"I have actively investigated your family."

"And you've found no evidence of anything shady," he said, obviously enjoying their exchange way too much.

"You're impossible."

"Now, I wouldn't say that. Difficult? Maybe. But not impossible. Not for you."

"I don't . . . .I mean . . . It's not . . ." Why did this man leave her so flustered? "Not a good idea."

Thankfully, she was saved from having to say anything else by the song coming to an end. She pulled out of his embrace, turned, and walked away, while ignoring the way he called after her.